The battles come fast and furious in this picaresque story. Teen-aged Bec is a boy determined to escape from his evil slave master, and with the help of a kung fu wizard, and a mysterious knight, the author provides all the key ingredients for a rollicking good adventure.

—Christine Welldon, acclaimed author of *Knight of the Rails* and *Kid Sterling*

Escape to Ponti *is a splendid medieval adventure about two boys running from danger in search of themselves. Brian Slattery is an expert storyteller. His plot races as fast as the eye can read, with a cliffhanger at the end of each short chapter. And his dialogue is as clean and natural as his prose is light and agile. A perfect book to hook the most reluctant Middle Grade reader.*

—Allan Stratton is the internationally award-winning author of *The Dogs* and *The Grave Robber's Apprentice*

Escape to Ponti

Brian Slattery

ILLUSTRATED BY
ANTONIO JAVIER CAPARO

Red Deer Press

Published in Canada by Red Deer Press,
209 Wicksteed Avenue, Unit 51, Toronto, ON   M4G 0B1.

Published in the United States by Red Deer Press,
60 Leo M Birmingham Pkwy, Ste 107, Brighton, MA 02135.

Red Deer Press acknowledges with thanks the Canada Council for the Arts and the Ontario Arts
Council for their support of our publishing program. We acknowledge the financial support of the
Government of Canada through the Canada Book Fund (CBF) for our publishing activities.

ONTARIO ARTS COUNCIL
CONSEIL DES ARTS DE L'ONTARIO
an Ontario government agency
un organisme du gouvernement de l'Ontario

Canada Council   Conseil des arts
for the Arts   du Canada

Library and Archives Canada Cataloguing in Publication
Title: Escape to Ponti / written by Brian Slattery ; illustrations by Antonio Javier Caparo.
Names: Slattery, Brian, 1942- author. | Caparo, Antonio Javier, illustrator.
Identifiers: Canadiana 2023022900X | ISBN 9780889957237 (softcover)
Classification: LCC PS8637.L385 E83 2023 | DDC jC813/.6—dc23

Publisher Cataloging-in-Publication Data (U.S.)
Names: Slattery, Brian, 1942-, author. | Caparo, Antonio Javier, illustrator.
Title: Escape to Ponti / Brian Slattery ; illustrated by Antonio Javier Caparo.
Description: Toronto, Ontario : Red Deer Press, 2023. | Summary: "A slave on the run from his vicious
master, Bec is desperate for money. But when he mugs Tien Nu, he gets more than he bargained for.
Tien Nu isn't just a superb acrobat and kung fu wizard. He's also killed his father — or so he thinks.
As the paths of the two boys become intertwined with the journey of a mysterious knight, mayhem
ensues when they head cross-country toward the safety of Ponti, with Bec's slave master in hot pursuit.
A medieval adventure in the Kingdom of Italia"-- Provided by publisher.
Identifiers: ISBN 978-0-88995-723-7 (pbk)
Subjects: LCSH Slaves — Juvenile fiction. | Kung fu -- Juvenile fiction. | Knights and knighthood –
Juvenile fiction. | Adventure stories. | BISAC: JUVENILE FICTION / Action & Adventure / General. |
JUVENILE FICTION / Historical / Medieval.
Classification: LCC PZ7.S638Es | DDC 813.6 – dc23

Edited for the Press by Beverley Brenna
Text and cover design by Tanya Montini
Copyedit by Penny Hozy
The illustrations by Antonio Javier Caparo were created with
a mix of graphite pencils on Strathmore paper,
and digitally using Procreate and Photoshop.
Printed in Canada by Copywell

To Mary Ann Yee-Sum,
Shannon Rei-Juh, and
Michael Rei-Fung

Contents

Map... 10

Chapter 1 – The Slave 11

Chapter 2 – The Forest 19

Chapter 3 – The Mountain............................ 27

Chapter 4 – The Town................................. 33

Chapter 5 – The Convent 42

Chapter 6 – The Abbess 50

Chapter 7 – The Tunnel 58

Chapter 8 – The Rooftop 63

Chapter 9 – The Church................................70

Chapter 10 – The Knight.............................. 75

Chapter 11 – The Accident 83

Chapter 12 – Quan Fa................................. 88

Chapter 13 – Catarina................................100

Chapter 14 – The Hideout............................ 106

Chapter 15 – A Visitor 116

Chapter 16 – The Graveyard. 120

Chapter 17 – Bandits. 127

Chapter 18 – The Bakery. 132

Chapter 19 – A Shock. 140

Chapter 20 – Trapped 146

Chapter 21 – Falco. 158

Chapter 22 – The Catacombs. 164

Chapter 23 – The Shrine. 169

Chapter 24 – A Robbery 172

Chapter 25 – The Dagger 177

Chapter 26 – Together Again 184

Chapter 27 – On the Road. 191

Chapter 28 – The Watcher 198

Chapter 29 – The Sausage 202

Chapter 30 – At the Gate. 211

Chapter 31 – The Valley. 216

Chapter 32 – Face to Face 224

Chapter 33 – The Steward. 228

Chapter 34 – The Inn. 235

Chapter 35 – The Chasm. 242

Chapter 36 – The Castle 247

Chapter 37 – The Rehearsal. 256

Chapter 38 – The Feast 260

Chapter 39 – Monkey Style. 268

Chapter 40 – The Escape 273

Chapter 41 – Scars. 279

Chapter 42 – Roast Pigeon 284

Chapter 43 – The Wall. 293

Chapter 44 – The Rescue 300

Chapter 45 – Adrift. 305

Chapter 46 – Fathers 311

Chapter 47 – The Spring. 319

Chapter 48 – The Ring. 328

Chapter 49 – The Gorge 332

Chapter 50 – The Bridge 338

Chapter 51 – The Village 342

Chapter 52 – The Amulet 350

Chapter 53 – The Hollow 356

Chapter 54 – The River 365

Chapter 55 – A Surprise 372

Chapter 56 – Surgery 377

Chapter 57 – The Peddler 381

Chapter 58 – Revenge 386

Chapter 59 – The Truth 396

Chapter 60 – The Tightrope 400

Chapter 61 – Death 405

Chapter 62 – The Dancer 410

Chapter 63 – Chess 416

Acknowledgments 422

Author Photo 424

Interview with Brian Slattery 425

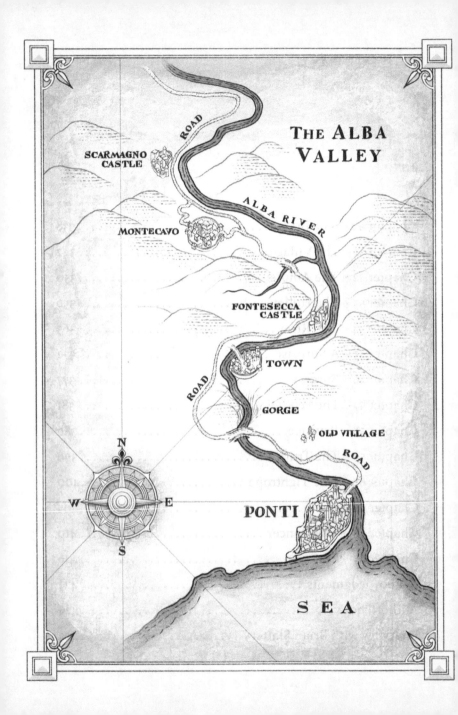

CHAPTER 1

The Slave

The branding iron hissed and spat in the burning coals, giving off angry wisps of smoke. Bec shrank into the corner, the bonds on his wrists and ankles biting into the skin.

The blacksmith drew the iron from the flames and held it up, then shook his head. He tapped it against the forge to knock off the crust and slid it back into the fire.

"Not ready yet?"

The blacksmith looked at the lean figure lounging by the wall.

"No, milord."

"How hot does it have to get?"

"White hot, milord."

Malaspina's gaze shifted to Bec.

"Why? He's just a boy. Tender skin."

"If it's not hot enough, it will take too long."

"The longer the better. Let him feel it."

"But it has to be quick, milord. Otherwise, the slave will thrash around and spoil the brand."

Malaspina stared at the blacksmith, the flames from the forge flickering in his eyes.

"All right," he said softly. "Have it your way. Just get on with it."

"Yes, milord."

The blacksmith gave a word to the man working the bellows and waited as the forge rose to a steady roar. Waves of heat rolled across the room, but Bec felt deathly cold.

The smith took another look at the branding iron—now an incandescent white.

"Ready, milord."

"And about time." Malaspina nodded to his bodyguard. "Take the boy outside. Everyone's waiting."

Nozzo released the bonds on Bec's ankles and dragged him upright. His feet were like blocks of wood. He stumbled on the uneven floor and pitched forward, hands tied behind his back. He came down hard, his head striking the flagstones.

He lay there unmoving.

"Get him up," said Malaspina, pointing with his cane.

Nozzo glanced at his master. He untied the ropes on Bec's

wrists and rolled him over, shaking him by the shoulder.

Bec let his head loll to the side, tracking the man through half-closed lids.

The bodyguard knelt down and held a hand in front of the boy's mouth, then sat back on his heels, rubbing his shaved head. "He's not breathing."

"Slap him about."

As Nozzo raised a hand, Bec rolled away and scrambled for the door.

The courtyard outside was packed with people summoned for the branding—servants, stable boys, slaves. They fell silent as Bec stumbled through the doorway. He plunged into the crowd, which parted to make way, then shuffled back into place, hiding him. Bec fell to his knees and crawled through the forest of legs, heading for the castle gate.

He heard Malaspina shout: "Drop the portcullis!"

Bec came to a halt, biting his lip. He'd never reach the gate in time. He reversed course and made for the lord's living quarters on the other side of the yard. He didn't know that part of the castle well, but it was his only chance.

"Where's the slave?" called Malaspina.

"Over there! There! There!" People pointed in all directions except the right one.

Bec spotted a wall ahead, then a narrow opening. He scuttled inside, finding a staircase that wound upward in semi-darkness. He climbed for what seemed like an eternity. At the top, he pushed open a door and entered a day-room—polished table, carpet, tapestries. A small book lay open on the table. The place was deserted.

Across the room was an open window, white curtains fluttering in the breeze.

He climbed onto the windowsill and leaned out, one hand gripping the side. Far below, dark shoals of sewage drifted in the moat where the privies emptied. The water was shallow—just a few feet deep—not enough to break his fall. It would be crazy to jump.

He turned his gaze upward, scanning the wall that rose to the battlements above. The castle was made of fieldstones, fitted roughly together. In places, the mortar had crumbled, leaving a network of cracks and crevices where the swallows flitted in and out. He wondered if he could climb all the way up. If he slipped, he'd be dead.

He recalled the branding he'd seen last winter—an old slave who had shrieked and struggled as they'd pinned him down. The smell of burning flesh still gave him nightmares.

No choice.

Bec wedged his foot into a gap in the stonework and pushed himself upward, grasping the narrow ledge on top of the window. He manoeuvred around until his knee found the ledge. He teetered there, grimacing as the rough stone pressed against the bone. A gust of wind caught his tunic and almost threw him off balance. He clung to the wall, breathing hard, then hoisted himself into a standing position on the ledge.

Behind him, he could sense a vast open space, billowing out across the valley. It sucked at his body, tugging at his limbs. The backs of his thighs tingled, as if a thousand ants were crawling there. He closed his eyes and held on grimly, while the wall seemed to sway back and forth.

Taking a deep breath, he groped upward and came across a hole with a bird's nest. He pushed the nest further inside, setting off a storm of cheeps. Baby swallows.

"Sorry, fellows!"

The mother swallow attacked him so suddenly that Bec yelped and nearly let go. The bird swooped around, making piercing cries, diving at him again and again. Bec hunched his shoulders as the wings thrashed against his head. He gently swatted at the bird, until she gave up and flew away.

That was better.

Bec wiped his palms on his tunic, one by one, then muttered a prayer and started dragging himself upward. His hands moved shakily from gap to gap, the muscles in his arms straining.

An outcrop crumbled under his right foot. His body dropped and his legs swung free. He hung from his fingertips, his feet flailing around.

A crack in the wall—just big enough.

God and all the saints! That was close. He flattened himself against the wall, chest heaving.

A head emerged from the window below.

Malaspina.

Bec held his breath. The man leaned out, looking down toward the moat.

There was still a chance. Bec eyed the dense patch of ivy that separated him from the battlements above. Quietly he slid his hand into the leaves and felt around for something solid.

Sweat streamed down his forehead, making his eyes sting. He blinked the sweat away and tugged at a thick vine. The branch lost its moorings and Bec swung out, almost falling. He clutched another vine, which held. Some leaves fluttered down into Malaspina's field of vision. Bec scrabbled for a foothold and thrust himself upward.

"Stop!"

Bec grabbed the edge of the battlements and hauled himself over, tumbling onto the inner walkway. He crouched there, thinking feverishly. He could hear Malaspina shouting as he raised the alarm.

The stables in back. His best chance.

He raced along the battlements to the rear of the castle enclosure. A wooden staircase on the inside of the wall led to a platform halfway down. He paused there, gazing about.

Not a soul in sight. Everyone was up front for the show—the branding of the slave. But there wouldn't be a show today—not if he could help it.

He lowered himself over the edge of the platform and dropped onto the roof of the kennels. Crawling to the front, he peered into the pen below. The dogs were pressed against the outer fence, yapping and baying, roused by the shouts spreading through the castle.

"Hey fellows," he said. "It's me."

The dogs stopped barking and turned to look, ears raised.

Bec leapt down into the pen. The dogs gambolled over, ready to play, licking his hands, pawing at his legs.

"Not now, my friends. Not now."

He pushed through the dogs, ruffling their fur.

"Good dog, Apollo. Down, Lupo, down."

He slipped out the gate and dashed across the narrow yard to the stables, where he eased open the door and peered into the long dim space.

No one there.

The horses nickered as they caught his scent. He crept past the stalls, quietly calling out their names.

He opened the shutters at the end and clambered onto the windowsill, gazing at the scummy surface of the moat a few feet below.

The door creaked. Bec spun around.

A figure stood there, black against the sunlit yard. A blade glinted in his hand.

"Don't move," said Malaspina. "Or I'll cut you down."

Bec stared at the man, momentarily paralyzed. Then a horse whinnied and kicked at its stall, and the spell was broken.

He sprang out over the moat, limbs splayed like a frog. There was a huge splash as he landed on his belly in the filthy water. Gasping for breath, he struggled to the other side and hauled himself up.

The forest was only yards away.

CHAPTER 2

The Forest

The shouts from Scarmagno Castle faded into the distance as Bec pushed through the heavy underbrush, ducking branches, stumbling over roots and stones. He stopped to catch his breath, hands on his knees, panting heavily.

His lungs burned and his arms and legs stung, lashed by nettles and thorns. He was soaked to the skin, and coated with a yellowish slime that stank to high heaven. He felt a strange mixture of euphoria and terror. The escape had left him almost drunk with elation, but he knew what would happen if Malaspina caught up with him.

He looked around, trying to work out exactly where he was. He wasn't familiar with this section of the forest. People rarely came up here except in groups—to hunt boars or search for truffles. Some said the place was haunted by ghosts and demons who could snatch your soul.

Don't think about that.

A search party would be setting out soon—and they'd have dogs. Once the animals caught his scent, very little would throw them off. They'd track him up and down rocky streams and through the thickest bush.

His best chance was to head for the mountain that towered behind the castle—away from the valley, away from the river, away from the road. Up through the dense forest that carpeted the lower slopes, until he reached the bare cliff-like screes that capped the summit. It would be a tough climb at the end, clambering over the loose stones and shale. But it would be a lot harder for the dogs, who were skittish on unstable surfaces and afraid of heights. Chances are, they'd balk at following him to the top. Once there, he could work his way south along the chain of mountains that overlooked the valley.

For south was where he had to go, aiming for the port of Ponti, where the Alba river met the Mediterraneo Sea. North of the castle, as far as the river stretched, were the vast territories controlled by various branches of the Malaspina family, of which his master, Adolfo Malaspina, was a minor member. Bec had often travelled north to jockey the castle's horses in local races, and he felt sure a runaway slave would be quickly spotted there. The area to the south was different—or so he'd heard—a sparsely populated land, as wild as any in the Kingdom of Italia. What little influence the Malaspina family had there died out completely at the walls of Ponti. The city was an independent republic, rich beyond imagining, and well known as a haven for wanted men of every description—criminals, deserters, runaway slaves.

Bec had never ventured south along the river more than a mile or two. Everything he knew about the area was gleaned from travellers passing through the castle. The road was said to be dangerous, full of bandits and outlaws, with only occasional towns and villages. People usually moved about in groups, often with guards. He didn't know how far away Ponti was—only that it would take him many days to get there.

Bec grabbed some leaves and did his best to wipe off the scum that clung to his hair and face and arms. He felt like a walking outhouse—an easy mark for the dogs. He'd have to find a stream where he could wash. But that was for later. Now he needed to put as much distance as possible between himself and the castle.

The forest was thick with small oaks and chestnut trees. Bec picked his way upward. He had no real idea where he was going. He relied simply on the fact that the land was steadily rising. In time, he came across an overgrown trail, which wound steeply up through the woods and emerged on a rocky ledge. Far below he could see Scarmagno Castle, perched on its hill above the river. Shouts and the baying of dogs came from the forest by the castle. The search was underway.

Bec hurried onward up the trail, cursing as a stitch seized his side. At the top of a wooded slope, he reached a grassy clearing surrounded by massive chestnut trees, as tall as church towers, their spreading branches intertwined. As he moved into the clearing, the back of his neck prickled.

He stared at the bushes on the other side. The leaves rustled and he caught a whiff of something very foul—a witch's brew of urine and turds.

A dark body shot from the underbrush.

Bec stared as the boar barrelled toward him. He fought the urge to run. A boar could outpace any man—but its eyesight was poor. He waited until the beast was almost on him before skipping out of its path. The boar hurtled past and Bec made a dash for the nearest tree. The animal turned, racing after him. Bec reached the tree first and leapt upward, grabbing hold of a branch as the boar's tusks grazed a dangling leg.

"Damn, damn, damn!" Bec scrambled onto the branch, blood dripping from his left calf. He gazed at the monster below, pawing and slashing at the trunk. It was the granddaddy of all boars—the biggest he'd ever seen.

There were voices in the woods not far away, along with the yaps of a dog. Bec felt a surge of panic. He had to get rid of the boar. He broke off some branches and hurled them down, only to infuriate the beast. Maybe if he moved higher, the boar would lose interest and wander off. Climbing steadily upward, he reached an area thick with leaves. The branch under him sagged alarmingly, and he scrambled to a bigger one. He stretched out along the bough, peering downward.

The boar had turned away and was gazing across the clearing, its nostrils quivering. The bodyguard emerged from the trees, his shaved head glistening with sweat, his hand on the leash of a straining dog. Behind him were several other men, who paused to glance around. They didn't seem to notice the boar, hidden in the waist-high grass. But the dog—Lupo—stood stock-still and stared in its direction.

Nozzo looked across the clearing. "What is it, Lupo?"

The dog gave several sharp barks. The bodyguard signalled to his companions, who drew their swords and waded into the grass.

The boar took off like a bolt, heading straight for the men. Lupo gave a howl and sprang to the side, ripping the leash from the man's hand. The bodyguard shouted when he spotted the beast hurtling toward him. He tried to fend it off, the tusks slashing at his leather boots. The other men struck haphazardly at the animal with their swords, prompting the beast to charge them in turn.

At last, the swords took effect and the boar backed away, giving the men the chance to escape into the forest, followed by the dog. The beast stared after them, then gave a grunt and trotted off in the other direction.

There were shouts from below as the men rejoined the others.

"Nothing up there—just a frigging monster of a boar."

Breathing easier, Bec inspected his calf. The tusk had torn through the skin, but the wound wasn't deep. He pressed it with a leaf until the bleeding stopped, then gently wiped it clean.

Just his luck to run into a boar, and a vicious one at that. But at least the beast had left his scent all over the clearing—a hundred times more powerful than Bec's, enough to throw off any dog.

What to do now? If he climbed down, he'd leave a new

trail for the dogs to follow. Better to wait until dusk, then make a dash for the top of the mountain. He wriggled into the cleft where the bough met the trunk, preparing for a long wait.

A soft noise came from the clearing below. Carefully, carefully, he parted the leaves and looked down. A man with a cane was standing at the foot of the tree, examining the gashes in the bark left by the boar.

CHAPTER 3

The Mountain

Malaspina took off his hat and gazed upward.

Bec held himself completely still.

He can't see me through the leaves. Not unless I move.

The man shifted position, head tilted back, pale eyes ferreting among the branches.

His gaze came to rest on the spot where Bec was hiding. He seemed to be looking directly at him.

Bec was struck with fear.

He knows I'm here.

Malaspina put down his cane and vaulted upward, grabbing the lowest bough in the tree. He swung up and straddled the branch.

Bec stared, not believing what he was seeing.

He can't climb any further. Not with his bad knee.

Malaspina stood up on the branch, steadying himself

against the trunk. He looked above him, once more training his sights on the leafy area where Bec was hiding.

A kind of numbness spread through Bec's body. He gazed in horror as Malaspina worked his way up through the branches, his powerful arms and shoulders dragging him ever closer. Bec could hear the sharp bursts of exertion as he hauled himself from one bough to another. But the man's leg kept giving way under him, prompting rounds of curses. Finally, he came to a halt about fifteen feet below.

Malaspina rubbed his knee and spat to the side, then stared toward the top of the tree.

"I know you're there," he said. "And I'll break every bone in your body when I get my hands on you."

He spat again and started moving back downward, staggering as he made the final drop to the ground. He picked up his cane and limped across the clearing, disappearing into the trees.

He's gone for help.

Bec took several deep breaths, trying to shake off his fear. It had always been this way with Malaspina. The man would come into the stables, shouting about one thing or another, striking out with his cane. And Bec would stand there frozen, powerless to shield himself from the blows.

He heaved a sigh and gazed at the neighbouring tree, a huge chestnut whose boughs were interwoven with his own. His eyes traced a path among the branches, then continued to the next tree and the one beyond that. It was his only hope.

He was several trees away when Malaspina returned, accompanied by a troop of men and dogs. Peering out through the leaves, Bec could see them gathering beneath the tree where he'd been hiding. The dogs milled around, sniffing the ground.

Voices rang out.

"Come on down, you little rat!"

"Don't make us go up there after you."

Silence.

"Is he really in the tree?" Nozzo asked.

"Don't just stand there," Malaspina said. "Climb up and see."

Bec watched as the big man hoisted himself into the tree and continued upward, directed by shouts from below.

"I can't see anyone," Nozzo called.

"Are you sure?"

"Sure as can be. There's nothing here."

Malaspina looked at the dogs, coursing back and forth across the clearing. "Have they picked up his scent?"

The kennel master shook his head. "The boar has spoiled the trail. The whole place stinks."

"All right, we'll keep on searching. He's got to be around here somewhere."

The men left the clearing.

Bec waited for several minutes, then continued along the chain of branches, moving slowly and carefully, stopping from time to time to listen. Eventually the grove of chestnuts came to an end. He slid to the ground and pushed his way through a stretch of small oaks and bushes, heading ever upward.

The sun had dropped behind the mountain when he reached the fringes of the forest. Above him rose the bare stony slopes of the summit, now cloaked in shadow. He kept moving, scrambling and clawing over the loose gravel and shale, acutely aware that he was in the open. Just beneath the peak, he found a small cave, barely more than a dimple in the face of the mountain.

He turned and gazed at the slopes below. There was no sign of the men—and not a sound. They must have returned to the castle for the night. But they'd be out again tomorrow—and for many days after that. Malaspina didn't give up easily.

Bec eased himself down by the mouth of the cave, watching as darkness flowed into the valley and crept up the slopes on the other side of the river. Exhausted, he leaned back and fell asleep.

When he awoke it was already night. He sat up, shivering with cold. The moon had risen—so bright it almost drowned out the stars. What had woken him?

Branches crackled in the patch of thorny bushes below the cave. Then came a weird sound—a low panting, hoarse and irregular—unlike anything Bec had ever heard. He shuddered and made the sign of the cross, thinking of the evil spirits that infested the slopes. He peered into the darkness, barely breathing.

The noises tapered off, then stopped. Whatever it was, it seemed to have moved on. Or maybe it was just hiding there, waiting for him to fall asleep before it pounced. Bec got up and collected several fist-sized rocks, retreating inside the cave. But rocks wouldn't be much help against a demon. He crossed himself repeatedly, resolving not to sleep until the sun came up.

He sat there, chilled to the bone, feeling lonely and miserable. He had no food or money, only a ragged tunic to his name. He thought of his warm burrow in the stable loft where he bedded down at night, while the horses snuffled in the stalls below and the other stable lads farted and made crude jokes.

Bec missed the horses—more than he missed the other boys, who looked down on him as a slave, even though they weren't much better than slaves themselves. He didn't have a single real friend among them, not one who gave a fig about him, not one he could count on when things turned bad. But he could always look to the horses and the dogs for affection and support. They were his truest friends.

All at once, he was overcome with regret—regret that he hadn't kept his mouth shut when Malaspina had provoked him, regret that he hadn't swallowed his rage and bowed his head, instead of lashing out at the man. It hadn't accomplished anything, except to almost get him branded.

Bec caught himself and shook his head fiercely. He was thinking like a slave, like someone who'd had every trace of hope beaten out of him. But he was not a slave—not in his heart, not in his soul. He'd always sworn that one day he'd be free. Now that day had come. Somehow, he'd find a way to get to Ponti, and there he'd be out of Malaspina's reach. He straightened up and squared his shoulders, renewing his resolve to stay awake until dawn.

In minutes, he was fast asleep.

CHAPTER 4

The Town

Sunlight streamed into Bec's face. He groaned and rolled over, every muscle protesting. He felt like he'd been trampled by a team of horses.

He opened his eyes and stared blankly at the walls of the little cave, then squinted at the sun shining through the entrance. Bit by bit, the events of yesterday came back to him, like fragments of a far-fetched story told by a minstrel. Could all these things really have happened?

He got to his feet and hobbled outside to relieve himself. He stood there, gazing down the steep rocky slope at the forest below. The sunlight hadn't yet penetrated the depths of the valley, where Scarmagno Castle lay. But the search party must already be gathering outside the walls.

He turned and looked southward, where the road to Ponti wound through the valley, following the course of the river. Something glittered on a distant mountainside.

He stared at it.

A roof. No, a whole cluster of roofs.

Montecavo, the nearest town to the south.

In the clear morning air, it didn't look that far away. Yet Bec knew better. It would take the entire day to get there.

He rubbed his arms and legs, trying to warm up. Then he set off, following the paths that snaked across the upper slopes of the mountains bordering the valley. The town remained in sight most of the way, growing ever larger, ensconced on a ridge high above the river.

The sun was low in the sky when Bec finally reached the winding track that climbed to the town from the river road below. He crouched in the scrub at the edge of the track, about halfway up. There wasn't a soul in sight, which seemed strange for a place this size.

He studied Montecavo's crumbling walls and towers looming above. They'd clearly seen better days. But at least it was a place to drum up some food—begging or stealing, whatever it took.

He was desperately hungry. All he'd eaten since escaping were a few berries and mushrooms, along with some glistening roots that tasted awful and made him feel sick.

He'd never imagined he could miss the food he ate at the castle—a grey sludge of bread and cabbage, with occasional scraps of gristly meat. Yet he'd found himself dreaming of it last night, as he huddled on the cold ground.

Above him, the track wound up to the town wall, then dog-legged to the left toward a pair of taller towers, half-hidden by the trees. That must be the northern gate. Bec gritted his teeth and tackled the track with fierce determination.

He had just reached the final bend when he spotted the guards. There were two of them, lurking in the shadows by the gate. He scrambled into the bushes beside the track and peered through the branches. One of the guards—a great shambling brute of a man—was propped against the wall, his eyes half-closed. A truncheon dangled from a cord around his wrist, and a sword poked from beneath his cape. The other guard—thin and pale, with a long nose—was hunkered down, gazing vacantly over the valley.

A fine pair, Bec thought. Wolf and Weasel. Bored and looking for victims. Bec had no intention of obliging them. But he didn't have enough time to circle around and find another gate. The day was coming to an end and the town would be locked up soon. He decided to hang about, in case something turned his way. If worse came to worst, he could always bed down in the olive groves below.

The sun dropped behind the mountains, and the countryside sank into a powdery darkness. A breeze came up, stirring the branches in the trees. Bec shivered and tugged up his frayed collar.

A bell in the valley started to toll, slowly and gravely. He peered down the hillside and spotted a church by the crossroads, where the track to the town branched off. The guards came to life. They paced back and forth in front of the gate, scuffing their boots in the dust. They seemed to be waiting for something.

From below came the faint sound of wailing. A light appeared by the church, then another, then a whole mass of them, bobbing and weaving about like fireflies. The lights left the churchyard and climbed the track in a long wavering line, winking and twinkling as they passed behind the branches of the olive trees. The wails grew louder, and a drum struck up a beat, accompanied by ragged blasts of trumpets. As the lights drew closer, Bec could make out a host of people with flaming torches in their hands.

The procession rounded a curve and headed his way. In front was a tall boy with a huge drum slung over his bony frame. He was scowling as he pounded on the drum, his long hair whipping back and forth. Bec grinned despite himself.

The poor fellow couldn't keep a beat to save his life. Behind him were several brown-robed priests, followed by some boys in rumpled tunics, clutching trumpets. Then came a cluster of men bearing something on their shoulders—a long box draped in black cloth.

A coffin. It was a funeral.

The pallbearers shuffled by with the coffin, followed by the mass of mourners, wailing and beating their breasts. Bec watched them move past. The entire town seemed to have turned out for the funeral. At the tail end of the procession was a horde of scruffy kids, jostling and joking among themselves.

This was his chance. Bec scrambled from the bushes and slipped into the unruly mob. As they approached the guards at the gate, the kids quietened down, huddling together. A boy collided with Bec, almost bowling him over.

"Hey, watch it," Bec said.

"Says who?" The boy glared at Bec, a mass of curly hair spilling over his grimy face. On his cheek was a small hooked scar.

"You!" came a hoarse shout.

Bec turned and stared at the guards. Wolf pointed in his direction, then pushed through the crowd, waving his truncheon.

"Thief! Muckworm! Out!"

Bec raised his arms to ward off the blow. But Wolf shoved him aside and nabbed the curly-haired boy by the ear.

"Thought we wouldn't remember you, eh?" Wolf roared.

He gave the boy a boot in the rear, sending him flying down the track.

The horde of kids scampered into town through the gate, and Bec went with them. The guards waved the last few stragglers inside and dragged the heavy gates shut.

Bec found himself at the base of a very steep street that was lined with tall shabby houses, shutting out the last light of day. The torches cast huge shadows on the walls, which flickered and shifted, as the mourners' cries echoed up and down the way.

Bec shuddered. He hated funerals.

The procession came to a halt. Somewhere up front, clouds of incense rose into the still air, and a priest launched into a high-pitched prayer. The crowd fell silent. It was so quiet Bec could hear his stomach rumbling.

Up ahead, he noticed a tall boy carrying a large pack. At his waist was a leather pouch.

Bec eyed the pouch, then sidled up and glanced sideways at the boy. He seemed to be a Tartar, with a gold earring glinting under a wild shock of black hair. Bec waited to see if the boy would notice him, but the Tartar continued to gaze ahead, over the heads of the mourners, as if lost in thought.

Bec reached out and delicately lifted the flap of the boy's pouch, slipping his hand inside.

Hallelujah! A treasure trove.

Scarcely breathing, Bec wrapped his fingers around the coins.

"What the devil ...?" The Tartar spun around and grabbed him by the wrist.

Bec stared into a pair of fierce black eyes. He tried to wrench his arm loose, but the boy's grip was so strong he couldn't break it.

"Give back my money," hissed the Tartar.

Bec kicked him in the shin. The boy gave a yelp, loosening his fingers, and Bec jerked his arm free. He skipped backward, stuffing the coins into his pouch.

He pointed a finger at the Tartar and yelled at the top of his voice. "Thief! Thief! He's a thief!"

"I'm not a thief!" cried the Tartar. "He is!"

"He's lying," Bec shouted. "He tried to rob me!"

People turned and stared—their faces pinched with suspicion.

"You can't fool us," growled a man. "We know your tricks. You're both thieves."

"Thieves! Thieves!" cried another.

"Grab them! Teach them a lesson!"

Wolf and Weasel peered up the street. They were starting to move when a loud banging came at the gates.

"Open up! Let us in, damn you!"

The guards exchanged glances, then returned to unbar the gates.

A man on horseback pushed through, followed by two others.

"There he is—the slave!" shouted Malaspina.

CHAPTER 5

The Convent

"Holy smoke!" Bec turned and raced up the steep street, dodging through the crowd of mourners. The Tartar pounded after him, his huge pack bouncing on his back.

As Bec neared the coffin, he glanced over his shoulder. Malaspina and his men were far behind, their horses mired down in the throng. But the Tartar was still on his tail. He'd have to shake him off, somehow.

Just ahead were the pallbearers, waiting for the priest to finish, their shoulders sagging under the weight of the coffin. Bec threw himself at the nearest man, tackling him about the legs. The pallbearer gave a cry and toppled over, losing his grip on the coffin, which slid backward and hit the ground with a great splintering crash. The lid burst open, and the corpse tumbled out and bumped down the precipitous street, its long white shroud unravelling.

The pallbearers rushed to recover the body, colliding with the Tartar, who stumbled and fell to his knees. Up ahead, the trumpeters were thrown into confusion and milled about, upending a fruit stall, which sent an avalanche of apricots and cherries bouncing down the road. Some urchins swarmed after the fruit, diving between the legs of the mourners and wrestling for the best prizes.

Bec scooped up a pair of apricots and stuffed them in his pouch. He spotted an alleyway where a beggar sat huddled on a mat. He leapt over the beggar and slipped inside.

The alley was pitch dark, running upward between tall windowless walls. The place reeked of cat pee and rotting garbage. Bec climbed up the slope, his hands pressed against the rough stone, his bare feet treading on nameless slimy things. All he could see was a thin slice of night sky above. The alleyway rose sharply for a distance, then levelled off. Something black loomed ahead. Bec reached out and touched a low archway that bridged the alley. Groping under the arch, he emerged into a flood of unearthly light.

He was on the edge of a small square that hung over the valley like a balcony. A full moon was rising above the mountains on the other side—glowing like a huge copper plate. Behind him came the hubbub of the main street.

"He's somewhere up ahead!" shouted a voice.

"No," cried another. "He must have gone back down."

Bec looked frantically around the square, whose sides were lined with high walls and buildings. There didn't seem to be any exit. At the far end was a low parapet, with the valley yawning beyond. He dashed over, hoping to find a pathway down. But the parapet bordered on a cliff that dropped to a maze of ruins far below.

More shouts from the main street. Bec turned and gazed at the massive building on his left, where a staircase led up to a porch sunk in darkness, sheltered by a low roof. It was the only place to hide.

He vaulted up the steps to the porch and crouched in a corner by the door. As he watched, a misshapen form emerged from the alley—a towering figure with a swollen head. He squinted at this strange creature, then let out a breath.

The Tartar with his immense pack.

The boy stood there, gazing around the square. He moved over to the parapet and looked down into the valley. Turning around, he stared at the porch where Bec was hiding.

Bec huddled in the corner, making himself as small as possible. The Tartar crossed the square and stood at the foot of the stairs.

"Filthy thief," he said. "I want my money."

Bec rose slowly to his feet.

The Tartar climbed the stairs, peering warily into the darkness.

"There you are!" He lunged at Bec, grabbing his tunic at the throat. Bec thrust his knee sharply upward. There was a groan and the hands let go. Bec lost his balance and fell back against the door, which swung ponderously open. He toppled onto the floor of a shadowy hall, where an oil lamp flickered at the foot of a staircase.

The Tartar shed his pack and flew after Bec, grappling him around the waist. Bec rolled over, trying to shake his attacker loose. But the Tartar's arms were like iron clamps. The two boys tumbled across the floor into the middle of the hall. There was a clatter as the coins in Bec's pouch spilled onto the floor. Bec paused and the Tartar seized the opportunity to pin him down, knee pressed against his chest.

"Give up!" The boy brandished a fist above Bec's nose.

"Take your bloody money," Bec panted. "It's on the floor."

The Tartar glanced around, then released Bec and started picking up the coins.

Voices came from the square outside.

Bec stared at the door, which had swung shut. He crept over and opened it a crack, peering out.

Malaspina and his two men were standing at the head of the alley, their swords glistening in the moonlight.

Bec closed the door and slid the bolt into place, locking it.

The Tartar continued to gather the coins, checking them one by one. Bec gazed at him, not saying a word.

"There's some missing," the boy said.

"Wha ... what?"

"My money. It's not all here. Fork it over."

Bec scowled and dug into his pouch. He fished out the remaining coins and handed them to the Tartar.

Heavy boots tramped up the steps outside. Steel rang on stone as swords poked about the porch.

"There's nothing here," said a voice. Nozzo, the bodyguard.

"Moron! I can see as well as you," said Malaspina.

The door shook as someone tried to force it open.

"Locked tight," Nozzo said.

Silence.

"Maybe the slave didn't come up this way after all." The voice of Pietro, the steward.

"But the beggar swore he saw him—him and the Tartar," said Nozzo. "They ran up here, one after the other."

"We'd better go back and check," Malaspina said.

There was the sound of retreating footsteps.

The two boys stared at each other in the dimly lit hall. The Tartar was nearly a head taller than Bec, with broad shoulders and long bony limbs. There was a stillness about him—like a creature of the forest.

"Who are those people?" the Tartar asked.

"Just some men that are after me."

"Why? Did you steal something?"

"No, I'm not a thief."

The boy's eyebrows lifted.

"I only took your money because I'm starving," Bec said. "That doesn't make me a thief."

"What does it make you then?"

"Desperate."

The Tartar's mouth curved slightly. "You're a knucklehead, that's what. Calling me a thief in that mob. You could have got me lynched."

"You and me both." Bec shrugged. "So, maybe it wasn't the smartest move."

"You're also a lousy pickpocket. You need some lessons."

"And you could teach me?"

"If I had the time."

The Tartar paused, looking Bec over. "You're a slave, aren't you? That's what the men said."

"They can say what they like. I'm on my way to freedom."

"Brave words. But you haven't told me yet who they are."

"My master and two of his bully-boys."

The Tartar tilted his head to one side. "What'll happen if they catch you?"

"Don't worry, they won't."

"Supposing."

"Well, they'll brand me for sure, and then ..."

"What?"

"Slit my nostrils, clip my ears. Either way, the girls won't like me as much."

"As much?"

"But they'd still like me."

The Tartar gave a guttural laugh. "You've got a mouth on you, *amico*. I hope you've got the wits to match."

He reached into his pouch and tossed Bec a coin. "Here's for your trouble."

Bec grinned and nodded his thanks. "What about the lessons?"

"Some other time." The Tartar heaved up his bag, adjusting the straps. "Well, I'll be on my way."

He was at the door when a voice came from outside.

"They must be in here," said Malaspina. "There's nowhere else to hide."

"But the beggar said it's a convent."

"So what?"

A fist hammered on the door.

Bec glanced at the Tartar, who put a finger to his lips.

The pounding continued. "Open up!"

From the rear of the convent came a clatter.

"Someone's on their way," Bec hissed.

He darted to the staircase. Partway up, he paused to look back.

The Tartar was still there, gazing at the front door. His eyes moved to Bec.

"Don't give me away," Bec whispered.

The boy gave him a scornful look. "What do you think I am?"

He let out a low oath and vaulted up the staircase after Bec.

CHAPTER 6
The Abbess

As Bec reached the top of the stairs, a door opened at the back of the hall below. A young nun hurried out, lamp in hand. She headed for the front door, which was shaking from the blows.

"All right, all right," called the nun in a singsong voice. "No need to break it down."

"This way," whispered Bec.

They crept down a long corridor with doors on either side and a shuttered window at the end. Moonlight poured through the slats, casting a barred pattern on the floor. Bec eased the shutters open and gazed out. The Tartar pressed in beside him.

The window overlooked the valley, with the mountains beyond. The moon had turned silver as it rose in the sky, bathing the scene in a clear, cool light. Bec leaned out as far as he dared, looking for a way to get down. But the wall was constructed of smooth stone blocks, which merged directly into the cliff below.

"Not a chance," Bec said.

The Tartar grunted his agreement.

They turned and gazed at the doors along the hallway.

Voices came up the staircase. Malaspina was insisting he had the right to search the convent. The young nun protested, her voice turning shrill.

Bec crept over to the nearest door and tried to open it. But it didn't budge.

More words from the staircase.

"These fellows are dangerous, Sister. Take it from me."

"Well ... we'll see what the Abbess has to say."

Bec skipped to the opposite door and threw his weight against it. It flew open without resistance, and he burst into a shadowy room. A tiny ancient nun was perched at a desk piled high with books that overflowed onto the floor. The nun was studying a chessboard in a space cleared between the books. She looked up as Bec tumbled inside. The Tartar followed, shutting the door behind him.

A small white dog trotted over to Bec, sniffing and wagging his tail. Bec extended the back of his hand, then scratched him behind the ears. The nun watched this in silence, moving aside the lamp on her desk to see better. She seemed quite unruffled. Her gaze shifted to the Tartar, lingered for a moment, then returned to Bec.

"And to what do I owe the honour of this visit?" she asked.

Bec gazed at her face and decided to take a gamble. "Mother, you've ... you've got to help us. I'm ... I'm a slave. I'm on the run."

"A slave? Good heavens! Where from?"

"Castello Scarmagno."

The tiny nun frowned. "That's Adolfo Malaspina's place."

"You know him?"

"Only by reputation, and that's quite enough."

There was a soft knocking at the door. The dog scurried over, barking sharply.

"Hannibal! Stop that!" The nun looked inquiringly at Bec.

"It's Malaspina," whispered Bec. "He's here searching for me."

The nun paused for an instant, then pointed to a low closet in the corner.

"You'd better hide in there—both of you. We'll sort this out later."

More knocking, this time louder.

The Tartar ran to the closet and crawled inside, pack and all. Bec squeezed in after him and tried to shut the door, but it refused to close completely.

The little white dog bounded over and stuck his nose in, nibbling at Bec's toes.

"No, no, Hannibal," said the old nun. "Leave them alone."

But the dog kept gnawing at Bec's feet as the knocks became more insistent.

Bec scooped up the dog and bundled him inside. He dragged the door shut as far as it would go.

The nun called: "Come in."

Through the gap, Bec saw the young nun enter the room while Malaspina and his men hovered in the doorway.

"Forgive me, Abbess," the nun said. "I'm so sorry to disturb you. Some men want to search the convent. Adolfo Malaspina and two others. They say a slave boy is hiding here—and a Tartar, too." She rolled her eyes. "I told them it was impossible, but they insisted."

"A search of the convent?" exclaimed the Abbess. "What an extraordinary idea!" She shook her head. "Definitely not, Sister Angelica. There'll be no such thing."

"Thank you, Mother. That's exactly what I said." Sister Angelica turned to leave.

"Not so fast!" Malaspina shouldered her aside and went over to the desk, where he rapped his cane on the surface, knocking over the chess pieces. "Don't think you can brush me off. I know they're here."

The Abbess gave him a cold stare. "My good man, how can you be so certain?"

"Some people saw them—the blond slave and the Tartar. They ran into the square outside. We've searched it, inch by inch, but we can't find them. They must have come in here. There's no other place to hide."

"That's all very interesting, I'm sure," said the Abbess. "But did anyone actually see them enter the convent?"

"Not exactly."

"So, you merely *suppose* they're here?"

"Any fool can see that must be true."

"Fools suppose all sorts of things," said the Abbess.

"Are you calling me a fool?"

"Dear man, it was you who brought up fools, not me."

"You can play with words all you like," said Malaspina. "But you can't stop me from searching this place. It's my right. The slave belongs to me."

"But this place does not belong to you. It belongs to God."

"The Devil take you!"

54

The Abbess gave a quiet laugh. "By God or the Devil, you will not search this place."

Pietro, the steward, took off his hat and stepped through the doorway. "It's not really a search, Mother. Just a quick look."

"And what, pray tell, will this *quick look* include? The nuns' private cells? The chapel? What about the pilgrim quarters, the refectory, the kitchen, the storehouse, the garden?" The Abbess let out a snort. "Oh, no! This foolishness has gone on long enough." She turned to Sister Angelica. "Kindly show these gentlemen out."

The young nun gave Malaspina a meaningful look.

The man scowled back at her, standing his ground. "You won't get rid of me so easily."

Bec's leg began to cramp up. He slid back to stretch it out, bumping into the Tartar, who shifted to the rear of the closet. The floorboards under him sagged, then gave way with a crash.

The Tartar fell backward into the hole and disappeared.

"What's that?" said Malaspina, staring at the closet.

"Must be my dog," said the Abbess. "He likes to root around for rats."

"Rats, eh? Let me check."

Sister Angelica reached out to stop him, but Malaspina was already at the closet. He stooped to open the door.

Hannibal squirmed from Bec's grasp and shot out through the gap, barking furiously. He sprang into the air and sank his teeth into Malaspina's arm.

The man jumped back. "God Almighty!"

He tried to shake Hannibal off, but the little dog hung on, stubby legs beating the air. Malaspina staggered about, jerking his arm, shouting curses.

Still Hannibal kept his grip.

Malaspina looked at the Abbess. "Call off your dog!"

"I warned you," the tiny nun snapped, "but you wouldn't listen." Then in a softer tone: "Enough, Hannibal. Let him go!"

At the nun's words, the dog released the man's arm and dropped to the floor. He pranced around Malaspina, letting out a torrent of piercing barks.

The man aimed a kick at Hannibal and caught him on the flank. The dog skittered across the room, yelping in pain.

The Abbess jumped to her feet. "Get out of here! Immediately!"

Malaspina shot her a poisonous look, then left the room, pushing Pietro ahead of him. There were bangs from the hallway outside, as if doors were being thrown open and closed.

The Abbess exchanged a look with the young nun. "We'd better make sure they actually leave."

She picked up the little dog, and the two nuns went into the hallway.

Bec turned and peered into the hole where the Tartar had disappeared. Dust billowed up, working into his eyes. He caught a glimpse of a dark floor somewhere below.

There was no sign of the Tartar.

Malaspina's voice came from the hall. "I'll look wherever I damn well please."

There was a sharp reply from the Abbess, then another bang.

Bec stared into the hole, repelled by the darkness. But the thought of Malaspina returning was far worse. He rolled onto his stomach and eased his legs over the edge, trying not to scratch himself on the jagged boards. He rested his weight on his forearms and let his feet dangle down. They didn't touch the ground.

How deep could the hole be?

He slid further down, little by little, until he was hanging from his fingers.

Still, he couldn't feel the bottom.

He closed his eyes and let go.

CHAPTER 7

The Tunnel

Bec's feet hit the ground with a bone-jarring crash. He looked up and realized he'd only dropped about a foot. But he'd expected a longer fall and his body was taken by surprise.

He stood there for a moment, shaking out his legs. Faint outlines emerged as his eyes adapted to the darkness. He found himself at the end of an old tunnel with rough stone walls. The passage extended some twenty feet, then turned a corner toward what seemed to be a source of light.

The Tartar was nowhere to be seen.

There was a chorus of squeaks and rustles—rats scurrying for cover. Bec shivered. He hated rats. The stables at the castle had been full of them.

He took a deep breath and started down the tunnel. Rounding the corner, he entered a gallery where milky moonlight seeped through a series of narrow openings along one side. Through the slits, he could see a line of mountains, black against the moon-washed sky.

The Tartar was at the end of the gallery, gazing through an archway.

He turned as Bec came up behind him.

"Are you okay?" Bec asked.

"Yeah, I'm all right." The boy grimaced and rubbed his rear end. "Do you often get into messes like this?"

"More than I'd like to. But this is worse than usual."

The Tartar glanced back along the gallery. "Is anyone coming after us?"

"I'm not sure. Malaspina's still skulking around."

"We need to keep going," said the Tartar. "With luck, this stairway will take us outside."

He stepped through the archway onto a landing, where a circular staircase descended from above and continued into darkness below.

Bec followed him onto the landing and looked down the stairs, wrinkling his nose.

"Something smells bad," he said.

"It's just damp and mouldy, that's all."

"No, no. It's something else."

"Sure it's not yourself you're smelling?"

Bec laughed. "You're not exactly a bunch of roses, either."

He peered down the stairs and shook his head. "I don't think we should go down there. It's pretty spooky."

"What's the matter? Are you afraid of the dark?"

"It's not the dark," Bec said. "It's what's in the dark. Ghosts, devils, ghouls …"

"I don't believe in ghosts."

"Well, bully for you. But that doesn't make them go away."

"What else can we do?" asked the Tartar.

Bec took a look at the stairs going up. They were just as dark. He gave a sigh and brushed some cobwebs from his hair. "Okay, tough guy, lead on. But don't say I didn't warn you."

The Tartar started moving slowly down the stairs. Bec followed, one hand on the wall, which was damp and slimy. The only light came from occasional slits that showed bits of starry sky. The steps were worn smooth and strewn with rubble. Several times Bec slipped and almost fell.

After a while, the slits came to an end. The darkness was complete, as thick and stifling as a blanket. The foul odour was getting stronger. Fragments of debris crunched beneath Bec's feet and skittered into the blackness below.

He gave a shiver. "Let's go back."

"We've come this far. We might as well keep going."

"All the way to hell."

"So, what's the problem? You'll feel right at home."

"Speak for yourself."

Something tickled Bec's cheek. "A breeze. Can you feel it? We must be getting close to the bottom."

The breeze picked up and the air turned cooler. The wall on the left side disappeared, leaving Bec's hand groping into empty space. The stairway stopped circling around and ran straight down.

The Tartar came to a sudden halt, and Bec bumped into him.

"What's going on?" he asked.

"Quiet."

Bec listened intently. At first, he could only hear the Tartar's breathing. Then he noticed something—the sound of trickling water. It echoed slightly, as if bouncing off unseen walls.

"Seems like we've come into the cellar," the Tartar said.

"It's a dungeon," Bec said. "I swear people have died down here."

"Just your imagination."

The boy started moving again, with Bec close behind him, hands resting on his pack.

Suddenly, the Tartar gave a shout and pitched forward.

Bec tried to grab him, but he slipped away into the darkness.

Bec stood there, aghast.

There was a moment of silence.

Then something clutched at his leg.

CHAPTER 8

The Rooftop

Bec gave a screech, trying to kick the ghoul away.

"Hold on," shouted the Tartar. "It's me!"

"Where are you?"

"Just down here. Give me a hand, will you? I'm barely hanging on."

Bec groped around and found the boy, who seemed to be dangling over the edge of the stairs. He helped him crawl back up.

"The staircase has collapsed," the Tartar said. "I nearly went all the way down."

"This place is a death trap!" Bec said. "Let's get out of here."

They climbed upward, soon reaching a slit in the wall where the moonlight poured through—incredibly bright after the darkness below. Moving faster, they came to the gallery.

The Tartar peered down the passage, which was quiet

and empty. "What do you think? Should we go back to the nun's room?"

"Too risky," said Bec. "Malaspina could still be around. Let's climb further up and see what's there."

They followed the staircase as it wound upward, emerging in a small round chamber with a high pointed roof. On one side was a door, topped by a tiny window.

"Looks like we're in some kind of tower," the Tartar said. "Should I try the door?"

"Just go easy. We don't know what's on the other side."

The Tartar drew the bolt and pushed the door open a few inches.

A cool breeze wafted through the gap. But not a sound.

The Tartar opened the door a little more, enough to squeeze through, then motioned for Bec to follow.

They were on the top of the sloping convent roof, high above the town. Spread out beneath them was a shadowy jumble of towers and gables, turrets and chimneys—all sleeping in the moonlight.

Voices came from the square in front of the convent. The two boys scrambled behind the ridge of the roof and peered over.

Malaspina and his men were standing there, talking in

low tones. After a while, Malaspina left the others and limped over to the parapet, where he stared down into the valley.

"That's your master?" whispered the Tartar.

Bec nodded.

"What's the matter with his leg?"

"It's the knee. He had a jousting accident when he was young, and it never healed right. Seems like he was quite the athlete in his day."

"And who's the big fellow?"

"His bodyguard—Nozzo. All-round flunky and fart-catcher. The closest thing to a friend he has."

"And the older man?"

"Pietro—the castle steward. No great love for Malaspina. But he does what he's told."

Malaspina turned and surveyed the square once more. His gaze shifted to the convent and flicked upward—first to the porch, then to the roof. The two boys ducked as his eyes swept along the ridge. When they looked again, the men were disappearing into the alley.

"Did he spot us?" asked the Tartar.

"Don't think so. He would have said something."

"Well, at least they're gone." The boy dropped his pack and sat down.

Bec remembered the apricots in his pouch and retrieved them.

"Want one?" he asked. "I picked these up at the funeral."

"You seem to have a talent for that."

"And why not?" Bec said. "They were right in my path. A gift from heaven. Look, do you want one or not?"

"Sure. Pass it over."

Bec weighed the apricots in his hands and tossed the bigger one to the Tartar. He polished the other fruit on his tunic and took a bite.

"Mmm ... sweet!" he said, dabbing at the juice trickling down his chin. "I'd have grabbed a few more, but I was in a rush. Mother of all the saints, weren't those people worked up, running around and squawking like a bunch of chickens."

"No wonder, after you knocked over the coffin. Did you do that on purpose?"

"Let's just say it was an inspiration."

"Like stealing my money."

"Exactly. Sometimes it works out, sometimes it doesn't."

Bec finished his apricot, sucking on the pit before throwing it away.

The Tartar glanced at him. "What's your name, by the way?"

"Albec. But everyone calls me Bec. And you?"

"Tien Nu."

"*Tien Nu.* Is that how you say it?"

"Close enough."

Bec eyed the Tartar's pack. "What are you, anyway? Some kind of peddler?"

"Not really. I'm a juggler, tumbler, conjuror, wrestler, boxer—what have you. All-round entertainer."

"Boxer. So that explains the hands."

"What? Oh, these." Tien Nu clenched his fist, displaying a row of giant knuckles.

Bec stared at them, then glanced at his own hands. "How do you get them like that?"

"Try punching trees a hundred times a day."

Bec laughed. "Not for me! So, what brings a primo juggler to an armpit of a town like this?"

Tien Nu gazed at the rooftops spread out below. "Actually, this isn't so bad. You should see some of the places we've stayed—me and my father." He paused. "Only now, it's just me. My father died last month. He ... we had an accident."

"I'm sorry." Bec tried to find something to say. "It must be hard losing your father."

Tien Nu shrugged. "I'm getting used to it."

There was a silence.

"What about you?" said the Tartar. "How did you come to be a slave?"

"Simple. My mother was a slave. But she was born free, in a place called Circassia. It's somewhere to the east—on the Mar Nero."

"The Mar Nero." Tien Nu mulled this over. "That's a long way off. How did your mother end up here?"

"Some slavers raided her village when she was young. She was taken with my grandmother to the market at Genoa. And that's where the Malaspina family bought them. My mother and *nonna* were servants in the castle."

"Are they still there?"

Bec shook his head. "My mother died when I was born. She was just sixteen. *Nonna* brought me up. But she passed away while I was still a kid. I hardly remember her."

"That's too bad," Tien Nu said. "What about your father? Is he still around?"

"No—at least, I don't think so." Bec chewed his lower lip. "You see, my mother wasn't married. And she never told anyone who my father was—not even *Nonna*."

"So, you don't have any idea?"

"Not really, except ..."

Bec picked up a bit of broken tile and pressed his thumb against the sharp edge.

"There was a slave who escaped not long before I was born. *Fiaccola*. That's what they called him. A real firebrand, always stirring things up. I think he may be my father."

Bec made a face. "Whoever he is, he sure doesn't care much about me."

They sat there, gazing at the dark mountains.

"So, where are you headed now?" Tien Nu asked.

"Down the river to Ponti. It's a free city, so I'll be safe there. And after that, well ... the world's a big place. How about you?"

Tien Nu ran a hand through his hair. "Actually, I was planning to stay here for a while—rest up, make some money. But now, I'll have to move on."

"So, why not come with me to Ponti? We can keep each other company."

Tien Nu gazed at Bec through hooded eyes, not saying anything.

Bec laughed. "I know, I know, I'm a walking disaster."

"More like a one-man plague."

"I admit it! But my luck is bound to change."

Bec clapped Tien Nu on the shoulder. "Think it over, brother. Rats like us—we'd make a great team."

CHAPTER 9

The Church

Bec stood up and stretched, looking around.

"The only question is how to get off this roof."

The answer wasn't very obvious. The convent stood on its own, with the cliff at one end and a garden at the other, the square in front and an alley in back, where a wing of the convent projected. It was a long drop to the ground—even to the porch in front—and the walls were too smooth to climb down.

"Over there," said Tien Nu.

He pointed across the alley to a church, whose roof was slightly lower than the convent's. In the corner was a tower, with bells showing through the arches.

"People need to reach those bells," Tien Nu said. "There must be a stairway or a ladder inside the tower."

Bec looked at the church, then at the gap between it

and the convent—about fifteen feet across. It wouldn't be a big jump by his standards. But his sense of mischief got the better of him.

He screwed up his face. "How do we get over there?"

"Jump. It's not far."

"I don't know if I can make it."

"Sure you can. It's easy."

"If you say so."

"Come on," Tien Nu said. "I'll show you."

He picked up his pack and tucked in the straps.

"I need to heave this across first. Can you grab the other side? That's it. Gently, gently. We don't want to break anything. On the count of three. One, two ..."

The pack went sailing across the alley and skidded onto the church roof.

"Now, watch." Tien Nu stepped back several paces and stood there, eyes fixed on the church. For a moment, he seemed to hesitate, frozen in place. Then, with a shake of the head, he took a short run and a flying leap, his arms thrusting powerfully forward. He arced through the air and landed neatly on the other side.

Bec stared across the gap. "It looks easy when you do it."

"Believe me, you won't have any problem."

Bec drew a breath and backed up a good dozen paces. He dropped into a half-crouch, then raced along the ridge of the roof and lifted off, going higher and higher.

He tucked in his legs and did a complete flip in the air. His feet found the roof of the church, where he finished with a fluid roll.

He jumped up and launched into a jig, one fist pumping the air. "How was that?"

Tien Nu gave a slow smile. "Not bad."

"Not bad! What do you mean, *not bad*. It was fantastic, unique, a jump for the ages!"

"You were pulling my leg, *amico*. You've done things like this before."

Bec grinned. "A bit, here and there. When tumblers came to the castle, I'd get them to teach me a trick or two. Then I'd practise on my own."

Tien Nu gazed at him for a moment, eyes flickering.

Then he turned. "Come on, monkey-boy. We're not there yet."

He went to the foot of the tower, where he reached up and grabbed a pillar, swinging himself into the belfry. He extended a hand and helped Bec scramble up after him.

They peered around the cramped space. There were

several bells on rockers, with ropes running through holes in the floor. And there, in the opposite corner, was what they were looking for—a small door.

Bec threaded his way through the bells.

"Watch your step," he said. "We don't want to wake up the whole town."

"Yes, granny."

Bec tried the door, which opened easily on well-oiled hinges. A ladder descended into a dark shaft. At the bottom was a faint glow.

Bec gazed down the shaft and gave a shiver. "You first."

Tien Nu looked at him.

"It's the darkness," Bec said. "It always gets to me."

Tien Nu tested the first few rungs in the ladder, then started climbing down. He waited for Bec at the bottom, where they stooped to pass under an arch.

They were in a long narrow gallery that overlooked the main altar of the church, where a raft of candles sent ripples of light shivering across the floor.

Beneath them, kneeling before the altar, was a gigantic man wearing a long black cape. A hood hung over his face, hiding it. On the ground beside him glimmered a huge sword.

CHAPTER 10

The Knight

Bec dropped behind the wooden railing, tugging Tien Nu down with him. He peered through the uprights at the altar below, then nudged the Tartar.

"He's a knight," he whispered. "See the sword."

There was a strange sound—a deep groan or sob. The Knight threw himself onto the floor, his broad shoulders heaving. A startled dove rose from its perch on a column and fluttered across the church.

The man lay there, face down, his massive body fully extended. He remained motionless as the minutes passed.

Bec pointed toward an archway at the end of the gallery. Tien Nu nodded and followed him down a stairway to a small chapel on the ground floor. Bec tiptoed to the chapel entrance and peered into the main body of the church. Twenty paces away was the Knight, still prone on the ground.

Bec darted out, heading for the side door of the church. As he passed the altar, he tripped on the cracked pavement and fell to the ground with a thud.

The Knight raised his head, then grasped his sword and pushed himself to his feet. He pulled back his hood, revealing a weathered face and deep-set eyes. A scar ran across his left cheek, vanishing into an unkempt beard.

The Knight held the sword lightly, as if it were made of straw. He turned around, staring into the darkness, his cape swirling about his legs. He looked in Bec's direction, then moved on, straining to see beyond the pool of light around the altar.

Bec wormed backward toward the chapel where Tien Nu was hiding. A loose bit of paving hopped across the ground.

The Knight swung about, squinting into the gloom.

"Who's there?"

Silence.

"Show yourself, or I'll kill you like a rat."

The huge man moved beyond the circle of light. His sword swept from side to side, hissing through the air.

Bec kept his head down. Another few paces and the Knight would trip over him.

Tien Nu stepped from the chapel, hands spread wide.

"We're sorry to disturb you, milord. My friend here tripped."

He came up to Bec and kicked him in the side.

Bec yelped and scrambled to his feet.

The Knight stared at them, eyes moving back and forth. Then he let out a sigh and lowered his sword.

"But you're just a couple of boys."

Bec drew himself up. "I'm not a boy. I'm ... I'm sixteen and as good a man as any."

The Knight eyed him, mouth curling slightly.

"Well now, sixteen. Pretty big. And a mouth to match, it seems. What's your name?"

"Bec."

"Well, Bec Good-As-A-Man, what brings you to church at this hour? You don't look much like the pious type."

"I'm ... well ..."

"We're just passing through," said Tien Nu. "Looking for a place to sleep."

"Travellers," said Bec. "Jugglers and tumblers."

"Are you now?" The Knight slowly shook his head.

"You!" He poked his chin at Tien Nu. "You're a traveller, all right. From the East if I'm not mistaken—China, Siria, Persia, thereabouts. But not you." He fixed his sights on Bec. "Your accent gives you away. You're a local boy—from somewhere up the valley. What brings you down this way?"

Bec hesitated, glancing at Tien Nu.

"Don't worry," said the Knight. "I won't give you away."

"I'm ..." Bec took a deep breath. "... The truth is, I'm a slave."

The Knight nodded. "As I thought."

"But in name only," said Bec. "In my heart, I'm free."

"We're all free in the eyes of God. But in the eyes of man ..." The Knight shrugged. "Who is your master?"

"Adolfo Malaspina."

The Knight's face went still. "He must be searching for you."

"He's already here in town. But he won't catch me. I'm on my way to Ponti."

The Knight stood there, swaying slightly. Then he made his way to a bench by the altar, where he eased himself down.

He motioned the boys over. "Let me see you more clearly."

Bec and Tien Nu moved forward.

"Closer still," he said, waving an enormous hand. "I'm not going to bite."

The Knight's eyes were bloodshot and underscored with dark circles. He stank of wine and sweat. For a long time, he scanned their faces in the dim light, stroking his beard. Bec noticed that the little finger on his right hand was missing.

"This is a strange coincidence," the Knight said at last. "I'm headed for Ponti myself, then onward to Roma and the Terra Santa. Escorting some pilgrims."

There was a silence.

Bec piped up. "If you need any servants, milord, we could travel with you. We're hardworking and reliable and ... and ... we can do all sorts of things."

"Is that so? Well, now ..." The Knight paused to think. "Can you, by any chance, play chess?"

"Chess," said Bec, somewhat startled. "No, milord."

"I can," Tien Nu said. "But not very well."

"Not very well. What does that mean?"

"I always lose."

"No shame in that. It's trying that matters."

"So, can we go with you?" Bec asked.

The Knight lowered his eyes, seeming to turn the matter over.

Bec winked at Tien Nu, and they waited while the guttering candles made the shadows dance. There was a strong scent of melting wax.

"No, I'm sorry," the Knight said abruptly, heaving himself to his feet. "I don't need any servants. You'll have to find your own way to Ponti. Now, if you'll excuse me ..."

He turned his back and resumed his place, kneeling at the altar, sword at his side.

Bec and Tien Nu stood there, staring at him.

He had shut them out completely.

"Let's go," the Tartar whispered. "He's not going to change his mind."

They crept to the side door and left the church.

A shallow flight of steps led into a walled cloister. There was the quiet splash of a fountain and the scent of herbs. At the far end of the cloister was an iron gate.

"Over there," whispered Bec.

They went to the gate and opened it, slipping through.

They were at the top of a hill that dropped sharply into the valley, forming a natural bowl. Clinging to the sides were the ruins of an ancient arena, glowing in the moonlight like the half-buried ribs of a gigantic dragon. Row upon row of mouldering stone benches descended to a sandy space at the bottom, which was backed by a tier of broken columns. Nestled among the columns was what looked like a small shrine.

They picked their way down through the arena to the shrine, where they paused to gaze at the carving of a tall saint with a child on his shoulder. A bunch of wilted flowers lay at the foot of the statue.

"It's San Cristoforo," said Bec.

He knelt down to pray, while Tien Nu gazed silently on. Then they pushed into the bushes surrounding the hollow, where they found a small grassy clearing.

"Let's sleep here," Tien Nu said. "It should be safe."

Bec nodded. "San Cristoforo will protect us."

"That statue?"

"The statue plus the saint, dummy."

"I have my own saint," Tien Nu said. "And I don't need a statue of him to protect me."

"Which saint is that?"

"*Zhen Wu*, the god of martial arts."

"Never heard of him."

"There's a lot you've got to learn."

Bec grinned. "Like how to pick a pocket."

"That, too."

Tien Nu dropped his pack and pulled out a cape.

Bec stood there, arms wrapped around his body.

The Tartar eyed him. "You can't go to sleep like that. You'll freeze to death."

He rummaged around in his pack and retrieved another cape. "Take this, *amico*. It belonged to my father."

"Thanks, brother," Bec said. "Just for the night."

He spread the big cape out on the ground and rolled up inside. It felt warm and comfortable.

"You look like a sausage," Tien Nu said.

Bec laughed. "I wish I were one. I'd munch on my fingers."

CHAPTER 11
The Accident

Tien Nu sat there, cape draped over his shoulders. He gazed at the blurry outline of Bec's body, listening to his steady breathing.

It was almost like being back with his father.

Ever since Tien Nu could remember, his father had been a big part of his life—energetic, exasperating, impossible to ignore—prodding him to get up in the morning, swearing in half a dozen different languages, cracking bad jokes, coaxing him to learn new tricks, conjuring meals out of nothing, telling improbable stories around the fire at night.

And then his father was gone. As if he had never existed. Tien Nu still couldn't quite believe it. He kept expecting his father to reappear—to step back into his life with a chuckle and a curse, as if nothing had happened.

"What's up, Tien Nu? You look like you've seen a ghost."

But there was no father, and no ghost. Nothing.

Tien Nu lay down and closed his eyes, trying to sleep. But strange images kept tumbling through his head, chasing after one another like feral cats.

And then, before he knew it, the terrible memory was back. He was standing at the end of the tightrope that stretched across the courtyard, gallery to gallery. Torches were blazing in the crowded yard below, the smell of burning pitch in his nostrils. They had already crossed the tightrope several times, juggling balls, tossing batons back and forth.

Now came the climax.

His father was stationed at the midpoint of the rope, back turned, slightly crouched. Tien Nu signalled to the drummer below, who started a low roll. The crowd grew silent, with all eyes turned upward. Tien Nu raised a hand, gave a dramatic shout, and danced out along the rope. He propped a foot on his father's calf and sprang onto his shoulders, toes curling into the slabs of muscle about the neck. His father steadied himself and straightened up, as Tien Nu widened his arms in triumph.

Cheers erupted from the spectators in the courtyard. His father began moving along the tightrope to the other side.

There was a sudden burst of noise, like a clap of thunder, then ...

Then ... nothing.

No sound, no colour, no shape, no movement. A sleep without dreams. A sleep that went on and on.

Much later, he became aware of vague noises—flutters, hums, whispers.

When Tien Nu awoke, he was lying in the infirmary of a pilgrim hostel. There had been an accident, said the nuns. A fall from the tightrope.

His father was dead.

Nobody at the hostel had actually seen the accident, and no one could tell him what had happened. And Tien Nu couldn't remember himself, no matter how hard he tried.

He was sure of only one thing. It must have been his fault.

A week passed before Tien Nu was well enough to visit his father's grave—an ugly slash of earth in a potter's field, where coarse blades of grass were already sprouting. Tien Nu had thrown himself onto the grave, burying his hands in the soil.

"I'm sorry, Papa ..."

The memory was so painful that Tien Nu sat upright and shook his head, trying to chase it away. It didn't serve any purpose. It wouldn't bring his father back. Tears sprang to his eyes. He tried to stave them off, but they kept coming. Worse still, groans welled up in his throat.

Tien Nu got to his feet and pushed blindly into the bushes, arms raised to fend off the branches. A steep path appeared from nowhere. He stumbled up the path until his sobs broke out in a great convulsive rush, driving him to the ground. He lay there, eyes shut, fists clenched.

It was the first time he had cried since his father's death.

Eventually the storm passed, and Tien Nu pushed himself up, wiping his arm across his face. The path had taken him up a slope that led away from the arena. In front, the cliff rose into the night sky. At the top loomed the convent, black and shuttered—all except for one window, where a light still gleamed. It looked like the Abbess's room.

Tien Nu pictured the old nun bent over her chessboard, with the little dog curled up at her feet. The thought was somehow reassuring—as if in this dark, chaotic world there was a point of stability and light.

He retraced his steps down the pathway to the clearing.

Bec stirred. "You're back."

"I couldn't sleep. So ... I went for a walk."

"I thought you'd taken off on your own."

"No, I'm still here," Tien Nu said. "Don't ask me why."

CHAPTER 12

Quan Fa

Tien Nu awoke just before sunrise. He gazed at the puffy clouds that scudded across the sky, like ships in a luminous sea. He remembered the day he'd arrived in Venezia, with the towers and domes of the city glittering in the distance, and the sunlight glancing off the waves. His father was hunched over the bow of the ship, squinting into the light. He turned to Tien Nu and smiled, the corners of his eyes crinkling into a thousand lines.

Tien Nu could see his father's face clearly, full of life and hope. Then the image faded, and he was left with a hollow feeling in his chest — the one that had taken up residence there ever since his father's death. He wondered how long it would stay with him, how long before it, too, faded away.

He struggled to his feet and glanced around.

Bec was gone.

Merda! The cape was gone, too—the one belonging to his father.

He stared at the depression in the grass where Bec had slept. There was fresh dew on the ground, and a track led into the bushes at the edge of the clearing. Bec must have gone to take a pee.

"Bec!" he called.

No answer.

"Where are you?"

Nothing.

"This isn't funny, Bec. Come on out."

There was a rustle in the bushes.

"There you are, you bonehead."

A young goat bounded into the clearing, almost colliding with Tien Nu. It gave a startled bleat and crashed back into the underbrush.

Tien Nu watched it disappear, rubbing his forehead. Where had Bec gone? Surely he hadn't decided to head off—without any food or money, not even proper clothing. He was the one who had wanted to stick together, who'd insisted they'd make a great team.

No, it didn't make sense. Bec must be out there somewhere, not far away, probably scrounging for something to eat.

It suddenly occurred to Tien Nu that this was his chance to slip away—to escape from the snake pit Bec had dragged him into. He could just pick up his pack and go. He wouldn't have to face Bec, explain why he was leaving, see the look in Bec's eyes.

But that was just the problem—the look in Bec's eyes. Tien Nu stood there, unmoving. He couldn't shake the feeling he'd be deserting Bec.

The boy was young and inexperienced—surely not sixteen, as he claimed to be. He had no clue about life on the road, and his survival skills stank. He was afraid of the dark and couldn't even pull off a simple theft. Malaspina would track him down in no time. Not unless Bec got some help— the kind that Tien Nu could give. If there was one thing he'd learned from his father, it was how to survive on the road.

Something else weighed on Tien Nu's mind. Although he didn't like to admit it, he felt lonely. For the first time in his life, he was completely on his own, and he found it tough going. He'd always dreamed of being free to choose where to go and what to do, where to stay, what company to keep. It had always been his father, with his opinions on everything under the sun, who had gotten to decide. Yet, now that Tien Nu was actually in charge of his own life, he found that he missed his father—missed his company, missed his dubious nuggets of wisdom, even missed his jokes.

The more he thought about joining forces with Bec, the more he warmed up to the idea. He hadn't had a real friend in years—not since leaving Alessandria. He and his father had always been on the move, never in one place long enough to put down roots. Tien Nu wasn't sure how far he trusted Bec, wasn't quite sure what to make of him. But at least he was funny and upbeat and scrappy—all things that would make for good company. Once they reached Ponti, he could always go off on his own. But until then, it made sense for them to stick together.

Tien Nu found his canteen and gulped down some water. It was time to get back to his morning routine, something he'd let drop since the accident. He walked over to the centre of the arena and stood there for a moment, gazing at the stone benches ranged up the side of the hill, all cracked and choked with vegetation. The sun rose over the mountains behind him, and rays of light struck the top row of benches and rippled downward, tier by tier—turning the dull grey stone a dazzling white.

He closed his eyes and let his mind go still and empty, invoking the spirit of *Zhen Wu*, his guardian and patron. He waited until he felt *chi* flowing into his body, making his arms and legs tingle. Then he eased into his warm-up, rhythmically stretching, bending, circling, mobilizing all his muscles. Gradually his body became more supple, and he broke a light sweat.

He stripped to his shorts and launched into a long-fist form, doing a fluid series of strikes and blocks and kicks, never stopping, each movement blending into the next. He jumped high, did a complete spin in the air, and landed low, his body spiralling downward. He lost his balance and toppled over, knocking his hip.

Swearing royally, he pushed himself up and tried the form again, this time finishing without incident. He repeated the sequence, again and again, until his heart was pounding and his body was drenched—each time improving on his rhythm and power.

Time for a break. He squatted down, sweating fiercely in the warm sun. It felt good to be training again, like in the old days. He could shut out the world, find a place where everything was simple and clear. Unfortunately, real life wasn't much like that.

He wondered if he'd ever find the courage to walk the tightrope again. Just thinking about it was enough to make him feel a bit sick. Heights had never bothered him before—

not from the time he'd started training as a kid. But the accident had changed that. He'd even had a bad moment last night on the convent roof, when he was about to jump over to the church—an unexpected lurch in his guts that had almost stopped him dead.

A fly bit him on the shoulder. He swatted at it, but the fly circled around and nipped him on the other side.

Pesky little beast!

Then something whizzed by his ear and skittered into the dust.

Not a fly.

Tien Nu pretended not to notice and resumed his training, keeping his eyes open. He spotted some leaves shaking in the bushes and marked the place. When another pebble flew his way, he spun around and batted it with his foot, sending it hurtling back to its source.

A sharp cry.

He plunged into the bushes and found Bec crouching down, too startled to react. Tien Nu caught him in a headlock and dragged him into the open. Bec flailed about, clutching at Tien Nu's legs, trying to upend him.

Tien Nu tightened his grip. "Say mercy!"

"Never! Not in a thousand years!"

He applied his knuckles to Bec's scalp.

"Mercy! Mercy!" squeaked Bec.

Tien Nu released his grip, and Bec dropped to the ground, shaking with laughter.

"Numbskull! Where have you been?" asked Tien Nu.

"You were snoring like a hog when I woke up, so I thought I'd take a look around."

Bec stood up and brushed off his clothes, then retrieved Tien Nu's cape from the bushes.

"What in God's name were you doing?" he asked Tien Nu. "All that twisting and turning and hopping around."

"It's called *quan fa*. Eastern-style boxing."

"*Quan fa*," Bec said, trying to imitate Tien Nu's accent. "But it doesn't look like boxing to me. It looks more like some kind of dance." He grinned. "Like the ladies do."

"I'll wear my veil next time," said Tien Nu.

"But really ..."

"That was just a drill—what's called a form. It improves your strength and technique. The fighting is different—fast and powerful."

Bec looked at him, head slightly tilted. "So ... let's say someone tried to jump you. A big guy, packed with muscle. What would you do?"

94

"Move Number One."

"What's that?"

"Run like hell."

Bec laughed. "Everyone knows that. But suppose the guy's got you cornered—no way to escape."

"Move Number Two. Ring the Temple Bells."

"Temple bells?"

Tien Nu pointed downward.

"Ouch!" said Bec. "I know that one, too."

"But there's lots more," said Tien Nu. "Kicks and strikes and grappling moves."

"So, where did you learn all this?"

"From my father. Fighting was a big part of our act. We called ourselves *The Immortal Fists.* We'd stage fights between the two of us and my father would let me win. Then he'd challenge anyone to take him on for a florin or two." Tien Nu laughed. "People thought he'd be a pushover. But he never lost."

"And now you're on your own."

"Now I'm on my own. It's going to be harder. But I'll get by."

"Maybe ..." Bec rubbed the back of his neck and smiled "... maybe you could teach me a few things—how to juggle and fight and do tricks. Then we could travel around and perform together. Like you and your father."

Tien Nu gazed at Bec's impish grin, his haystack of blond hair. People would like him. And he was small and light—good for a partner.

"Didn't you say you already know a few tricks?" he asked.

"Just some basic things. But I learn fast."

"I guess we could give it a try. See how it goes."

Bec grabbed Tien Nu's hand and pumped furiously. "Thanks, Scraps! I know I can do it."

"Scraps?"

"Because you like to fight."

"Only when I have to."

"Sure. Tell that to my neck."

"So, what should we call ourselves?" Tien Nu asked. "We need a name."

"*The Immortal Fists* sounds good to me."

Tien Nu paused to think.

"Let's go for something different," he said. "Like ... let's see ... *The Young Dragons*."

"Dragons." Bec stared at him. "Aren't dragons bad?"

"Not to me they aren't. As far as I know, they're good, powerful."

"But don't they rampage around, eating people? What about San Giorgio and the dragon?"

"Well, I suppose some dragons are good and some are bad—just like people."

"Which are we?"

Tien Nu grinned. "A bit of both, I guess."

Bec grinned back. "All right. *The Young Dragons*. That's us."

Tien Nu's stomach gave a growl.

"Did I hear something?" Bec cupped a hand to his ear. "There it is again. A voice. Speaking some strange language."

"The universal language," Tien Nu said. "The language of starvation."

"Not the language of the Tartars?"

Tien Nu shook his head. "Anyway, I'm not really a Tartar—though I don't mind when people call me that. I'm a mix of things. My father's family came from China, but he was born in Samarkand. He left when he was young and somehow reached Africa. That's where he met my mother. And that's where I was born—in Alessandria. We lived there until my mother died. Then we went travelling again and ended up here."

"I've heard about some of those places," Bec said. "But honestly, I don't have a clue where they are."

"Samarkand is far to the east, and China's even farther—across a big desert. But Alessandria is closer, south of here across the sea."

Bec gazed at Tien Nu. "You're lucky. You've travelled all over the world. I haven't seen a thing beyond the tip of my nose."

Tien Nu grinned. "Knucklehead! Your nose goes with you no matter where you travel."

"So, you must speak all sorts of languages," Bec said.

"Bits and pieces," Tien Nu said. "I grew up speaking Arabic at home, but I always talked to my father in Chinese. He wanted me to learn it."

"So, your name is Chinese?"

Tien Nu nodded. "It means something like 'Striving for Heaven.'" He wrinkled his nose. "My father's idea of a joke, I guess. I'll show you how to write it in Chinese."

He picked up a stick and traced a figure in the sand.

"That's the word for *Tien*—the first part of my name. It means 'sky' or 'heaven.'"

"It looks like a man walking," said Bec, peering at the figure. "I can see his legs and arms. And he's wearing a hat with a wide brim."

Tien Nu smoothed out another patch of sand. "And here's the second part—*Nu*."

98

He started to draw, and then paused.

"No, that's not right. I always mess this one up."

He wiped it out and started over.

"There," he said finally. "That's the word for *Nu*. It means 'try hard.'"

"It looks like someone doing *quan fa*," Bec said. "He's leaping into the air and whirling swords above his head."

"So, maybe it's a good name for me, after all," Tien Nu said.

His stomach gave another growl.

"The beast speaks again," Bec said. "Say, have you got any food? I don't have a scrap to my name."

"There's some in my pack. Not much, but enough for breakfast."

"Excellent!" said Bec. "Let's head to this place I found. It's the perfect spot to hide out."

CHAPTER 13

Catarina

The Knight made his way down the stairway to the main room of the inn, which was flooded with early morning light. There was no one there except the landlady, clearing the tables from the night before. She glanced up as he approached.

"Morning, Cristofo."

"Morning, Catarina." The Knight dragged a stool over to the counter.

"Something to eat?"

The Knight yawned and scratched his beard. "Maybe a bit of wine and bread."

"The baker's boy hasn't come round yet. But there's some bread left over from yesterday."

"That'll do."

Catarina went behind the counter and took out a half-loaf, then poured a cup of red wine.

The Knight downed the wine in a single draught and broke off a chunk of bread.

"So, when are you leaving?" Caterina asked.

"Tomorrow morning. Crack of dawn—that's if I had my way." He gave a rueful smile. "But the pilgrims howled when I mentioned the idea. So, we settled on mid-morning."

He shook his head. "What a pampered group! They've even hired a wagon with horses, for the baggage. Don't know how they'll make it over that road."

"Where are they staying—the pilgrims?"

"The women are at the convent. My friend the Abbess has them well in hand. But the men are scattered all over town. We're meeting at the south gate. God knows what time they'll all show up."

Caterina picked up a stack of platters and stored them on the shelf behind her.

"We're going to miss you, Cristofo. Especially Jaco. You know how that boy looks up to you. Ever since his father died ... well, he needs someone."

"I'll miss him, too—miss all of you. You've been very good to me these past months."

"So, you're really travelling all the way to the Terra Santa?"

"God willing! Roma first—and then onward to a port down

south, where we'll find a ship to Alessandria. From there, it's overland to Gerusalemme."

"And you won't be coming back?" said Catarina.

"Not likely. Once we get there, I'll stay."

"And how will you keep body and soul together?"

"I'll find something. Like I always do."

"Something ..."

"Soldier. Retainer. Bodyguard. There's always work for people like me."

"So ... we'll never see you again."

"Who knows? They say only mountains never meet."

"And are you a mountain?"

Cristofo smiled. "Maybe."

A little boy tumbled into the room and tugged at the Knight's leg. "Cri-Cri! Come, come! The grey cat had kittens last night. Come and see."

The Knight tousled Jaco's hair. "In a minute. I'm just talking to your mother."

"But come quick! They're really cute." Jaco went dashing out.

Catarina started wiping the counter with a damp cloth. "Did you know that Adolfo Malaspina came by here last night—while you were away?"

The Knight frowned. "What was he doing here?"

"Looking for a slave boy—a runaway." She paused and shook her head. "That man! Ordering me around in my own house. I nearly smacked him."

"But you didn't …?"

Catarina laughed. "Don't worry. I know how to deal with men like him."

Cristofo reached for the wine jug and poured himself another cup. "What did he say about the slave boy?"

"Not much. Gave a description. Offered a reward."

The Knight took a draught of wine. "I ran into him last night."

"Adolfo? I thought you were in church."

"No, not him. The slave boy. He told me he'd run away from the estate at Scarmagno. At first, I thought I might recognize him, but of course that's not possible. He said he's sixteen, so he was no more than a toddler when I left—now fifteen years ago."

He rubbed the stump of his little finger, momentarily lost in thought. "He was with another boy—a Tartar—some kind of travelling juggler. The slave asked if they could come along with me—said they'd make good servants."

"And what did you say?"

Cristofo shrugged. "I turned him down."

"You turned him down?" Catarina stopped and stared at the Knight. "How in conscience could you do that? You know what Adolfo will do if he catches the boy."

"You think I was wrong?"

"Of course, you were! Here you are, playing the pious one, setting off for the Terra Santa. And you can't even lift a finger to save a boy. Shame on you!"

"Maybe you're right. But I had my reasons."

"Such as?"

"Something like this happened before—when I was living in the Terra Santa. I took a couple of boys under my wing. Daud and Bakr. Orphans. Street boys. I brought them up, treated them like my own."

The Knight gave a sigh and drew out an ornate dagger, laying it on the counter.

"They gave me this on my name-day. Said they'd pooled their money." He raised an eyebrow. "Scoundrels. More likely stole it. But I was glad to have it."

Catarina picked up the dagger, fingering the intricate carvings on the handle.

"They must have loved you a lot."

"Perhaps. But it didn't turn out well."

"What do you mean?"

Cristofo heaved himself to his feet and walked over to the window, gazing into the street.

"One night, I was ambushed by a gang of thugs—just outside my door. Some dirty business I'd got myself mixed up in."

He lowered his head.

"Go on," said Catarina.

"Not much to tell. It was a hot night, so Daud and Bakr were sleeping outside in the courtyard. They heard my shouts and came running. Tried to help." He turned to look at her, shaking his head. "They never stood a chance. Slaughtered like lambs, throats slit, tossed in the gutter."

Catarina put a hand to her mouth. "How terrible! I'm sorry. What happened to you?"

"I was carved up nicely and left for dead. But somehow, I survived."

The Knight took a breath. "God knows why. I should have died that night. I should have died instead of them."

CHAPTER 14

The Hideout

Bec led the way along the base of the cliff, whistling softly, bouncing off his toes. For the first time since escaping, he had the feeling that maybe Ponti was more than just a dream.

The path wound through mounds of ancient rubble, covered with thistles and patches of yellow broom. Eventually, it veered away from the cliff and passed into a thickly wooded area, where stunted trees and bushes pressed in on either side.

"We're pretty close now."

Bec slowed down, looking carefully around, then stopped and pointed to an opening in the underbrush, so faint it was hardly noticeable.

"It's through there."

He ducked under the branches and scrambled ahead on hands and knees, with Tien Nu following behind. Soon they emerged in a sandy clearing at the base of the cliff. The space was roughly oval, with the worn surfaces of old paving stones peeping through the sand.

Bec spread out his arms and smiled. "Malaspina will never find us here."

They were completely cut off from the outside world. In the back of the clearing, the cliff towered into the sky, draped with vines. To their left a rocky ledge, a dozen feet high, extended from the cliff like a protective arm. The other sides were hedged about with trees and shrubbery.

Bec clambered up the ledge, his toes finding places to grip in the crumbling layers of rock. The top was almost perfectly flat—as wide as it was long.

"Come on up, Scraps," he called.

Tien Nu shrugged off his pack and climbed up after Bec. He screened his eyes and gazed out over the surrounding scrub.

"The beauty of it is you can see in all directions," Bec said. "We'd spot anyone coming miles away."

"Pretty good, *amico*," Tien Nu said.

"But you haven't seen anything yet."

Bec jumped back down into the clearing and stood there, hands on his hips. "It's somewhere around here. See if you can find it."

Tien Nu sighed. "All right, all right. But only if we eat soon."

"In a minute, Scraps. Just play along."

Tien Nu got down from the ledge and took a look around the clearing, gazing at the rocks and bushes, the cliff soaring overhead.

"I'm stumped."

"Listen," said Bec.

Tien Nu held still, head cocked. Then he smiled.

"Water."

"You're on the right track."

Tien Nu went over to the cliff, trying to locate the source of the sound. He pushed aside some vines that hung down like curtains.

Hidden behind them was a rectangular opening, like a doorway, cut into the face of the cliff. A little stream of water burbled from a fissure below the opening and disappeared into a hole in the ground that was overgrown with ferns.

"Wait until you see what's inside." Bec wriggled through the opening, holding the vines for Tien Nu.

The cave was dark and cool. After the bright sunshine outside, it was hard to see anything. Bec released the vines, which swung back into place, covering the entrance. Fingers of sun poked through the leaves, shedding a soft light.

The cave slowly came into focus. It was about twenty paces wide and very deep, sloping steeply upward into the darkness. The walls were covered with paintings in faded tones of red and brown, showing horses and bulls and stags with spreading antlers. There was a narrow channel in the ground beside the right wall, where the stream of water gurgled as it hurried through the cave and passed outside.

"How did you ever find this place?" asked Tien Nu.

"I was walking along the path, when I stopped to look at a jay that was fluttering above the bushes. It flew in close to the cliff and disappeared. So, I figured it had a nest somewhere up there in the rocks. I crawled through the bushes to take a look and found the clearing. Then I heard the sound of water. I searched around in the vines and, lo and behold, there was the opening in the cliff."

"Nice place, Bec."

"I thought you'd like it. We can hide out here for a while— at least, until things cool down. It's not safe to set off for Ponti right now. Malaspina and his men will be watching the roads."

Tien Nu nodded, gazing around.

"But there's more," Bec said.

He went over to the left wall, where a cubbyhole was carved into the rock. Tien Nu followed, stumbling over a ring of blackened stones. He bent down and picked up some cinders, which crumbled to ash at his touch.

"Look at this," said Bec, tugging a dusty sack from the cubbyhole. He untied the cord and started hauling things out.

"A plate, a jug, a spoon. Some rope. Also, a tinderbox." He gazed at Tien Nu. "Somebody used to live here."

"So, that explains the fireplace." Tien Nu poked at the

110

embers. "But it looks like it hasn't been used for years."

Bec sniffed the mouth of the jug. He yelped as a spider scuttled out. "Smells really musty. I wonder who left all this behind?"

"Hermits live in caves like this," said Tien Nu. "Bandits, too."

"Whoever it was must have left here ages ago," Bec said.

Tien Nu looked at the stream running down the channel. "Is the water good to drink?"

"Try it, Scraps, you'll see."

Tien Nu went over and scooped up some water. "Good enough."

"Do you want something from the sack?" Bec asked.

"Maybe the rope," said Tien Nu. "It could come in handy."

Bec tossed it over. "Anything else?"

Tien Nu shook his head.

"Then I'll take a few things myself." Bec stowed the spoon and the tinderbox in his pouch, before returning the sack to its hiding place.

"So ... how about breakfast?" he said.

Tien Nu grinned. "At last."

He retrieved his pack from the clearing and dug out some cheese and a few shrivelled sausages, along with a loaf of dark bread.

He prodded the loaf. "It's a bit squashed."

"Squashed is good. Adds that special something."

Tien Nu took a knife from his pack and divided the food into equal portions.

Bec watched him. "Why don't you keep that knife in your belt, where it's handy?"

"My father was dead against it. He said a knife was like a crutch—a dangerous one. If you got into a fight, you should rely on your fists and feet. Otherwise, there'll be blood for sure."

"But what if the other guy has a blade?"

"That's where *quan fa* comes in."

Bec didn't say anything. But he thought he'd choose a knife any day.

They ate silently, breaking off hunks of bread, and washing everything down with water from the stream.

Bec finished the last of his food and wiped his greasy hands on his tunic. "Ah! That feels better."

He leaned back against the wall and stretched out his legs. He was starting to doze off when something tickled his hand. He opened his eyes and saw a lizard scurrying away. It stopped not far off and waited, head poised.

Bec gazed intently at the lizard. The little creature looked back at his hand, its tongue flicking in and out, then scuttled onto the fingers. Bec raised his hand and gently stroked the lizard, which lifted its head to meet the strokes. Bec smiled and deposited the lizard on his shoulder. The creature darted inside his collar.

"A new friend," said Bec. "He'll bring us luck."

"How did you do that?" asked Tien Nu.

"Don't know. Animals just like me."

"So, you'll carry him around inside your clothes?"

"Until he gets bored or hungry and scoots off. Some of them disappear after a day or two. Others stay on for weeks, and I have to catch flies to feed them."

"Sticky little feet crawling all over your body!" Tien Nu shook his head. "Not for me."

"I don't mind it," Bec said. "It makes me feel ... less alone. Not that I'm lonely or anything. It's just that animals have always been my friends. My best friends, really. You can't trust people. Turn around and they stab you in the back."

Tien Nu smiled. "So, you should be happy my knife is safely stowed away."

The lizard peeped from Bec's sleeve.

"Hungry, are you?" Bec salvaged some crumbs from the ground and fed them to the creature. "I had a dog once," he said. "Named Fracas. We were together all the time, day and night, always getting into trouble. He died last year. I still miss him."

"It must be nice to have a dog," Tien Nu said. "I've never had one. My father didn't like them much." He paused. "Actually, maybe we could get ourselves a dog. Teach him some tricks."

"Tricks? What kind?"

"Oh, I don't know. We could think of something. Actually, there was a juggler I saw once. He had floppy yellow pants, and every time he bent over, his dog bit the pants and pulled them down. The juggler had a huge hairy bum—so people loved the act."

"It wouldn't be hard to teach a dog a trick like that," said Bec. "But I'll leave the hairy bum to you."

Tien Nu grinned. "My speciality."

He got up and wandered around, looking at the paintings on the walls. He paused and peered into the murky interior of the cave.

"Did you hear something?"

Bec shook his head, prompting the lizard to scurry back up his sleeve.

Tien Nu listened for a while, then shrugged.

"Thought I heard a noise." He nodded toward the back. "I wonder what's up there?"

"Don't know. I didn't check."

"Let's take a look."

Bec glanced at the shadowy interior and made a face. "Why don't you go?"

Tien Nu collared Bec and dragged him to his feet. "Come on! The darkness won't kill you."

"How about maimed, blinded, mutilated?"

"Won't happen."

The cave narrowed as they made their way inside, climbing upward. In no time they came to a tunnel, black as pitch, where the stream emerged on the side.

At the mouth of the tunnel was a scattering of bones.

"Look at this," Bec said, squatting down.

Tien Nu bent over. "Must be the remains of a rabbit."

He picked up a bone, sniffing. "Pretty fresh. Could be the work of a fox."

"Or a wolf."

"Not this close to town."

A scuffling noise came from the tunnel.

Bec looked up.

Something sprang from the darkness and struck him in the face.

CHAPTER 15

A Visitor

Bec toppled backward, hitting the ground. The beast lunged at him again and again, grazing his mouth and nose. Bec grabbed it by the throat and tried to fend it off.

"Stop! Stop!" cried Tien Nu. "It's that dog. The one from the convent."

"Hannibal!" said Bec, loosening his grip.

The little white dog wriggled out of Bec's hands and went into a fit of delight, tail thrashing, body switching back and forth. He leapt onto Bec's chest and licked his face.

"Hannibal! All right, all right, that's enough!"

Tien Nu peered into the black tunnel. "I wonder ..."

"Wonder what? Easy there, Hannibal. Sure, sure, I love you, too."

"Maybe this connects with the tunnel under the old nun's room. That's how Hannibal found his way down here."

At the mention of his name, the dog bounded over to Tien Nu and began nipping at his ankles.

"Hannibal, don't be such a pest! Hey, let go. That hurts!"

Bec scooped up the dog and held him fast. Hannibal lay happily in his arms, licking his chin.

"Well, Bec, looks like you've made another friend. Come on, let's go outside."

They left the cave and climbed onto the ledge, where they let down their tunics to the waist, soaking up the sun. Hannibal squeezed in between them, tongue lolling.

Tien Nu stared at Bec's back. "Those bruises. You're black and blue all over."

"Are they still there?" Bec reached around and rubbed the skin. "It's Malaspina. He gave me a thrashing the day I escaped."

"There are some older scars, too. Those white things. Looks like you've been beaten more than once."

"I've had my share. Mostly from Pietro—the steward. The old crow. He hates it when I make fun of him. But often from Malaspina, too." Bec shrugged. "Pietro only does it when he's really angry. But Malaspina does it just because he likes to. Well, he won't get his hands on me again."

Tien Nu was silent for a moment. "You know, the only problem with staying here is that we're all out of food."

"Maybe we can find some berries and mushrooms and other things."

Tien Nu shook his head. "Not as easy as it sounds. You can't live on that sort of stuff for long. You get the runs."

Bec laughed. "Tell me about it."

"I'll have to go to the market in town," Tien Nu said.

"Just you? Not both of us?"

"It's too dangerous for you, *amico*. I'll be better off on my own. They're looking for you, not me."

"Are you sure? I feel like I'm loading everything on your shoulders."

"Nothing I can't handle."

"Tough guy, eh?"

Tien Nu smiled. "As tough as they come. Now, what should I buy?"

Bec ticked off his fingers. "Sausages, cheese, bread."

"How about some meat pies?"

"Even better. I've never actually had one."

"All right, I'd better be off." Tien Nu got to his feet and pulled up his tunic, then gazed out over the bushes. "I wonder what's the best way to get into town."

Bec pointed in the direction away from the arena. "If you keep going along that path, you'll reach the track that

118

leads up to the north gate. I went exploring over there this morning."

"Were there any guards?"

"Not that I saw."

Tien Nu fetched his pack from the cave. He took out his crumpled hat and tried to punch it into shape, but soon gave up and jammed it down on his head.

He glanced up at Bec, who was watching from the ledge. "I'll be back soon."

"Take your time, Scraps. I'm not going anywhere. Just be careful."

Tien Nu heaved up his pack and busied himself with the straps.

"Why lug that thing around?" Bec asked. "It must weigh at least a ton."

"I need it to carry the food."

"You could take your things out and leave them here."

"It's not worth the trouble. I'm used to carrying it."

"Tough guy."

Tien Nu grinned and tapped his head. "Like a rock."

CHAPTER 16

The Graveyard

Bec gazed at the Tartar as he made his way along the path, tunic flapping in the breeze. He waited for him to turn around and wave. But Tien Nu just stared doggedly ahead, soon disappearing around the face of the cliff.

Bec wondered if he'd ever see him again. The Tartar had insisted on taking his pack with him—carrying everything. Why would he do that unless he had other plans? Maybe all this talk about buying food was just a cover, an excuse to slip away.

Tien Nu had said they'd travel together to Ponti. But people didn't take promises very seriously. Why should you when it didn't serve your own interests? The best thing was to look out for yourself. The only thing. That's what everybody did.

Bec picked up a rock and tossed it high over the bushes, watching it rise into the bright sky, then drop into the dust. He could hardly blame Tien Nu if he decided to leave. Bec knew he'd been nothing but trouble to the boy. And more of the same lay ahead, what with Malaspina on his tail. There was nothing in it for the Tartar—no reason for him to stick around. If he were in Tien Nu's place, he wouldn't stick around, either.

Hannibal pressed against Bec's legs, whining slightly. Bec bent over and mussed him about the neck.

"How long are you going to stay, little fellow? You'll be heading off soon, won't you? That old nun must be missing you. But for the moment, we're friends."

He gazed at the mountains on the other side of the valley, where sunlight glittered on the snow that lingered on the peaks. All at once, he felt a longing so strong, he thought his chest would burst. A yearning for something—he couldn't say exactly what. Freedom, yes, but not just that. Something more. A sense of who he was, of where he belonged in the world. He knew so little about his family. His mother and grandmother were both gone, taking with them everything they could have told him about his past. And his father ... well, sometimes he believed it was better not to know.

He thought about what had happened in the graveyard two days ago—the day he had escaped from the castle. The incident was so strange and disturbing it had sunk hooks deep into his mind. Now the memory came flooding back, as vivid and painful as if it were happening again. The day had started with him hurrying down the track below the castle, as the early morning sun slanted across the meadow. On reaching the chestnut grove, he had turned as usual onto the sunken lane that ran beside a high stone wall to the gate at the end.

Inside was a neglected graveyard, its tombstones cracked and stained, tilting in all directions, as if planted by a careless giant. Shaggy mounds reared like islands above a sea of grass, with tangled bushes crowding along the walls. Here lay the graves of criminals, paupers, heathens, slaves— outsiders of every stripe.

Closing the gate behind him, Bec followed the path to the other side of the graveyard, where a straggling row of tombstones led him to the plain grey slab that marked his mother's grave, next to that of his *nonna*. He knelt down, crossed himself, and said a prayer that his grandmother had taught him, stumbling over the words in a language he barely understood. There was a fluttering in the air, and a raven landed on his shoulder and nibbled at his ear.

Bec smiled. "Don't worry, I haven't forgotten you."

He tapped the raven on the beak, then reached into his pouch and found the dry crusts he'd stored inside. He broke them into bits and held them up in his palm for the bird to peck at, wondering where the rest of the ravens were. When the bread was finished, the bird flew up into the yew tree by the wall, watching with bright eyes as Bec set about the business of cleaning the graves of his mother and grandmother—sweeping away the dead leaves and branches that had gathered since his last visit.

He was almost finished when he heard voices. Men on horseback were approaching along the lane outside, their hats bobbing above the high wall. He scrambled into the bushes behind him, crouching down. Slaves were forbidden to leave the castle without permission. But he was friendly with the guards at the gate, who let him slip out from time to time.

"Wait here with the horses," said a voice. "I won't be long."

Malaspina pushed open the gate and paused for a moment, surveying the graveyard. He had a bunch of white flowers in one hand, and in the other his cane—slim as a rapier.

What was the man doing here? No one he cared about could possibly be buried in a place like this.

Malaspina fixed his gaze on the area where Bec was hiding and made his way across the yard. Bec's stomach tightened as he approached. The man reached the final row and moved slowly along it, examining each grave in turn. Finally, he stopped and gazed at the gravestone of Bec's mother.

Bec held himself still, hardly breathing, his heart beating wildly. Malaspina was so close he could smell the lavender scent on his clothing.

The man knelt down and laid his flowers by the gravestone. He lowered his head and murmured something, as if praying.

Bec caught some words: "… so angry, so very angry … how could you do this to me …"

The man let out a jagged sob, his shoulders shaking.

A raucous cawing came from the yew tree behind Bec. He glanced up. The entire mob of ravens had arrived, settling in tiers along the branches like a black-robed choir. A few bolder birds swooped down to flutter impatiently overhead.

Malaspina turned and looked at the birds in the tree, then focused on the ones above the bushes. He got to his feet.

Bec hunched over, head to the ground.

He felt a hand on his collar.

Malaspina dragged him into the open and wrenched him to his feet.

"You little snake!" he hissed. "Why are you spying on me?"

Bec gazed at Malaspina. The man's cheeks were streaked with tears.

"I'm ... I'm visiting my mother's grave."

Malaspina gave a choked laugh. "You, of all people! Don't you know how your mother died?"

Bec was silent.

"Well, I'll tell you," Malaspina said. "You killed her."

Anger welled up in Bec's throat. "That's not true! You're a liar!"

Malaspina turned pale.

"No one calls me a liar," he said. "And for that you'll pay."

Bec stared at Malaspina's face, which was twisted in fury and contempt. He felt the urge to punch the man. But he was paralyzed with fear.

"You'd like to hit me, wouldn't you?" Malaspina said. "But you can't do it. You're nothing but a coward."

He shouted: "Nozzo, over here! On the double!"

The bodyguard peered through the gate at his master.

"We need to teach this boy a lesson," Malaspina called.

Bec was stripped and pinned to the ground, while Malaspina applied his cane to Bec's back—more than a dozen strokes, each one searing the flesh. Bec clenched his teeth, determined not to cry out. But by the end, he couldn't help himself.

Malaspina hauled Bec up and threw his ragged clothing in his face.

He turned to the bodyguard. "Take him back to the castle. This afternoon we'll have a little show for everyone. A branding."

⌣

Something scratched at Bec's legs. With a start, he came back to the present. Hannibal was gazing at him, a mournful expression on his face.

"What's the matter, boy?" Bec asked.

Hannibal whined and shifted gingerly from paw to paw.

"Ledge too hot for you? All right, let's go inside."

He picked up the little dog and retreated to the coolness of the cave, where he settled near the entrance, with Hannibal snuggling close.

Bec gazed at the motes swirling in the beams of light that shot through the vines. He felt like one of those specks of dust, spinning randomly about, bumping into other specks, not knowing what might happen next.

CHAPTER 17

Bandits

Bec dozed through the morning, his arm wrapped around Hannibal. By the time he awoke, the sun had almost reached its peak and the sunbeams were slanting steeply through the vines.

He rubbed his eyes, gazing around the cave. He must have been asleep for hours. Tien Nu should be back soon—if he came back at all.

Hannibal's ears pricked up. He raised his head and stared at the entrance. Bec listened but, at first, couldn't hear anything. Then came the crackle of leaves and twigs. Someone was pushing through the thick barrier of bushes around the clearing.

Bec grinned. The Tartar was keeping his promise after all.

A voice. Deep and booming—nothing like Tien Nu's. And now another voice—high and nasal. Hannibal bared his teeth and growled. Bec clamped a hand over the dog's mouth and waited.

The voices grew louder, until they were just outside the cave.

"Shut up for a moment, will you Falco?" said the deep voice. "I'm trying to find the opening. I know it's around here somewhere."

Bec grabbed Hannibal and scrambled up the rocky slope to the back of the cave, where he crouched in the darkness just inside the tunnel. The vines over the entrance were swept aside. A flood of light poured in, blocked almost immediately by a huge form. A heavy man squeezed through the narrow opening, grunting prodigiously from the effort. He plodded across the cave to the nearest wall, panting as he wrestled off his pack.

Immediately behind him was another man, even bigger than the first, who sat down beside his companion. A skinny fellow followed, venting a stream of curses and complaints as he paced about the cave.

Bec stared at the men. They looked like bandits.

"For God's sake, Falco, give us some peace," said the first big man. "You'll get your share. Lord above, what a shambles! A miracle we got away. No thanks to you, Falco, tripping like that."

He let out a long wheeze. "I'm getting too old for this.

Burglary's a young man's game. We should stick to what we do best. A nice quiet ambush—a knock on the head, and we're off like the wind."

His arms fell limply to the side. "Now I need some rest, Falco. We'll split up everything later."

"But you shorted me last time, Bosco."

"What a load of crap! Fact is, you're never happy, no matter how I make the split."

The skinny man twisted his mouth but said nothing.

Bosco glanced around the cave. "Lucky I remembered this place. It's been years. Three, maybe four?" He nudged the big man beside him. "What do you think, dear brother?"

The brother smiled, gazing silently at him.

There was a rustle at the entrance. Bec's heart skipped a beat. The Tartar—showing up at the worst possible time.

A boy slipped into the cave and folded himself against the wall. Bec peered at him. Grubby face beneath a tangle of curly hair. The boy from the funeral procession—the one Wolf had booted down the road.

"About time, Curly!" said Bosco. "Where the devil have you been?"

"What's it to you?" said the boy. "Since when do I have to account for my every move?"

"Oh, dear Lord, preserve me!" said Bosco, rolling his eyes. "Where are your manners, Curly? If I wasn't so tired, I'd get up and teach you some respect."

"Not a chance, Bosco. You couldn't lay a finger on me, not in a thousand years."

The big man stared at the boy, then let out a rumbling laugh. "On that point, I suppose you are correct, Curly. I'm not as quick on my feet as I used to be. But enough of this chatter." Bosco nudged his brother. "How about some shuteye, Beppe?"

The two big men wrapped themselves in their capes and made themselves comfortable against the wall of the cave, followed by Curly. There were mutters and grunts as they settled in.

Falco continued to shuffle about, grumbling to himself. Then he retrieved his cape and stretched out across the mouth of the cave.

Bec gazed at the man's skinny body, blocking the entrance.

Watchman. That was his job.

There was no way to leave the cave without waking Falco up—and no way to warn off Tien Nu.

He was trapped.

CHAPTER 18
The Bakery

Tien Nu trudged through the gates of Montecavo, avoiding the fresh piles of donkey dung steaming in the sun. There were no guards on duty and the morning bustle was over, with the main street almost empty.

He paused for a moment, adjusting the straps on his pack that cut into his shoulders. He wished he could have left some of his belongings at the cave. But he still wasn't sure how far to trust Bec. There were things in his pack he couldn't afford to lose—precious family things that were irreplaceable.

Tien Nu let out a sigh and looked around, wondering where to find the market. A small boy appeared at the top of the steep street, swooping downward, arms spread, mouth rounded: "Who-o-o-o-h-h! Who-o-o-o-h-h!"

Goosebumps rose on Tien Nu's arms. He stared at the boy. He'd never laid eyes on him before. So why this feeling of dread—as if something awful was about to happen?

The boy came closer, dodging the few passers-by, shrilling at the top of his voice.

"Who-o-o-o-h-h!"

Tien Nu pressed his hands over his ears and stumbled to the side of the road—sounds and images clashing in his head. Strange pulsations, throbs, whirrs. Earth and sky tumbling.

A terrible silence.

He leaned against the wall, his forehead dripping with sweat.

The small boy stopped to gawk.

"You all right, mister?"

Tien Nu glanced at him.

"Yes. Go away."

The boy stared.

"You heard me. Beat it!"

The boy backed off, still staring, then resumed his swooping flight down the street.

Tien Nu took off his pack and sat down on a doorstep, trying to understand what was going on. He was sure it had something to do with his father's death. But what? He sorted through the jumble of sights and sounds, yet couldn't make any sense of them.

He pulled himself together and resumed his journey up the street. With the help of a garrulous old lady who virtually took him by the hand, he finally found the market. He bought a large supply of bread and cheese and haggled for some sausages with a friendly butcher, who told him where to find the best meat pies in town.

He set off for the shop, which was on the other side of the marketplace. As he walked up the street, he saw a beggar at the corner ahead, his crutch propped against the wall. The beggar lifted his hand in greeting, murmuring some stock phrases. Tien Nu dropped a coin in his bowl, then turned the corner into a narrow lane. The smell of fresh pastry came drifting from a doorway not far off. This was the place. As he entered the shop, he glanced back and saw the beggar talking to an urchin, who raced off.

Inside, a broad-shouldered woman was serving a customer at the counter. While Tien Nu waited, two girls emerged through a beaded curtain over a doorway at back, carrying steaming trays of pies. One of the girls looked at Tien Nu, poked her companion, and whispered. The second girl, who had black hair and very red lips, stared boldly at him.

Tien Nu could feel his face flushing. He took off his battered hat and tried to smooth down his hair, which was sticking up in all directions. The girls continued to whisper and giggle, throwing glances at him as they arranged the pies on racks along the wall. The woman turned and spoke a few sharp words, and the girls scurried off.

The other customer finished paying and Tien Nu took his place. The woman gave him a swift appraising look, then smiled broadly, showing a gap between her two front teeth.

"Yes, my little duckling."

Tien Nu blushed even more and asked for two meat pies. The woman took her time serving him, wrapping the pies in a clean scrap of cloth and tying it up securely. As Tien Nu handed over the money, she gave his fingers a squeeze. Tien Nu's cheeks burned. He mumbled his thanks, stored the pies in his pack and went outside.

The lane in front was blocked by men unloading barrels from a cart. Tien Nu peered around the cart toward the corner, and caught a glimpse of a lean man conversing with the beggar.

Bec's master, Malaspina.

Tien Nu ducked back inside the bakery and asked if he could use the privy. The woman nodded, indicating the doorway at the back. He pushed through the curtain into a courtyard, where the two girls were sliding freshly made pies into a large clay oven.

They turned and stared.

"What's through there?" Tien Nu pointed to a passage at the end.

"Just the privy," said the dark girl, wiping a strand of hair from her eyes.

"Is there any way out?"

The girl shook her head. "Not unless you're a bird."

From the front came a loud voice. Malaspina was arguing with the woman.

"What's going on?" asked the girl.

"A man is after me," said Tien Nu. "I have to hide."

The girl's eyes widened. "Are you an outlaw?"

"Not at all."

The girl gave a knowing smile. "You wouldn't say so, even if you were. All right, over here."

She opened a door at the side, revealing a deep storeroom with bags stacked high against the walls on either side.

Up front, the woman cried: "That's private! You can't go back there ..."

Her voice broke off in a scream.

Tien Nu ran into the storeroom and shut the door. The room was dimly lit by a small opening high in the back wall. There was no way to bar the door and no other exit.

He groped his way down the middle aisle and squeezed behind some stacks of bags at the end. He waited, peering through a gap, the blood throbbing in his temples.

A chorus of squeals sounded from outside, followed by a clatter.

Then a long silence.

Tien Nu counted to himself: ... *eighteen ... nineteen ... twenty.*

Malaspina must be gone. They had gotten rid of him, somehow.

The door flew open with a bang.

Malaspina stood there, perfectly still. Behind him, the two girls huddled with the woman.

"Show yourself," the man said.

Tien Nu held his breath.

"It's not you I'm after. It's the slave boy. Tell me where he is and I'll let you go. There's a reward. Thirty florins."

Tien Nu said nothing.

Malaspina drew a knife from the holster on his chest and took a step forward, blade in hand.

Tien Nu pressed his back against the wall.

The man moved slowly down the aisle, jabbing his cane behind each stack of bags, first on one side, then the other.

Tien Nu plucked at the seams of a bag in front of him. The thread gave way and rivulets of flour trickled out.

Malaspina moved steadily closer.

He was some three stacks away when he came to a halt, peering into the gloom.

"This can go two ways," he said. "Easy or hard. Either way, you'll end up giving me what I want. People always do."

He paused.

Tien Nu was silent. He gazed at the man's knife, calculating its distance from the ground.

"Foolish boy," Malaspina said. "What is the slave to you?"

He sighed and took another step forward.

Tien Nu gave a shove to the stack of bags in front of him. It swayed, then toppled over. Malaspina shouted and leapt back. The bags hit the floor, splitting at the seams. A dense cloud of flour burst into the air, filling the entire space, making it impossible to see.

Tien Nu plunged low, his pack just grazing the outstretched knife. He caught Malaspina about the ankles and threw him down.

The man gave a deep grunt, then lay there groaning.

"Was that easy or hard?" Tien Nu said.

He struggled to his feet and made for the door. By now

the courtyard was full of people. He pushed his way through and in a moment had reached the lane outside.

The beggar was up at the corner, staring at him. Tien Nu gave him a dirty look and raced in the opposite direction. He turned into an alley and cut across a yard, where a woman was hanging out her laundry. Her mouth dropped as he fought his way through the sheets and scrambled over a wall. Panting heavily, he passed through a maze of alleys until he reached the main street, where he joined a boisterous group of peasants heading home from market.

"Doing some baking, laddie?" laughed one.

Tien Nu looked down at himself.

He was covered with flour from head to toe.

The clearing in front of the cave was empty. Tien Nu checked the top of the ledge, thinking Bec might still be there, but found nothing.

He went over to the cave, swung aside the vines and crawled inside, blinking into the darkness.

There was Bec, curled up on the ground—fast asleep.

Tien Nu smiled and gave him a poke. "Wake up, lazybones! It's time to eat!"

The body rolled over. It wasn't Bec.

CHAPTER 19

A Shock

Tien Nu gaped at the strange man. He started to wriggle backwards from the cave, but the man grabbed him by the shoulders and held on tight.

Tien Nu struggled furiously. His hat went flying as he thrashed around. He seized the man's wrists, trying to break his grip.

From the darkness at the side of the cave came a slurred voice.

"What the devil is going on, Falco?"

"Help! Help!" shouted the skinny man. "I've got him!"

"Got what, you nitwit?"

"Hurry up! I can't hold on."

Tien Nu found the pressure points on the man's wrists and dug in his thumbs.

Falco howled with pain.

"Bosco! He's killing me."

A small white dog came hurtling from the dark and sank his teeth into the man's arm.

Falco gave a startled shriek. He let go of Tien Nu and grappled with the dog, shouting frantically.

A low voice mingled with Falco's cries.

"Hannibal!"

Tien Nu froze. It sounded like Bec.

On hearing his name, Hannibal let go of Falco and raced into the back of the cave.

Tien Nu slipped outside to the clearing, where he scrambled up onto the ledge and flattened down.

He could hear Falco's shouts and groans inside. Another voice broke in, deep and weary, leading to a lengthy argument.

Tien Nu listened for Bec. But his voice didn't come again.

His head whirled, trying to make sense of things. Who were these men? And what had happened to Bec? Why had he called Hannibal just once, and then gone silent? And why wasn't Hannibal barking and jumping around? It wasn't like him to stay quiet for very long.

He inched closer to the rim of the ledge, where he had a better view of the cave. After some time, the vines parted and a big man pushed out. He was followed by another man, who had difficulty squeezing through the opening. The first man assisted his companion and for a moment the pair stood there, side by side, blinking in the sunshine.

They looked so much alike, they must be twins—brothers at the least. Scruffy beards, bulbous noses, bellies drooping over their belts. But the first man had a sly face and quick eyes, while his brother wore a strangely vacant expression. He seemed to be unarmed, whereas the first man had several weapons stuffed in his belt.

The brothers were now joined by the skinny man who'd been sleeping at the entrance. He slouched into the middle of the clearing, where he pinched his nose and blew its contents onto the ground.

The first big man twisted his lips in disgust. "Not here, Falco! My God, what a pig you are!"

Falco gave him a disdainful look and wiped his nose on the back of his hand. "I'll do as I damn well please, Bosco. I'm fed up with the lot of you. As soon as I get my share, I'm off."

"And Godspeed!" said Bosco. "But I've heard that one before."

He looked around the clearing with exaggerated care. "So, where is this Tartar of yours?"

"He's cleared out, of course," snapped Falco. "What did you expect—that he'd hang around, waiting for us to grab him?"

"If he really exists, that is. I don't see any sign of him."

Falco shook his head in frustration. He paced restlessly around the clearing, staring at the ground.

"What are you looking for?" said Bosco. "Tracks? Ghosts don't leave tracks."

Falco scowled, picked up a stick, and poked about in the bushes.

Bosco watched him for a moment, then turned to his brother. "Let's go back inside, Beppe. It's too hot out here. There's nothing much to see, anyway."

He collared his brother affectionately and helped him climb back into the cave.

Falco continued to prowl around the clearing, beating the bushes with his stick. Suddenly, he turned and looked up at the ledge.

Tien Nu ducked down, his cheek pressed against the scorching rock.

Scraping noises, followed by an oath. Falco was trying to climb up.

Tien Nu wriggled backwards across the ledge and dropped over the other side, where he squatted under the bushes, holding his breath.

More scuffling, then soft footsteps. Tien Nu looked up

through the leaves and glimpsed Falco standing directly above him, shading his eyes, staring out toward the ruins of the arena. The man mumbled something to himself and spat into the bushes, spraying Tien Nu's face. He turned around and disappeared. There was a clatter and a burst of curses. Then silence.

Tien Nu took some leaves and wiped the slimy stuff off his face. He listened for a moment, then climbed up the side of the ledge and peered over the rim. No one was there. He crawled across to look over the other side—in time to see Falco disappearing into the mouth of the cave.

Tien Nu gazed at the vines as they swung back into place. What had happened to Bec? He was sure he'd heard him calling Hannibal. His voice was unmistakable. But what could Bec be doing with this gang of thugs?

Maybe they were holding him prisoner. Maybe he was lying inside the cave right now, bound and gagged. But in that case, how had he managed to call Hannibal? And where did the dog go, anyway?

It was a real puzzle. And the more Tien Nu thought about it, the less he understood. There was nothing to do but wait and see.

The ledge was burning hot. He squinted up at the brilliant

ball of the sun, then moved to the patch of shade by the cliff. The shadows crept over the rocky shelf as the sun slowly dropped into the western sky.

CHAPTER 20

Trapped

Bec watched in horror from the back of the cave as Tien Nu struggled with Falco, his hat flying into a corner. Hannibal shot from between Bec's legs and launched himself at the skinny man, giving Tien Nu the chance to escape.

"Hannibal!" Bec hissed.

The little dog came scurrying back. Bec swept him up and held him tightly.

At the side of the cave, Bosco turned over and squinted at Falco through bleary eyes.

"What in God's name is the matter? Can't you let a man sleep?"

"Me?" Falco screamed. "Why do I always get the blame? Here I am, fighting with the Tartar. But do I get any help?"

He paced furiously around, massaging his hands and wrists. "The Tartar did something to me! I can't feel a thing."

"Tartar? What are you talking about?" asked Bosco.

"The Tartar boy! Pale as a ghost! He jumped me while I was asleep. I grabbed him but he paralyzed my hands. And ... and ... then a dog bit me."

"A dog? Along with a Tartar?" Bosco gave a coarse laugh. "Sounds like one of your nightmares, Falco."

"No, you moron! How could a nightmare cripple my hands? How could it bite me?"

He rubbed his wrists vigorously.

"Well, my friend," said Bosco. "All I can say is, I didn't see a thing. Just you jumping about and screaming like a madman. Like you always do when you have those dreams of yours."

"Nitwit! Lamebrain!" cried Falco.

Bosco sighed. "All right, Falco. Calm down, calm down. Where did this famous Tartar go?"

"Outside," Falco said, pointing to the entrance.

"Let's take a look, then—just to keep you happy."

Bosco called to his brother, and they squeezed out through the opening, followed by Falco. As soon as they'd left, the curly-headed boy got up and scuttled over to Bosco's pack, where he found a sausage. He broke off a chunk and stuffed it into his mouth, then crept back to his place.

The two big men returned through the entrance and

eased themselves down, fanning their faces. After a while, the skinny man made his appearance.

"Are you happy now, Falco?" wheezed Bosco. "No phantom Tartar out there, lurking in the bushes?"

Falco made a sour face and shrugged. Suddenly he spotted Tien Nu's hat in the shadows and pounced on it.

"So, where did this come from?" he crowed, waving the hat in the air. "Tell me that!"

"What have you got there? Let's see."

Falco tossed the hat to Bosco, who turned it over in his hands, pursing his lips.

"Where did you get this?"

"It was here on the floor, you imbecile! You saw me pick it up. The Tartar was wearing it."

Bosco's brow creased in thought. For the first time, he seemed to be taking Falco seriously.

"And what did you say about a dog?"

"There *was* a dog, I tell you! A nasty little brute. It bit my arm and then ran away. I think maybe someone called him."

Bosco sat up straight. "Called him? Who? You mean the Tartar?"

"No. Somebody else. From back there." Falco gestured toward the rear of the cave.

148

Bec shrank against the wall of the tunnel as the big man peered into the interior.

"Maybe we should settle this, once and for all," Bosco said finally. "If somebody's hiding back there, we'd better find out."

Bec gazed into the tunnel behind him, his chest tightening. It was completely black—not a glimmer of light.

The big man fished around in his bag and pulled out a tinderbox and some candles. He lit one for himself and another for Falco, then called to the boy lying at the side.

"Don't pretend you're asleep, Curly. Get up."

The boy rolled over and raised his head, yawning ostentatiously.

"That's better," said Bosco. "Now, listen to me, Curly. You stay here and keep an eye on my brother. Don't let him follow us. Sometimes he gets into a panic when I'm not around."

The big man turned to Beppe, speaking gently. "Falco and I are going away for a while. He wants me to check on something. But we won't be long. Curly will look after you."

He patted his brother on the shoulder and gave him a confidential wink. Beppe gazed back, nodding and smiling.

Bec gritted his teeth and began moving into the tunnel, one arm cradling Hannibal, the other feeling its way along the wall, which was slick with moisture. He could hear the men's voices behind him and the gurgle of the little stream as it ran down the channel at the side.

The tunnel veered to the left and seemed to narrow. Bec glanced back and saw some light glistening on the damp wall at the bend. The voices were getting louder. Another sharp turn and the tunnel began a steep climb. Bec nearly slipped on the slimy surface and slowed down to keep his footing.

The tunnel came to an end. He groped around but couldn't feel anything. This seemed to be another cave. There was the sound of falling water.

He took several steps forward, then turned and stared back into the tunnel, clutching Hannibal.

He could see a glow where the tunnel bent to the right. The light got steadily stronger, and two men appeared around the corner. They paused and looked ahead, their faces wreathed in shadow. They began climbing up the steep slope. Halfway up, the big man stopped.

"This is a wild goose chase, Falco," he panted. "What's the point?"

He pulled out a cloth and wiped his face.

"They've got to be up here somewhere," said the skinny man.

"It's all in your head, Falco. Let's face it. There's nobody here."

"It's all in my head, is it?" shrilled Falco, raising his wrist. "Look! You can still see the marks where he bit me."

He spat on the ground and began moving forward.

Hannibal gave a throaty growl. Bec clamped his hand around the dog's muzzle.

Falco stopped and squinted into the darkness. "Did you hear that?"

"What now, Falco?" said the big man, coming up behind him.

"Shut up. I heard something."

Hannibal squirmed around, trying to work his jaws free.

"I don't hear a thing," said Bosco. "Your imagination again, Falco."

"There was a noise, I tell you!"

Hannibal arched his back and pushed his legs against Bec, who was struggling to hold him. All at once, between compressed jaws, the dog let out a long, strangulated yowl. Bec tightened his grip but was powerless to stop the dog, who released a stream of unearthly wails.

The two men stood there transfixed, mouths drooping, eyes showing white. Long moments passed, as Hannibal's cries reached a dreadful crescendo.

"I'm getting out of here," said Bosco.

He lumbered back down the tunnel, skidding on the

slick surface and colliding with the walls. He disappeared around the bend, and the sounds of his unsteady progress slowly faded.

Falco remained stock-still, the wax from the candle dripping onto his hand. He stared into the darkness as Hannibal's moans petered out. He drew his dagger and took a couple of steps, then paused to listen.

Bec edged backward into the cave, his eyes fixed on Falco's blade. His heel bumped into something and he almost tripped, saving himself just in time. He felt around with his foot. Behind him was a low stone ridge, forming the rim of a pool of water, cold as ice.

He stood there, backed against the rim. Falco resumed his slow progress up the tunnel, the candle making hollows of his eyes. Bec waited for the man to spot him, but Falco seemed to be dazzled by the light.

Just as the man reached the entrance of the cave, Hannibal dug his claws into Bec's arm and catapulted out. He tore across the space and bit the man on the calf. Falco gave a cry and dropped his candle, which rolled back into the tunnel and sputtered out.

Complete darkness.

Bec felt the dog brush against his legs.

152

A string of curses from Falco. Then a fit of coughing that trickled off into silence.

Bec waited tensely.

Faint noises. The man was entering the cave.

The sounds got closer. Bec shuffled sideways, following the rim of the pool. He could hear Falco breathing, taking in shallow gulps of air.

Then a voice came from the darkness. "I'll get you, you little rat."

Bec went rigid with fear. The man seemed to be directly in front of him.

"I'll teach you not to bite me," said the voice. "I'll slit your bloody throat."

A flurry of barks and a ripping sound. The man howled with fury.

Something rushed past Bec, grazing his leg. A wild cry and a splash—water spraying all over. There was a gurgling noise, then silence. No thrashing about, no stream of oaths. Just the steady splash of falling water.

Bec waited, hardly daring to breathe.

The silence continued.

Something clawed at his leg. Bec jumped in terror.

A low whimper. Hannibal!

Bec picked him up and hugged him. The dog was trembling, but his fur was dry.

Still no sound.

Bec thought about the candle the man had dropped. If only he could find it. The entrance to the tunnel was somewhere out there, not far away. He put Hannibal down and started moving quietly forward, hands extended.

He touched something. The wall. He followed it to the right and came to the tunnel, where he stumbled over the channel of water. Crouching down, he groped around inside the mouth of the tunnel. The candle must be here somewhere.

He crawled slowly down the tunnel, searching feverishly. Still no candle. He reversed course and plunged his hands into the channel, his fingers numbed by the frigid water. Hannibal hugged close to him, shivering and whimpering. Bec tried to push him away, but he kept nosing back.

Finally, Bec encountered a stick-like object, half-submerged in the stream. The candle. He wiped it on his tunic and squeezed the wick. He waited in the darkness for a while, listening. But there was only the quiet gurgle of water.

Maybe Falco had climbed out of the pool. Maybe he was standing there in the cave, dripping wet, biding his time. Bec pictured the man, blade in hand, peering around.

But the silence went on and on. Surely Falco would have spoken by now—or at least made a sound. Something must have happened.

Well, he had to take the risk. Bec dried his hands on his tunic and extracted some tinder from the little box he'd stored in his pouch. He spread it on the ground with trembling fingers, then located the piece of iron. But where was the flint? It seemed to be missing. He fumbled around in the box. There it was. He struck it against the iron. A shower of sparks briefly lit up the tunnel, but the tinder didn't catch.

Bec paused to listen. The sparks were intensely bright in the tomb-like darkness. Surely Falco would have noticed them. Yet he didn't say a word.

Bec struck the flint again and the tinder burst into fire. He grabbed the candle and held it to the flame. But the wick was still damp and the tinder flickered out. He rolled the wick between his fingers, squeezing out the last drops of moisture, then struck the flint one more time, trying to stop his hands from shaking.

The tinder flared up and he thrust the candle into the flame. This time the wick hissed briefly and caught fire. He sheltered the tiny flame with his hand, nursing it to life.

Once the candle was burning steadily, Bec got to his feet

and crept back up the tunnel to the cave. Hannibal squeezed between his legs, almost tripping him up. He stopped at the entrance and held the candle out in front of him, looking inside.

It was not a cave after all, but a large underground chamber with a high vaulted ceiling. The walls were covered with mosaics, showing boats and fish in a pale blue sea. Embedded in the right wall was an ancient fountain, where water spouted from the mouth of a stone lion and tumbled into a sunken pool on the floor below. The pool stretched into the middle of the chamber, taking up almost half the space. The overflow from the pool emptied into the channel that ran across the floor and down the tunnel.

There was no sign of Falco.

Bec moved warily into the chamber, gazing around, candle in hand. The man had vanished. On the far side of the room was an elaborate archway leading into another tunnel, which seemed to run upward. Bec peered at the tunnel, wondering if Falco was hiding there. It was too dark to see anything.

He tiptoed across the floor to the pool, then gave a cry, almost dropping the candle.

Falco was floating just beneath the surface of the water, his eyes and nose exposed. In his hand was a dagger.

Bec staggered back, waiting for the man to spring from the pool. But he just bobbed up and down. A dark red ribbon curled away from his head, drifting to the side of the pool, where it slid over the spillway.

Blood.

And there was more blood smeared on the opposite rim of the pool.

Bec crept closer and gazed at the man, gently rocking in the water. Long strands of hair were wrapped across his face, clinging to the skin.

A bubble emerged from his purple lips, slowly swelled, and burst.

The man was dead.

CHAPTER 21

Bec's stomach heaved. He turned quickly away, staring at the mosaics on the wall. Boats with billowing sails. A boy riding a sea monster. Schools of fish — big and small.

He felt Falco's eyes crawling over his back.

He gave a shout and whirled around.

Falco stared back at him.

Stared but saw nothing. Bobbing in the water.

Bec gave a shudder, his whole body quaking.

The lizard he was carrying scuttled onto his collar.

"Sorry, little fellow," said Bec. "I think it's time for you to go."

He picked up the tiny creature and deposited it on the ground, where it flicked its tail and scooted into the shadows.

Bec dripped some wax onto the floor and pressed the candle into it. He gazed at the wavering flame, trying to steel himself.

There was something he had to do. But he could hardly bring himself to do it.

He went back to the pool, where he reached out and grabbed one of Falco's legs. It was as slippery as a fish. He dropped it, splashing water all over.

Gritting his teeth, he grasped the leg again and manoeuvred the body until it floated alongside the rim of the pool. He grasped the man's dagger, but it slipped from his fingers and sank to the bottom, well out of reach. It gleamed at him wickedly from beneath the water.

Bec gazed at the plume of blood coiling from Falco's head. He would not go into that water for all the daggers in the world.

There was still the pouch. He reached out and unfastened it from the man's belt. Inside was a store of money—some florins and lesser coins. He weighed them in his hand, hesitating. It was surely wrong to steal from the dead. But he really needed the money. If he left it behind, it would only go to waste—or be appropriated by the next person who happened to come along.

He quickly pocketed the coins and sorted through the other items in the pouch—a battered razor, a rusty key— useless stuff. At the bottom, wrapped in a swatch of linen, was a silver ring, delicately worked—a woman's ring. On the inside was an inscription. Bec recognized a few letters but couldn't read well enough to know what the inscription said. He wondered if the ring had been stolen, or if it had belonged to someone Falco cared about—mother, wife, daughter.

He gazed at the man's crumpled face. What had gone on behind those hollow eyes? Where had he come from, and how had he ended up an outlaw? Then, with a sharp intake of breath, he noticed something on the man's arm. Two crude letters seared into the skin.

A M

He knew what the letters stood for. *Adolfo Malaspina*. It was the brand they gave to rebellious slaves—the one they'd planned for him.

Falco had once been a slave on Malaspina's estate.

Bec stared at the man. He didn't look at all familiar. He must have escaped from Scarmagno many years ago.

Bec stopped breathing.

Fiaccola.

Falco must be Fiaccola.

The slave who'd escaped just before Bec was born.

The one he believed was his father.

A deep groan escaped from Bec's throat.

Hannibal trotted over to tug at his tunic, then lick his hand.

"Cut it out, Hannibal."

He pushed the dog away and looked again at Falco, studying the man's features. His face was deeply lined, and his long greasy hair was streaked with grey. His lips were parted, showing big gaps between his stained and chipped teeth.

Could this bony wretch really be his father?

Bec gave a shiver. He seemed much too old. Fiaccola had been a young man when he'd escaped. Could he have aged so much since then?

Bec bit his lip, thinking over what he knew about the slave. People on the estate often told stories about him— his run-ins with Malaspina, the beatings he'd received. But no one had ever said Fiaccola might be his father. It was a conclusion he'd come to on his own.

Bec shook his head. It was hopeless. He had no way of knowing who his father really was.

He turned the silver ring over in his hand and looked again at the inscription. He'd have to find someone who could read.

He put away the ring and gazed at Falco's body. If he left it in the pool, it would rot away, fouling the water. He couldn't let that happen.

Swallowing hard, he grabbed an arm and a leg and tried to drag the body up over the rim of the pool. The man felt incredibly heavy. His clothes were drenched and he flopped about, resisting every effort to lug him out of the pool. Bec shunted the body around and put his hands under the armpits, pulling as hard as he could. He slipped on the wet floor and almost went slithering into the pool. He recovered, tried again, and finally managed to drag the man up onto the floor.

He stood there panting. Water trickled from Falco's nose and mouth, making a puddle on the ground. He stared at the man in horrified fascination, half-fearing, half-hoping that he would suddenly cough, sit up, and look around. But Falco just lay there in a sodden heap, blood leaking from the wound on his head.

Bec straightened out the man's legs and folded his arms across his chest, like he'd seen people do with the dead. He tried to close Falco's eyes, but they kept popping open, staring at him. So, finally, he gave up. He knelt down and made the sign of the cross, murmuring fragments of a prayer he'd heard at funerals.

It felt strange to be praying for someone who had tried to kill him. But now that Falco was dead, he seemed almost like a comrade—an escaped slave like himself.

Perhaps his father.

162

CHAPTER 22

The Catacombs

The candle on the floor had already burned halfway down. Soon it would go out and the chamber would be plunged into darkness.

Bec wondered what to do. It wasn't safe to go back to the cave in front—the other bandits would be there. Yet he couldn't stay here, either. His only option was to try the archway on the other side of the room.

He eyed the murky tunnel. All his instincts spoke against going in. He stood rooted to the spot, unable to will his legs to move.

In the end, Hannibal decided for him. The little dog had been wandering around the chamber, sniffing here and there. All at once, he came up to Bec, whining and rubbing against his legs, then set off toward the archway. He stopped at the entrance and looked back at Bec, his ears raised. He gave a single sharp bark, turned away, and trotted through the opening, disappearing into the darkness.

Bec hated the idea of following him. But he was terrified at the thought of being left alone.

"Well, here goes nothing," he muttered.

He picked up the candle and entered the archway, in time to see Hannibal's white rump vanishing into the gloom ahead, beyond the candle's range. The tunnel ran steeply upward, with rough steps carved into the floor. Hannibal led the way, glancing back from time to time to make sure Bec was still there.

As Bec clambered up the tunnel, he noticed a foul smell—like the one he'd encountered on the stairway in the convent. The odour grew stronger as he moved along, until he was forced to breathe through his mouth.

The tunnel levelled out, leading him into a circular chamber. The walls were honeycombed with cells hollowed into the rock, row upon row, extending from floor to ceiling.

Bec stared.

The cells were full of skulls and bones. From every direction, empty eye sockets and broken jaws gaped at him. It was some kind of underground graveyard—catacombs— perhaps where the nuns used to be buried.

Bec stood there, petrified, certain that the skeletons would pounce on him, tearing off chunks of flesh with hungry mouths and lapping up his blood. The candle shook in his hand, sending shadows dancing around the room, as the eyes of the skulls flickered with life.

The smell was awful.

Hannibal was standing in the centre of the room, gazing back at Bec with a puzzled expression. He went over to a cell, sniffed at the bones inside, and lifted his leg, propelling a yellow stream onto a skull. Bec watched in dismay, waiting for the dog to be torn to shreds. But nothing happened. The skull just sat there, pee trickling into its eyes and mouth. Hannibal moved on to another skull, which he baptized in similar fashion.

Bec burst out laughing. He leaned against the wall and laughed until his stomach ached, and tears ran down his cheeks. He wiped his face and looked again at the skeletons. Their power over him was gone. They were just a bunch of old bones. He walked into the middle of the room.

"Boo!" he shouted at the skulls.

Hannibal looked up, quite startled. The skulls gazed on silently.

"Boo! Boo!" Bec turned in all directions.

Hannibal didn't seem impressed by Bec's performance. He resumed his circuit of the chamber, sniffing and leaving his mark.

Bec kept whirling around, shouting at the bone-filled cells, until the candle started to sputter. He quickly stopped and shielded the flame with his hand.

Hannibal had completed his tour and was now waiting by the exit on the other side, gazing at Bec with bright eyes, his tail whisking back and forth. He turned and vanished inside the tunnel. Bec hurried to catch up.

On both sides were tiers of cells stuffed with skeletons. In some places, the bones were scattered on the ground, and he had to skip over them. Finally, the tunnel led to a high cave, where water trickled from a rough fountain, and a stone stairway ran up the wall into darkness. A section had collapsed and was choked with rubble.

Bec gazed at the stairway. This was the same one they had come down yesterday. He could identify exactly the spot where Tien Nu had fallen.

Hannibal bounded over the rubble, leaping from spot to spot, until he reached the stairs that were still intact. Bec gazed upward, then scrambled after the little dog. The stairway rose through an opening in the roof of the cave and began winding steeply upward. Soon Bec came to a slit in the wall. He looked out, almost blinded by the light. He could see the mountains on the other side of the valley, hazy in the afternoon sun.

He breathed a sigh of relief and kept climbing, until he arrived at the gallery leading back to the old nun's room, where he blew out the candle.

Hannibal was there waiting. As soon as he saw Bec, he turned and scurried ahead to the place where the floorboards in the closet above had collapsed. Bec helped him scramble into the closet, then leapt up and did the same himself. He lay on the floor for a moment, catching his breath.

The closet door was ajar. Bec got to his feet and peered into the Abbess's room.

The shutters on the window were closed and a soft light filtered through the slats. The desk was empty and the room was silent.

Bec tiptoed from the closet.

"Well, look what the dog dragged in," said a voice.

The tiny nun was seated on a stool in the corner, cradling Hannibal in her arms.

CHAPTER 23

The Shrine

The Knight closed the cloister gate behind him and climbed down through the crumbling rows of the arena, as the setting sun etched the ruins in lines of black and gold. He crossed the sandy hollow to the shrine, where he knelt before the statue of the huge man with a child on his shoulder.

San Cristoforo, his namesake. A knight and swordsman like himself. A man who had once served the devil.

"San Cristoforo," began the Knight. "Help me ..."

He stumbled to a stop.

"Help me become the man I want to be ..."

But there lay the problem. He didn't know what that was. Once he had thought he did. He'd believed in the code of the knight and tried to follow it. But he'd never gotten very far. Little by little, he became like most of the other knights— proud and greedy and violent.

The Knight began again. "San Cristoforo, help me understand what kind of man I ought to be. Help me see my way."

He made the sign of the cross, pushed himself stiffly to his feet, and found a seat on the base of a shattered column.

He wondered if he should have returned to Castello Scarmagno. He remembered his favourite room at the top of the stairs, its window overlooking the river, the dark forest beyond. As a child, he'd spent hours there with his cousin, Bernardo. They'd gaze out the window, imagining what lay beyond the mountains that ringed the castle, talking about what they'd do when they grew up, where they'd go, the adventures they'd have.

But returning to Scarmagno with Adolfo in charge ... no, it was impossible.

He thought of Bernardo, his oldest, dearest friend. They'd grown up together, closer than brothers. He'd heard that Bernardo had left the estate not long after himself— headed down the valley to Ponti. Maybe he was still there and they'd meet again.

The sun set and the features of San Cristoforo softened into obscurity. All that remained was the outline of the saint's body—a warrior's body like the Knight's, battered and torn. He wondered if the saint had ever ached so badly, he could hardly sleep at night, whether he'd been haunted by the lives he'd ruined, the deaths he'd caused.

The Knight sat there for a long time, thinking about San Cristoforo, wondering if he'd ever felt the same hopelessness and despair. Then, overcome with weariness, he leaned back against the column and fell asleep.

CHAPTER 24

A Robbery

A loud sneeze broke the air, followed by an oath. Tien Nu awoke with a start, feeling chilled. The ledge was already in darkness, and shadows were gathering in the folds of the mountains across the valley.

Another sneeze. Tien Nu crept to the rim of the ledge and saw Bosco standing by the mouth of the cave. A pair of legs protruded through the vines.

"Hold on, Beppe," he said. "Stop kicking and I'll give you a hand."

Bosco helped his brother from the cave, dusted him off, and patted him on the shoulder. The pair pushed through the bushes and moved along the path toward the arena.

A small, hooded figure slipped from the cave.

Tien Nu was about to call out: "Bec!" But something held him back.

He stared at the figure as it hurried after the men, then shook his head. It didn't look much like Bec after all.

His eyes turned back to the cave. Long minutes passed and no one else appeared. What could have happened to his friend? And what about the skinny man?

Tien Nu climbed down to the clearing and quietly approached the cave. He stood there listening. There was nothing but the sound of the little stream. He moved the vines to one side and peered through. The outlines of the cave gradually emerged from the gloom.

"Bec!" he called softly.

No reply.

Tien Nu crawled cautiously through the entrance.

"Bec! Where are you?"

Still nothing.

He moved further inside, straining to see.

"B–E–C!" he called.

His voice echoed back, followed by a wave of silence.

Tien Nu thought about the hooded boy he'd seen leaving the cave. Could that have been Bec, after all? He'd better make sure.

He exited the cave and made his way along the path. Soon, he spotted three figures ahead, crouched behind some bushes, staring down into the sandy hollow at the base of the arena. He worked his way closer, moving from bush to bush, until he could see what they were looking at.

Slumped against a pillar by the shrine was an enormous man in a faded black cape, sound asleep.

The Knight.

Bosco whispered something to the boy, then took his brother by the arm and disappeared into the woods nearby. The boy waited until they'd gone, then crept down to the hollow and approached the sleeping man. He paused, then snatched something from the Knight's belt and raced off.

The Knight awoke with a roar and staggered to his feet. The boy sprinted up the path in Tien Nu's direction, while the Knight stumbled after him.

Tien Nu shouted at the boy as he ran by. The boy gave a start and slowed down, glancing through the bushes at Tien Nu. Then he picked up speed and tore along the path. Tien Nu shrugged off his pack and sprinted after him. The boy was running full out, his legs pumping, his bare feet throwing up spurts of sand. Tien Nu gained steadily on the thief, until he could hear his breath rasping in his throat.

The boy glanced over his shoulder, then wheeled around to face him.

They stared at each other, chests heaving. The moon had

risen over the mountains and the light streamed into the boy's face, showing a small, curved scar on the cheek. His mouth was twisted in a scornful smile.

The thief raised his hand and hurled something at him. A glittering object hissed past Tien Nu's ear, slithering into the long grass.

Tien Nu dove at the boy, dragging him down.

The two tumbled through the grass, the boy thrashing like a wildcat, scratching and clawing.

Tien Nu punched him in the face and a red flower bloomed under his nose. The boy gave a shrill cry and kneed Tien Nu, sending shivers of pain up through his belly. Tien Nu rolled away, gasping. The boy hobbled to his feet and made for a clump of trees, one hand pressed to his nose. Tien Nu pushed himself up and staggered after him.

The boy turned around, ropes of blood drooping from his nostrils.

"What more do you want?" he cried. "I've given it back!"

Tien Nu stared at the boy. His eyes were strangely liquid and alive, like those of a small, trapped animal.

The boy plunged forward and rammed him in the chest. Tien Nu fell back. There was a sharp pain at the rear of his skull, and then a burst of light.

He sank into darkness.

CHAPTER 25

The Dagger

The smell of garlic and wine. Tien Nu gagged and opened his eyes, to see the face of the Knight peering down at him.

"Ah, that's better," said the man, leaning back. "For a moment, I thought you'd decided to pack it in."

Tien Nu struggled into a sitting position. "Did he get away?"

"Into the trees," said the Knight. "I tried to follow him, but he was much too quick for me. How do you feel?"

"I'm all right."

Tien Nu touched the back of his head, which felt wet and sticky. "I must have hit a rock or something."

He tried to get up, but his legs buckled under him.

"Steady now," said the Knight. "Let's take a look."

He parted Tien Nu's hair and prodded, none too gently, at the skull.

Tien Nu set his jaw, trying not to wince.

"It's a bit bloody," said the Knight. "And you'll have a nice goose egg. But I think you'll live."

Tien Nu took a deep breath and pushed himself unsteadily to his feet. He looked around, searching for whatever the thief had thrown at him. In the deep grass he found a dagger, its silver hilt elaborately wrought in the Eastern style.

"I think this may belong to you," he said.

The Knight took the dagger and gazed at it.

"Thank you," he said. "This means a lot to me."

He slid the dagger into the loop at his waist and stood there, absent-mindedly massaging the stump of his little finger.

"I'm in your debt," he said quietly. "How can I repay you?"

Tien Nu paused. "Didn't you say you're travelling south?"

"That's right, with some pilgrims. I'm the guard. We're headed for Ponti, then onward to the Terra Santa."

"That's where we're going—to Ponti," said Tien Nu. "Maybe ..."

His voice trailed off.

"You'd like to come along as servants—you and your friend?" said the Knight. "That's what he asked about earlier."

Tien Nu nodded. "We're strong and reliable, and we know how to fight."

"As I saw."

Tien Nu's cheeks burned. "I can do better than that."

"You did all right." The Knight gazed at Tien Nu. "Where is your friend, anyway?"

"Bec? I'm ... I'm not sure. He went off on his own somewhere. But he'll show up."

The Knight shrugged. "Then come along, if you like."

"To Ponti?"

"As far as you want—Roma, Alessandria, the Terra Santa. Just show up tomorrow. We leave mid-morning from the south gate."

"Thanks, milord. But I'll have to find Bec first. I can't go without him."

"Understood."

"Actually ... I don't have a place to stay tonight. Is there any room where you are?"

"At the inn?" The Knight thought for a moment. "There's a spare room where I store my things. But I guess you could use it."

"If it's not too much trouble, milord."

"What's your name?"

"Tien Nu."

"Are you a runaway slave like your friend?"

Tien Nu shook his head. "That's just Bec. I only met him

last night. We got into a bit of trouble and ended up hiding in the convent. An old nun helped us."

"The convent up there?" The Knight glanced at the building high above them, pale in the moonlight.

Tien Nu nodded.

"Which nun helped you?"

"I think she's the Abbess."

"The Abbess! It so happens, she's a friend of mine. We play chess. Beats me all the time." The Knight gave Tien Nu a sharp look. "You're sure you're not making this up?"

"Yes, milord. I mean no, milord. She has a little white dog."

"So she does. Hannibal. A real rascal. Well, well! Come along, then."

Tien Nu fetched his pack and followed the Knight up through the arena to the cloister. They passed through the church to the street outside. Nearby was an inn, where a lantern creaked in the breeze. They entered through the door in the yard, climbed some stairs, and went down a dimly lit hallway. The Knight stopped and pushed open a door.

"Here we are. You can have this place to yourself."

He found a candle inside and went to light it from the lamp in the hallway.

The room was small, with some luggage and a huge sword

in the corner. On one side were a table and a three-legged stool. On the other, a rough-hewn bed hugged the wall.

"Make yourself at home," said the Knight. "I'm just next door."

There was a pounding of feet along the hallway and a small boy burst in.

"Cri-Cri," said the boy breathlessly. "My mama ... my mama ..."

He stopped short when he saw Tien Nu.

"Hello," he said.

"Hello," said Tien Nu.

"The landlady's son," said the Knight. "Name of Jaco."

Jaco stared at Tien Nu for a moment, then turned to the Knight. "My mama says ... says ..." he spun around on one foot, "she says there's a message from the Ab ... Ab ..."

"The Abbess," volunteered the Knight.

"Yes, the Abscess. It's about tonight." He jumped on the bed and bounced up and down.

The Knight smiled. "The chess game?"

"Yes, yes! She says to come right away!" Jaco hopped off the bed and made for the corner, where he tried to tug the huge sword from its scabbard.

The Knight put a hand on the boy's shoulder. "Swords aren't

for you, Jaco. Not yet. Tell your mama I'll be coming soon."

Jaco dashed from the room, then popped his head back in and looked at Tien Nu.

"Goodbye," he said.

Tien Nu grinned. "Goodbye."

Jaco was gone.

The Knight glanced at Tien Nu. "Now, if you'll excuse me, I've been summoned. And when the Abbess calls, I've learned it's wise to obey. If you need the latrine, it's out in the yard. Just follow your nose."

Tien Nu closed the door after the Knight, then eased off his pack, suddenly aware of the hole in his stomach. It seemed like years since he'd eaten.

The meat pies were still at the top of his pack. Tien Nu unwrapped them carefully and set them out on the table. They were crumbling at the edges but otherwise fine. He gazed at them. One was meant for Bec.

He sat down and nibbled at a pie.

Delicious, full of spicy meat.

Once he'd started, there was no holding back. He wolfed the pie down, then eyed the second one. It would be soggy by the morning. And there was no telling when Bec would show up.

The second pie disappeared almost as fast as the first. Tien Nu leaned back and let out a belch, feeling pleasantly full. He yawned and stretched, then went outside to use the latrine.

When he got back, he loosened his tunic to get ready for bed and found something snarled in a hook—a tiny leather bag on a frayed cord. He untangled the bag, kneading it with his fingers. It was sewn up tightly, but there was something inside—perhaps an amulet or medallion. He tried to think where it could have come from, but his mind refused to work.

He stored the bag away in his pack, wrapped himself in his cape, and stumbled into bed, falling into a deep sleep.

Hours later, someone pushed in beside him.

"Goodnight, Papa," Tien Nu muttered.

"So, I'm your father now?"

Tien Nu's eyes fluttered open.

"Shove over, will you?" said Bec. "You're hogging the whole bed."

CHAPTER 26

Together Again

Light filtered through the window, just enough to see by. Tien Nu raised his head and peered around the cramped room.

He had a muddled memory of Bec showing up in the middle of the night. But it must have been a dream. There was no sign of him now. Anyway, how could Bec have known where he was staying?

Tien Nu rolled to the side of the bed and planted his feet on the cold floor. He ran a hand through his hair and winced when he grazed the wound on his scalp. His cheeks burned as he recalled his fight with the thief—and the way it had ended. He wondered what the Knight had made of him. He knew what his father would have thought.

The sound of splashing came from outside. Tien Nu went to the window and looked down into the yard of the inn. A half-naked person was crouched by the well, spluttering and snorting as he dumped water from a bucket onto his head.

So, it hadn't been a dream after all.

"Bec," he called quietly.

The figure gave a start and looked around the yard—then up at the window.

"I'm coming down," Tien Nu said.

Bec nodded and went on with his washing.

Tien Nu got dressed and made his way down the dark stairway. When he reached the yard, Bec was perched on the rim of the well, his hair plastered to his skull, his eyes dancing.

Tien Nu grabbed him and wrestled him to the ground, pommelling him in the chest and stomach, until Bec was laughing so hard he gave up defending himself.

"Idiot!" Tien Nu said. "Where did you disappear to? You really had me worried."

"Which makes you an idiot, too, for worrying about me," Bec said. "Nobody in their right mind does that."

It took some explaining, but eventually the two stories got pieced together. Bec related his side with gusto, explaining what had happened to him inside the cave, and how Hannibal had led him up to the old nun's room.

"But how did you know where to find me?" Tien Nu asked.

"I didn't! Not until the Knight showed up to play chess

with the nun. He brought me back here afterward."

Bec grinned. "He also told me we can go to Ponti together."

Tien Nu's story was more straightforward, or it would have been if Bec hadn't kept on interrupting.

At the end, Tien Nu shook his head. "That master of yours is a nasty piece of work. He was ready to carve me up if I didn't turn you in."

"Sorry to drag you into all this crap," Bec said.

Tien Nu shrugged. "Not to worry. It's what friends do."

"Drag you into crap?"

"No, no! I mean ..."

Bec laughed. "I know what you mean."

He paused, gazing at Tien Nu. "Actually, when you went into town, I didn't expect you to come back. Not when you left with your pack and all your things."

"Well, I did come back," Tien Nu said. "Pretty dumb, eh?"

"As dumb as they come."

Tien Nu scooped some water from the bucket and splashed it on his face.

"Oh, I forgot to tell you," he said. "There's a price on your head. Malaspina's offering a reward."

"How much?"

"Thirty florins."

"Not enough!" Bec said. "I'm worth at least double that."

The Knight was waiting for them when they returned to the room. Bread and cheese and a cruet of olive oil were spread out on the table.

"I brought these up from the kitchen," he said. "You need to stay out of sight until we're on the road."

"There's more food in my pack," Tien Nu said. "Sausages and other things I got at the market yesterday."

Bec's eyes lit up. "What about the meat pies?"

"Don't worry. They didn't go to waste."

"You mean ...?"

"I was hungry last night."

"Holy smoke, Scraps! How many pies?"

"Two."

"That's disgusting."

"I thought so, too. But not enough to slow me down."

As they ate, the Knight explained his plans. "We'll be leaving from the south gate later this morning. The pilgrims have organized everything themselves. All we need to do is show up."

He scratched his beard. "But we'll have to be careful. I hear Malaspina and his men are roaming around."

He studied Bec for a moment.

"The problem is you're too easy to spot. We need to change your looks. Some new clothes wouldn't be a bad start. Those rags you're wearing—holes in all the wrong places. The girls must blush to look at you."

"What's wrong with my clothes?" Bec said. "Anyway, the girls are free to look."

"And that mop of blond hair," the Knight said. "It's a dead giveaway."

"Why not shave it off?" Tien Nu said.

"Hold on!" Bec said. "Whose side are you on?"

"Not a bad idea." The Knight glanced at Tien Nu. "In fact, it might work for both of you."

Bec smiled. "Now there's a plan."

The Knight rummaged around in his chest and pulled out a razor.

Bec eyed the long thin blade. "Are you sure you know how to handle that thing?"

"As if my life depended on it," said the Knight.

"But it's my life, not yours."

The Knight secured a pitcher of hot water and some soap from the kitchen, then sharpened the razor on a whetstone.

He nodded to Tien Nu. "Let's start with you."

The Knight set himself to the task, humming cheerfully.

"Oh, I almost forgot." He peered at the scabby lump on Tien Nu's head. "I'll have to go easy here."

"*Ecco!*" he said eventually. "How's that?"

Tien Nu rubbed his head. It was perfectly smooth, except for a bristly area around the scab.

"How do I look?" he asked.

"Like an egg," said Bec. "A cracked one."

The Knight waved the razor at Bec. "Your turn now."

The blond hair came off in swathes, exposing a pale dome of untanned skin.

Bec turned his head from side to side. "I can feel the breeze around my ears."

"Does the breeze go right through—ear to ear?" Tien Nu asked.

Bec grinned. "Funny man."

The Knight stepped back to admire his work. "Now, if you'd only wipe that smirk off your face, you might pass for a pilgrim."

CHAPTER 27

On the Road

"Turn it the other way, Scraps," Bec said. "A bit higher. That does it."

Tien Nu gave a grunt. "How did he get this thing up the stairs in the first place?"

They were carrying the Knight's wooden chest down to the yard of the inn, no easy feat on the narrow twisting staircase. Eventually, all their belongings were piled in a handcart, ready to be transported across town to the south gate.

Catarina and Jaco were there to see them off, along with the Abbess. Hannibal raced madly around, yapping with excitement.

The old nun picked up the dog and gave him a hug. "Goodbye, you little rascal. I'll miss you."

Bec stared at her.

"Yes, yes," said the Abbess. "I'm giving Hannibal to you.

I talked to the Knight about it, and we agreed the dog needs a new master, someone as young and frisky as himself. He'll be good company on the pilgrimage."

"Thanks, Mother," Bec said. "It's the best present I've ever had."

Hannibal wriggled from the old nun's grasp and dashed over to Bec, who scratched him behind the ears, then hoisted him into the handcart.

"And here's something to carry him around with," the Abbess said.

She handed Bec a long piece of cloth, to be used as a sling.

"Why don't you fellows go on ahead," said the Knight. "I'll catch up in a minute."

Bec and Tien Nu said their farewells and set off across the yard with the handcart. Bec was in front between the long wooden handles, and Tien Nu was pushing from behind.

"Don't keep stopping," Tien Nu said.

"I can't help it," Bec said. "It's this new tunic Catarina gave me. It's a bit too long and I'm tripping over it."

When they finally reached the gate to the street, they paused to look back.

The Knight was saying goodbye to the Abbess, who handed him a string of rosary beads, which he hung around his neck. Catarina kissed him on both cheeks and gave him a long hug, quickly turning away to wipe her eyes. The Knight mussed up Jaco's hair and said a few words, then came tramping across the yard.

Tien Nu waved to the Abbess, who smiled and waved back.

"Hey, watch out," said Bec. "The cart nearly went over."

"Shall I lend a hand?" asked the Knight.

"No, no," they said together. "We're doing fine."

They turned into the street and started up the steep slope.

The Knight took one look at their red faces and laughed. "Let me help. I think the baggage weighs more than the two of you together."

He took the chest from the cart and heaved it onto his shoulder.

"That's better," said Bec. "What have you got in there, anyway?"

"All sorts of things," said the Knight. "Bits and pieces of a wasted life. I should throw most of it away, but I can't bring myself to do it."

People hurried past, wrapped in cloaks to ward off the morning chill. A knot of ragged boys emerged from an alley, chattering at the top of their voices as they kicked a makeshift ball back and forth. Bec recognized some of them from the funeral procession and signalled for Tien Nu to keep his head down. But the boys hardly gave them a second glance as they passed, reserving their attention for the huge Knight.

After some time, they reached a crossroads at the top of town, where a long straight road led down to a square just inside the south gate. A market was getting underway—rows of untidy stalls with all sorts of produce, as well as crates of chickens, ducks, geese, rabbits, pigeons, piglets—all squealing and squawking and hissing. Vendors called out their wares and children raced around, shrieking with delight as they dodged through the maze of stalls.

Bec noticed someone staring at them from behind a wagon.

There was a spark of recognition.

"Look!" he said. "It's Curly—that bandit boy from the cave. Over there."

Tien Nu turned to look.

The boy gazed steadily at them for a moment, then melted into the crowd.

"Up to no good, I'll bet," Tien Nu said. "Picking purses and filching from the stalls."

Bec looked around for the other bandits and noticed a group of rough men headed for the gate. Sure enough, Bosco and Beppe were among them, their broad-brimmed hats pulled low. Bec nudged Tien Nu, and they watched as the men disappeared through the gate.

The Knight led them to a corner where the pilgrims had gathered, their luggage piled in heaps. He talked to the leader of the group—a slight man named Federico—while Bec and Tien Nu unloaded their bags.

"What about the handcart?" Tien Nu asked. "Shall we run it back up to the inn?"

"No need," said the Knight. "Catarina said to leave it with the cooper. His place is around here somewhere. Ah, there it is." He pointed to a workshop bearing the sign of a barrel.

At the shop, a man in a leather apron came out to meet Bec and Tien Nu.

"For the Three Bells inn?" he said, glancing at the cart. "I'll make sure it gets there. I've got some barrels to deliver anyway. So, you're travelling today?"

Bec nodded. "To Ponti—with some pilgrims."

"Ah! Ponti." The man's brow furrowed. "Another group of pilgrims went down that way not long ago. Seems they had a spot of trouble. Bandits, you know. The road is full of them." He shook his head. "Well, I won't trouble you with the story. With God's grace, you'll have better luck."

Bec saw the Knight beckoning from the corner. They thanked the cooper and hurried back to the pilgrims.

A wagon came rumbling up, driven by a burly man with deep circles under his eyes.

"Ponti!" he droned in a mournful voice. "All for Ponti!"

The pilgrims surged toward the wagon.

"Baggage goes in back," the driver said. "No room for anything else. Everyone walks."

Bec and Tien Nu climbed into the wagon and helped to load the bags. The leader, Federico, hopped up beside them and did a head count.

"Eleven ... twelve ... thirteen ...." He frowned and counted the pilgrims again, then ran a hand through his wispy hair.

"Thirteen. Unlucky number. Someone's missing." Federico cast an eye over the group. "I should have known. It's that fool of a boy, Emilio. Does anyone know where he's gotten to?"

A couple of pilgrims looked at each other, smirking.

"He went off on his own last night," said one. "Well ... not exactly on his own."

Federico shook his head and muttered to himself. His eye lighted on Hannibal, who was nosing around the wagon.

"No one said anything about a dog," he grumbled. "Keep him away from the horses."

"Not to worry," said Bec. He jumped down and grabbed Hannibal.

After a while, Federico declared they couldn't wait any longer. He said a word to the driver, who picked up the reins and lightly slapped the horses. With a jolt and a clatter, the heavy wagon began moving across the square. The pilgrims fell in behind, walking in clusters of two and three.

Bec pulled on his hood. "This is it, Scraps."

As they approached the gate, a young man with red hair and freckles came flying from a laneway, his clothes in disarray, a bag slung over his shoulder. He ran after the wagon, tossed in the bag and trotted alongside, smiling broadly.

"Nice of you to join us, Emilio," said the leader.

"Some pilgrim!" snorted a lady.

"Fine weather," said Emilio, ignoring her. "Seems like spring is here for good."

Bec and Tien Nu kept their heads down as they passed through the gate. But the guard on duty only glanced at the wagon and gave the driver a friendly wave. There was no sign of Malaspina or his men.

The horses picked up speed, and the wagon lurched down the stony track.

They were off.

CHAPTER 28

The Watcher

On reaching the valley, the wagon turned onto the main road, which followed the river southward toward the sea. On either side, heavily forested hills rose to steep slopes above, with snow-capped peaks glittering in the distance. Tien Nu took a deep breath, relishing the fresh morning air.

Bec threw back his hood and trotted along in front of the wagon. Hannibal gambolled around him, barking and nipping at his feet.

The horses shied sideways, spooked by Hannibal's antics.

"Hey, you!" shouted Federico. "Didn't I tell you to mind your dog?"

"Sorry!" said Bec.

"Come on, Scraps," he shouted. "Race you to that rock ahead."

He dashed off, with Hannibal keeping pace. Tien Nu

followed, loping along in their wake. But whenever he tried to pass, Hannibal got in his way, tripping him up. Bec darted past the rock just ahead of Tien Nu. He collapsed on the grass at the side.

"Not bad for a little guy, eh?" he said.

Tien Nu dropped down beside him. "You had some help from your friend."

Bec gazed back at the town of Montecavo, perched on its rocky throne, its walls and towers bathed in the morning sunlight.

"I can't believe we've finally left that place," he said. "Now all we need to do is keep out of Malaspina's way."

"Do you suppose he'll come searching down the road?" Tien Nu asked.

"Probably. But only once he figures out we've left town— which may take a while. Until then, we're safe. How about another race?"

"Sure, but let's try something different. Can you do handsprings?"

"Can a fish swim? Can a lark sing? Can a ..."

"Okay, monkey boy. Let's say we race to that cypress tree."

"Nothing but handsprings?"

"Exactly! No steps in between."

They hung their pouches in the bushes by the road, then got into position.

"Ready?" said Tien Nu.

"Ready."

"*Pronti, partenza, via!*"

Bec took the lead, his body spinning around like a hoop, with Hannibal bounding alongside. But he couldn't keep up the pace. Tien Nu soon passed him, moving steadily forward, each handspring exactly like the one before it. He was far ahead by the time he reached the tree.

"Whew!" said Bec, swiping his face with his arm. "How do you do it, Scraps? I couldn't keep up."

"Actually, you're not bad," Tien Nu said. "You just need more practice."

"And a longer pair of legs."

Tien Nu grinned. "That wouldn't hurt."

He gave Bec a quick glance. "Say, I've been meaning to ask. Are you really sixteen, like you told the Knight? To be honest, you don't look it."

Bec shook his head. "Actually, I'm fourteen. I was trying to impress the Knight. How old are you?"

"Just turned fifteen and still growing. Almost half a foot since last spring."

"I haven't grown much yet," Bec said. "But I've got big feet. They say that's a sign."

"That your feet will get even bigger?"

Bec laughed. "Something like that."

Tien Nu glanced at the road behind them. "The wagon's starting to catch up. I'll go back and fetch our things. You stay here with Hannibal."

As he approached the place where the pouches were hanging, there was a sudden crash in the underbrush and something scuttled away to the safety of the forest beyond, leaving a trail of trembling leaves. Tien Nu peered after the animal—if that's what it was—but he couldn't see anything.

He scooped up some pebbles and tossed them at the trees where the thing had disappeared.

Silence. Not a leaf moved.

But Tien Nu had the feeling he was being watched.

CHAPTER 29
The Sausage

It was late afternoon, with the sun casting spidery shadows over the road. The pilgrims had spent most of the day moving southward along a plain beside the river. Now the valley narrowed, and the road climbed into the foothills, passing over a series of ridges.

Bec had hitched a ride in the wagon, wedging himself in among the bags, while Tien Nu practiced *quan fa* at the rear of the group—punching and feinting and kicking. After a while, Bec drew a sausage from the store of food in Tien Nu's pack and slipped it up his sleeve. He turned to look at the Knight, who was in front, chatting with the driver. Then he hopped down from the wagon and waited for Tien Nu at the side of the road, as the pilgrims trudged by.

"Interested in a wager?" he asked. "Just to pass the time."

"A wager?" said Tien Nu. "About what?"

Bec lifted up his sleeve, showing the long black sausage—
stiff as a truncheon.

"Bet you I can switch this with the Knight's dagger
without him noticing."

Tien Nu looked ahead at the ornate weapon hanging
from the Knight's belt.

"Switch it? Are you serious, *amico*?"

Bec nodded. "I'll take the dagger and put the sausage in
its place."

"The Knight will skin you alive if he catches you."

"Don't worry. He won't catch me."

"All right. But you've got to bring the dagger back here to
show me, then return it to the Knight's belt."

Bec grinned. "No problem. One florin says I can do it."

"Deal."

Bec moved ahead to the wagon, where he fell in beside
the Knight, engaging him in conversation. As they talked,
Bec began walking more slowly. The Knight slowed down
with him, until all the other pilgrims had moved ahead, save
only Tien Nu. Bec's left hand was hanging casually at his
side while he kept up a stream of chatter. He reached out
and tugged gently at the Knight's dagger, which slid upward
out of the loop in his belt.

The Knight continued to gaze ahead, not noticing anything. Bec passed the dagger behind his back and exchanged it for the sausage. Still talking, he inserted the sausage in the loop and nudged it down into place.

After a while, Bec excused himself and sauntered back to Tien Nu, barely able to conceal his glee. With his back to the Knight, he pulled up his sleeve and showed Tien Nu the dagger.

"Now you have to put it back," Tien Nu said. "That's the bet."

"Watch and weep!"

Bec headed back toward the Knight and then stopped in his tracks. *"Porca miseria!"* he muttered.

There was Hannibal, trotting along at the Knight's side, gazing up at the sausage dangling from his belt.

"Hey there, little fellow," said the Knight, noticing the dog. "What's up?"

The dog barked sharply, looking into the Knight's eyes.

"What is it, Hannibal? What's the matter?"

The dog barked again and started pawing at the Knight's leg, trying to nibble the end of the sausage.

Bec ran up. "Hey, Hannibal, don't be such a pest."

He bundled the dog into his arms. The little dog whined and wriggled, his eyes still fixed on the sausage.

Bec was caught between two poles. He couldn't return the dagger while he was holding Hannibal. But if he put Hannibal down, the dog would head straight for the sausage.

He glanced back at Tien Nu, signalling for him to come and take Hannibal.

Tien Nu only grinned and shook his head.

Bec gave him a dirty look, then turned around, keeping close to the Knight so as to hide the sausage from the pilgrims.

They were coming to a small town situated at the top of a ridge. The driver pointed ahead to an inn just outside the walls.

"Here we stop for the night," he announced.

As they approached the place, Bec could hear the sound of raised voices. The front door of the inn flew open and a young soldier in dirty livery staggered drunkenly out. He was followed by an older soldier with a ratty beard, who stumbled over the doorstep and fell headlong into the road.

"And don't come back!" cried an aproned woman, who appeared in the doorway, hands on her hips.

"*Vai al inferno!*" roared the bearded soldier, who was struggling to get up.

The landlady stared scornfully at him, tucking up her hair. The man lurched back toward her, letting out a stream of curses. The younger soldier tried to restrain him, but the other threw him off. He dragged out his sword and waved it at the landlady, who stood her ground, eyes flashing. A bare-bottomed child toddled from the inn and clung to her skirts, gazing wide-eyed at the man.

The wagon came to a stop, with the pilgrims clustered

in the road. The Knight moved toward the bearded soldier.

"I'd put that sword away if I were you," he said.

The man turned to stare at him through rheumy eyes. His mouth hung open, a thread of saliva glistening on his beard.

"Who says so?"

The Knight didn't bother to reply. He slowly drew his sword from its scabbard and held the huge weapon in front of him, gazing evenly at the man.

The younger soldier yanked at the other's arm. "Come on, Lucio. The game's not worth the candle. Let's get out of here."

He tried to drag his comrade toward their horses, which were tethered nearby. But the bearded soldier swore and struggled free. He moved unsteadily toward the Knight, clutching his sword with a wavering hand.

People appeared at the windows of the inn, drawn by the noise.

The Knight gazed at the unkempt soldier in front of him. The man stared back and spat on the ground. Then, without warning, he launched himself at the Knight, slashing out wildly with his sword.

The Knight stepped to one side, avoiding the onslaught. The soldier spun around and squinted at him, watery eyes trying to focus. He fumbled at his belt and found his dagger.

Now the sword was in one hand and the dagger in the other. His lips were parted in a lop-sided grin, showing long yellow teeth.

The Knight reached for his own dagger. He grasped the sausage and pulled it out. The soldier stared at the Knight, then gave a loud guffaw.

"Wha-a-zz-at?"

The Knight looked at the long black sausage in his hand and muttered a curse. He vaulted at the soldier and struck him about the head with the sausage, again and again, until the man stumbled back and fell to the ground, dropping his weapons, hands over his head. The Knight kicked the weapons toward the younger soldier.

"Get your friend out of here, and we'll pretend this never happened."

The young man nodded, avoiding the eyes of the enormous Knight, who was still brandishing the sausage. He went over to his fallen comrade and helped him up. In a minute, they had ridden off.

The Knight watched the horses disappear down the road, then turned and gazed at Bec and Tien Nu, who were standing there, not saying a word.

"And who do I have to thank for this?" He dangled the sausage from his fingertips.

"It's me," said Bec. "It was just a prank. I switched the sausage with your dagger. I never thought ..."

"It's my fault, too," Tien Nu said. "I bet him he couldn't do it."

The Knight stared at them. "A bet? How much?"

"One florin," they said together.

"So, who won?"

"Tien Nu did," said Bec. "I was supposed to put the dagger back without you noticing."

"Then pay him."

Bec and Tien Nu exchanged glances. "But ... but ..."

"You heard me, pay him. A debt is a debt."

Bec dug into his pouch and sheepishly handed over one of the coins he'd taken from Falco, which Tien Nu just as sheepishly accepted.

The Knight followed the transaction with hooded eyes. Then he held up the sausage and studied it.

"Quite a handy weapon."

He broke off a chunk and tossed it to Hannibal, who caught it mid-air and wolfed it down.

Most of the pilgrims went straight up to bed after supper, worn out from their first day of travel. The Knight stayed downstairs for a while, gazing into the fire, nursing his wine. Bec and Tien Nu, cowed by his silence, eventually excused themselves and retired to the long stuffy room set aside for the men, where they got into bed. Bec quickly went to sleep.

After a while, there was a noise. Bec opened his eyes. A little moonlight shone through the window. The huge shape of the Knight loomed in the doorway, then moved into the shadows as the door closed.

Bec rolled over, drifting off.

Something was in his hands—something wet and floppy. Bec squeezed it, then gave a shriek and jumped out of bed. The other pilgrims sat up, staring blearily around. Bec lurched into the centre of the room, screeching like a madman. A shapeless item dangled from his outstretched hand.

He gave a shudder and dropped it on the floor.

Tien Nu came over and peered at it. He picked it up gingerly and took a long careful sniff, then showed it to Bec.

A piece of calf's liver, wet with blood.

"It was in my hands," said Bec. "Sick! Disgusting! I don't know how it got there."

He glanced over at the Knight's bed. The man's face was shrouded in darkness, but his shoulders were shaking.

CHAPTER 30

At the Gate

The Knight rose before dawn, brimming with good humour. He made a special point of asking Bec how he'd slept, an innocent smile playing about his face. Bec mumbled something, all the while watching the Knight's eyes. Then he ventured a grin.

"Are we even?"

The Knight's mouth was hidden as he fingered the scar on his cheek. But his eyes crinkled at the edges.

"Just don't try it again."

The sky was still dark when the pilgrims set off from the inn, pausing for fresh *focaccia* at a bakery in the main street. As they passed through the gate on the other side of town, the sun broke over the mountains and the light streamed into their faces.

Bec stopped for a moment, shielding his eyes to look ahead. The road zigzagged down through some vineyards to the river, then climbed back into the hills. A line of ducks passed overhead, honking loudly.

Tien Nu came up beside him, munching on some bread. They gazed at the pilgrims plodding down the road behind the wagon.

"Ponti must be over there somewhere." Bec pointed to a notch in the mountains where the river disappeared. "Another week—that's what the driver says."

Tien Nu watched the ducks winging southward. "If only we could fly."

"I do sometimes—in my dreams," Bec said. "Fly, that is. Do you?"

Tien Nu shook his head. "My dreams are all about falling."

Bec glanced back toward the town.

A man was standing at the gate, squinting at the pilgrims.

"*Merda!*" Bec ducked and pulled on his hood.

"What's the matter?"

"It's Pietro—the steward. At the gate."

Bec sidled ahead, slipping in among the pilgrims. Pietro peered in his direction, then gave a shrill cry. He ran over to the guard, who was drowsing on a bench by the gate. He shook his shoulder, shouting and pointing.

The guard sat up and looked down the road. Eventually,

he got to his feet and came hobbling after the pilgrims, with the steward beside him.

"Hey there!" called the guard. "Pull up! Stop!"

He came alongside the horses, catching at the harness. The driver pulled up the reins and the wagon creaked to a halt. Bec edged to the other side of the wagon, his head down. But the steward had already pointed him out.

"You!" the guard said to Bec. "Come over here and show your face."

Bec did not move.

The Knight looked at Bec. "Do as he says."

Bec moved slowly around the wagon.

"Off with the hood," said the guard.

Bec pulled back his hood and gazed at the man.

"That's him!" said Pietro with a nasty smile. "He's cut off his hair, but I recognize him, all right. He's a slave—a runaway. He belongs to Adolfo Malaspina."

"There must be some mistake," said the Knight. "This boy belongs to me. He's my servant. Perhaps this gentleman is confusing him with someone else."

Pietro scowled. "I know him well enough. His name is Bec."

The guard looked from the Knight to the steward and back again.

"So, you say this boy belongs to you?" he asked the Knight.

"He's my servant. I can vouch for him. This gentleman is making a mistake."

The guard stared at the huge Knight, who was leaning against the wagon, thumb hooked in his belt. The guard dropped his eyes and turned to Pietro.

"This fellow says the boy is his servant. That's good enough for me. He ought to know."

Pietro spluttered: "But ... but ... I recognize him. I've known him for years. There's no mistake."

"Let's get moving," said the driver. "We've got a long way to go."

There was a chorus of assent from the pilgrims. The guard nodded to the driver, who slapped the reins, and the wagon creaked into motion.

Pietro grabbed Bec by the shoulder. "You'll come with me."

The Knight's hand moved to his sword.

"Hold on," said the guard. "There's no need for that."

He pulled Pietro back. "Leave the boy alone."

The steward watched as Bec walked away beside the Knight.

He glanced at the guard. "Idiot!" he hissed.

The guard stared. "What did you say?"

"Nothing."

The wagon picked up speed and rounded a bend in the road. When Bec turned back to look, Pietro was still standing there, gazing steadily after him.

CHAPTER 31

The Valley

As the day wore on, Tien Nu noticed that Bec became steadily quieter—constantly glancing over his shoulder.

Tien Nu waited until they were alone at the rear of the group.

"What's the matter, *amico?*" he asked.

Bec made a face. "It's no good. I have to head off on my own. It's not safe for me to stick around."

He kicked at a pine cone, sending it bouncing along the track. "The steward won't give up that easily. He'll be back, and this time Malaspina will be with him."

"But won't the Knight protect you?"

Bec shook his head. "Why should he? Malaspina will claim me as his own, and the Knight will have to turn me over."

"Then I'll head off with you."

"You don't have to, you know. Malaspina doesn't care about

you. He only wants me. You'll be fine here with the Knight."

"No choice, bonehead. I'm coming."

They walked along in silence.

"What should we tell the Knight?" Tien Nu asked.

"Nothing. He'll try to persuade us to stay—and then everyone will know what's going on. We should just sneak away when we get the chance."

Tien Nu frowned. "That doesn't seem right, after what he's done for us."

Bec gave him a sideways glance. "Look, Scraps. I don't like this any more than you, but what else can we do?"

"What about Hannibal?"

Bec looked at the little dog, who was nosing about the roadside, his fur tangled with burrs.

"He'll have to come with us. I promised the old nun I'd take care of him. Anyway, he wouldn't stay here with the pilgrims. He'd follow us and give us away."

The wagon reached the top of a hill, where the driver stopped to let the horses rest. The two boys caught up with the wagon and gazed ahead.

The road dropped precipitously into a narrow valley, where it crossed a bridge over a rocky stream, and climbed an almost vertical slope on the other side. Bushes crowded the banks of the stream and spread up the sides of the valley.

The wagon started moving again, bumping slowly down the road. It rumbled across the stone bridge and came to a halt on the other side. The driver turned in his seat.

"All right, my friends. Take out your bags—as much as you can carry. Otherwise, we'll never make it up this hill. And I'll need some people to help push the wagon."

The pilgrims began unloading their baggage, grumbling among themselves.

Bec whispered: "This is our chance."

Tien Nu nodded and went to retrieve his pack.

The Knight joined some men who were putting their shoulders to the wagon. On the driver's word, they gave a concerted shove and the wagon started lurching up the steep road.

"Hey, Giacomo!" panted the red-haired youth to the driver. "How come you get to sit up there while we slave away?"

"What's the matter, Emilio?" said the driver. "Still recovering from the other night?"

Bec corralled Hannibal and stuffed him into the sling the old nun had supplied.

He told the Knight: "Back in a minute. Call of nature."

The Knight nodded. He gave a mighty heave and the wagon jolted forward.

The red-haired youth glanced at the boys as they went to relieve themselves in the bushes by the stream. Tien Nu kept one eye on the wagon as it laboured up the track, with the pilgrims straggling behind, loaded down with bags.

"Now," he said. "No one's looking."

He slipped into the thick underbrush, with Bec close behind. They scrambled up the hillside until they came to a narrow path.

"Wild goats," Bec said, pointing to some droppings. "They come down here to drink."

They followed the path as it wound up the hill. There was a sudden explosion, as some partridges burst from the bushes ahead and rose into the air with rapid wing beats. The sound reverberated in Tien Nu's ears, and he felt his chest contracting. The sky tilted abruptly, and the ground slid out from under him, sending him careening forward. He fell onto the path, face down in the sandy soil.

He pushed himself into a sitting position and took a deep breath, feeling dazed.

Bec was staring at him.

"Holy bones, Scraps. What happened?"

Tien Nu brushed some grit from his face, trying to stop his hands from trembling.

"Bloody birds. Scared me half to death."

But Tien Nu was aware that something else was going on. Something connected with his father's death. But he didn't know what.

After a hard climb, they finally reached the top of the slope, where a clearing was shaded by a stunted tree. Looking out over the bushes, they could see the entire valley.

"This is as good a place to hide as any," said Bec. "If Malaspina comes along, we'll spot him right away."

Tien Nu nodded and dropped his pack.

Hannibal whined, wriggling around in his sling. Bec took pity on him and let him jump to the ground.

"Lie down, boy!"

Hannibal shuffled from side to side, then stretched out on his belly, tongue lolling, looking up at Bec.

"Smart boy!" said Bec, tickling him behind the ears.

Tien Nu watched as the wagon crawled up the hillside. At the top, it stopped to let the Knight and the other men go back to fetch their baggage.

After stowing away his things in the wagon, the Knight stationed himself on the brow of the hill, gazing back into the valley. From time to time, he cupped his hands to his mouth and shouted something, but the breeze carried his words away.

Tien Nu felt a pang of guilt. The Knight had befriended them, taken them under his wing. And they'd left without a parting word. He looked at Bec, whose eyes were fixed in the opposite direction, watching for any sign of Malaspina. He wondered if Bec felt as bad as he did.

The driver came to talk to the Knight, gesturing broadly. But the Knight stood his ground, his arms folded across his chest, eyes on the valley. The driver shrugged and retreated to his seat in the wagon.

Bec prodded Tien Nu. "Look! Over there!"

Three riders had appeared on the road from Montecavo, dark against the low-lying sun. They paused on the ridge above the valley. One of them raised an arm and pointed at the wagon on the opposite side.

Tien Nu looked back at the Knight, in time to see him turn and join the other pilgrims. The wagon jolted to life, and in a minute the group had disappeared over the top of the hill.

The riders picked their way down the steep track into the valley. Malaspina was in the lead, wearing a sky-blue tunic. He rode his horse fluidly, with an air of arrogant ease. Behind him came Nozzo, the bodyguard—easy to spot with his shaved head and barrel chest. Pietro, the steward,

brought up the rear. He was having trouble controlling his horse, which tossed its head and skittered sideways.

On reaching the bottom of the valley, the riders stopped by the bridge. Malaspina took off his hat and swivelled in the saddle to talk to his companions, the slanting rays of the sun illuminating his features.

Tien Nu gazed intently at him.

A chill trickled down his back.

Something about Malaspina reminded him of Bec.

The man shifted back to inspect the road ahead and the resemblance faded, eclipsed by the expression on his face— as cold and rapacious as a hawk.

Malaspina gave the word and the riders set off again. They climbed the hill on the other side of the valley and vanished over the crest.

CHAPTER 32

Face to Face

The Knight turned to gaze at the riders as they rode up behind him. Malaspina looked much as he remembered him. Still as spare and sinewy as ever—at ease in the saddle.

He wondered if Adolfo would recognize him. He thought it unlikely. He'd been barely more than a boy when he'd left, skinny and beardless as an egg. Since then, he'd grown a foot or more and doubled in girth, with his face hidden by a bushy beard. Not that it mattered to Cristofo whether the man recognized him or not. He was no longer part of that world.

Malaspina came to a halt and surveyed the disorderly band of pilgrims in the road ahead. He glanced at the older man beside him. "So, where's the slave, Pietro?"

Pietro screwed up his mouth and muttered something. He trotted forward, then slowed down as he reached the pilgrims, who parted to give him a wide berth. He passed through them, looking right and left, examining their faces. When he reached the front of the group, he tugged on the reins and managed to get the horse to turn around. He scanned the pilgrims one more time.

"He's not here. He must be hiding somewhere."

Malaspina's face hardened. He cantered up to the wagon and shouted to the driver.

"Hey, you! Hold on! You heard me. Stop! You've got a slave boy here. A slave who belongs to me."

"Not again!" said the driver wearily.

He pulled the horses up and sat slouching in his seat, massaging the folds at the back of his neck.

Malaspina turned and scrutinized the pilgrims, who were spread out behind the wagon, muttering among themselves. The Knight felt the man's eyes pick him out, pause for a moment, then move on. Malaspina manoeuvred his horse closer to the wagon, his glance ferreting among the bags. He pointed to some bulging sacks in the corner.

"Those bags over there—the big ones. What's in them?"

"They're mine," wheezed a stout woman, who, despite the heat, was swathed in several layers of wool. "Bolts of cloth. Dry goods. I'm selling them along the way."

"Dry goods. Is that so?" said Malaspina. "Let's see."

He extracted his cane from its case and jabbed the iron tip at the bags.

"Careful!" said the woman. "Those things are delicate."

Malaspina ignored her and kept prodding at the bags.

Eventually he glanced at Pietro. "So? Where's the slave?"

Pietro pointed at the Knight. "Ask that fellow. The slave was with him."

Malaspina turned to the Knight. "My man here says you had a slave boy named Bec—a slave who escaped from my estate."

The Knight offered a shrug. "I did have a couple of boys. Servants. But they ran away. Shifty little beggars!"

Malaspina gazed at the Knight. "So, when did this happen?"

"Earlier today sometime—can't say exactly when. I wasn't paying them much attention."

Malaspina pointed his cane at the driver. "You, there! When did the boys leave?"

The driver gave a deep sigh. "How should I know? I had my eyes on the road. Now, if you don't mind, milord, we need to keep moving. We're already late. We've got a town to reach by nightfall."

Malaspina looked at the group of pilgrims. "Anyone notice when the two boys left?"

He took out some coins, which he held up for all to see.

There was an uneasy silence.

"At the bridge in the last valley," piped up a voice. "They went into the bushes and never came back."

"Where, exactly?"

The red-haired youth gestured. "Up beside the stream, this side of the bridge."

Malaspina tossed the coins to Emilio, who grinned as he caught them one by one and dropped them into his pouch.

Malaspina stowed his cane away and started to head back. As he passed the Knight, he pulled up and stared.

"It seems we've met before."

The Knight returned Malaspina's gaze. He no longer feared the man, no longer cared whether he feared him or not.

"It's possible," he said. "The world's a small place. Perhaps in the Terra Santa?"

Malaspina shook his head, continuing to stare at the Knight.

"You remind me of someone," he said. "Someone I hope is dead."

He kicked the flanks of his horse and rode back toward the valley.

CHAPTER 33

The Steward

"They're here again," Tien Nu said.

He watched as the three riders emerged over the brow of the hill. Malaspina was in the lead, his eyes sweeping the land above the road. The other two men trailed behind, slouched in their saddles, looking hot and bored.

When they reached the bridge, the bodyguard and the steward dismounted and glanced around. Malaspina remained on his horse and issued instructions, gesturing up the stream.

"They must know where we left the road," Tien Nu said. "Somebody told them."

"Shouldn't we take off?" Bec said.

Tien Nu turned to look. Behind them the underbrush gave way to open pasture, where they'd be visible from the road. "Let's stay here for the time being. If they spot us, then we'll have to make a run for it."

The steward and the bodyguard clambered up the edge of the stream bed, slipping on the wet rocks and splashing through pools of water.

Tien Nu crouched down beside Bec, who pulled Hannibal close.

"I don't think they'll come up here," Bec whispered. "They're both as lazy as sin."

They could hear the scuffling of boots as the two men drew near. After a while, a voice floated up.

"This is a hopeless task," said the steward. "We'll never find them in this godforsaken place. They must be miles away by now."

Tien Nu peered down through the bushes. Pietro was standing by the stream below, wiping his face as he gazed at the underbrush on the other side of the valley. The bodyguard was resting on a boulder beside him, his heavy shoulders rounded.

"Malaspina wants us to search—so we search," Nozzo said. "It's as simple as that. Don't push your luck, my friend. Anyone who crosses Malaspina regrets it."

Tien Nu was aware of movement at his side. Bec was down on his hands and knees, peering under the bushes.

"What's the matter?" he whispered.

"It's Hannibal. He's gone."

"I thought you had him."

"I did. But he's disappeared."

Tien Nu gazed around. There was no sign of the dog.

Pietro was complaining to the bodyguard, reciting a long list of grievances against Malaspina. The big man listened, not saying a word. Meanwhile, Malaspina waited by the bridge, looking impatient. He started to cough—a jagged cough from the depths of his lungs. He hawked and spat, then pulled out a handkerchief to wipe his lips.

Tien Nu saw a flash of white in the underbrush, not far from the road.

"Hannibal!" he breathed. "Down there!"

Bec shifted to look, dislodging a stone, which tumbled down the slope, triggering a shower of pebbles and dirt.

Pietro gave a start and turned.

"What's that?"

"Something up there."

They both looked upward, setting their sights on the small tree in the clearing.

"We'd better go and see," said Nozzo.

The men began climbing up the steep incline, clutching at bushes and slipping in the loose soil.

Tien Nu glanced at the pasture behind. "We've got to take off," he hissed. "Keep as low as you can."

Some yelps came from the road, followed by shouts and curses. Hannibal was dancing around the horses. He barked furiously, keeping just out of range. The horses shied away, neighing and twisting their heads. Malaspina yelled at the little dog, provoking further torrents of barks.

"Come back here!" Malaspina called to the men. "There's a dog."

"Now what?" said Pietro.

"Clumsy fools!" Malaspina shouted. "You'll never find anything up there. Come on down! This dog's spooking the horses."

The two men retreated down the slope, swearing and stumbling over the stones. Hannibal glanced at them as they approached, then scurried off into the underbrush.

Malaspina dismounted, leaning on his cane as the others joined him by the bridge.

Pietro spoke to his master, gesturing at the surrounding countryside. Malaspina swore and poured abuse on the steward, who stood there silently, head bowed.

Malaspina prodded him in the chest. Pietro still said nothing. Malaspina gave him a shove, making him stumble back.

"Look at me!" he screamed.

Pietro slowly lifted his head, and Malaspina slapped him across the face.

For an instant, the man was still. Then he struck out at Malaspina, catching him on the chin.

Malaspina gave a roar. He swung his cane and hit Pietro on the temple.

The man dropped to his knees, one hand groping upward. The cane rose again and came down on the back of his neck. There was a shriek and Pietro collapsed onto the ground, where he lay motionless.

Malaspina nudged him with the toe of his boot, then said something to Nozzo. The bodyguard squatted down beside Pietro and rolled him over, shaking him. He looked up at Malaspina, who shrugged and turned away, limping back to his horse. He put away the cane and swung himself up into the saddle.

The bodyguard shook Pietro one last time, then took the man's pouch and stood up. He tied the steward's horse to his own mount, and the two men rode off in the direction of Ponti, soon disappearing over the hill.

The steward remained on the road, a dark stain spreading in the dust.

"Do you think he's dead?" whispered Bec.

Tien Nu let out a long breath. "Don't know, *amico*. Your master hit him pretty hard."

"Shouldn't we go down and check?"

"They might double back. We'd better wait."

The two boys sat there silently, gazing at the road. There was a rustle in the underbrush. Hannibal emerged and scooted over to Bec, who ruffled him about the neck.

"Good boy! You saved us, just in the nick of time."

The sun dropped lower in the sky. A vulture circled above, then landed on the road and hopped over to Pietro, pecking at his face.

"Let's go down," said Tien Nu.

They made their way to the bridge, scaring off the bird. Hannibal went up to the body and sniffed, then turned away, whimpering as he rubbed against Bec's leg.

The steward's eyes were blank, and blood trickled from one ear. A fly crawled over his cheek.

Tien Nu knelt down and shooed the fly away. He opened the man's collar and placed a hand on his bony chest.

No sign of life.

Tien Nu gently freed an arm that was pinned beneath the body, then looked up at Bec. To his surprise, tears were spilling down his cheeks.

"He was a miserable old crow," Bec said. "But he didn't deserve to die like this."

He turned away, roughly wiping his face. "We'd better get going."

Tien Nu got to his feet. He didn't like leaving the body in the open, but there was no time to bury it.

"Give me a hand, Bec. Let's move him off the road. You take the feet. I'll take the shoulders."

They laid the steward out in the grass at the roadside. Eventually someone would come along and find the body— or whatever was left after the vultures had done their work.

"We can't use the road," Bec said. "Malaspina will be prowling around—moving back and forth. He knows we're here."

Tien Nu gazed at the stream tumbling down below the bridge.

"This must flow into the river. And the river leads to Ponti, doesn't it?"

Bec nodded.

"So why don't we follow the stream down? There may be some kind of path along the river."

Bec glanced at the setting sun. "Let's get moving, then. We'll need all the light we can get."

CHAPTER 34

The Inn

The Knight sat alone at a table in the corner of the inn. He nursed his drink, gazing with narrowed eyes at the red-haired youth across the crowded room, his anger slowly coming to a boil.

Emilio was installed at a table with some newfound friends. He was telling a story to the innkeeper's son, who was standing alongside, arms folded, belly shaking as he laughed. The others were hanging on Emilio's words, mouths open, faces flushed. Jugs of beer sat on the table, which was strewn with chicken bones and crusts of bread.

The Knight gripped his cup of *grappa*—one of many he'd drunk. The inn was the only place to stay in the town, which was hardly more than a walled village lost in the mountains. The pilgrims had stowed the baggage in their rooms, then trooped downstairs to eat.

The Knight took another sip of the fiery liquid, feeding his dark mood. He blamed himself for letting Bec and Tien Nu slip away. He should have realized what would happen—talked to the boys, persuaded them to stay. He'd never have allowed Malaspina to take Bec, not in a thousand years. But how was Bec to know that? And now the boys were on their own, with Malaspina scouring the countryside.

A peal of laughter came from across the room. The Knight peered through the smoky air. The red-haired youth was laughing at his own joke, his eyes bright with drink. The jackass. If only he'd had the sense to hold his tongue, Malaspina wouldn't have known where to look. None of the other pilgrims would have said a thing. But the youth had been too dazzled by the silver in Malaspina's hands to keep his silly trap shut. If Malaspina found the boys, it'd be his fault.

Emilio noticed the Knight staring at him. He raised his cup and called across the room.

"Come and join us, friend. I'll stand you a drink."

The Knight stumbled to his feet, banging his head on the low rafters.

"And how will you pay for it?" he shouted back.

The red-haired youth was too drunk to notice the expression on the Knight's face.

"Don't worry, friend. I've got lots of money."

"Judas money!"

Emilio looked startled. For the first time, he seemed to realize that the Knight might not be friendly. His smile wavered.

"Surely, no hard feelings!" he said. "What did those boys mean to you, anyway? Little beggars! You said it yourself. Come and have a drink!"

The Knight lunged across the room, knocking over benches and tables in his path, sending the crockery flying. The other customers scattered to get out of his way. He shoved Emilio's table aside and grabbed the young man by the throat, throwing him to the ground. He fell on top of him and punched him in the face—once, twice. Blood came spurting from Emilio's nose and a dark welt bloomed on his cheekbone. The Knight was about to hit him again when he saw the terror in the young man's eyes. In a flash, he remembered something that had happened years ago— something that still haunted him.

He was passing through a town he hardly knew, on a mission of no importance. He stopped at a tavern to eat and stayed on to drink. He got into an argument with a local man, a young blacksmith with colossal arms, who was almost as drunk as the Knight. Insults were exchanged, and the blacksmith jumped the Knight and dragged him down.

The two men rolled across the floor, locked in a wild struggle. The blacksmith, his stomach full of ale, fought bravely but unskilfully. In the end, he was no match for the Knight, who pinned him on his back, legs astride his body, one hand gripping his hair. The Knight's heavy fist smashed into the blacksmith's face again and again, until it was a mass of blood and splintered bone, and the man fell limp. Some other patrons dragged the Knight off the body, and he got away before the constables arrived. He never knew what happened to the young blacksmith, whether he lived or died. But he was haunted by the expression on the man's face, the look of naked fear as the Knight's fist struck relentlessly home.

All this passed through the Knight's mind as he saw Emilio's eyes, wide with terror. He gave a low sigh and let go of the young man's hair, allowing himself to be pulled away by the other pilgrims. Emilio stumbled to his feet, blood streaming from his nostrils, his left eye puffing up. He pulled out a handkerchief and covered his nose, looking fearfully at the Knight with his one good eye. When he realized the Knight wasn't going to hit him again, he dropped onto a bench and started sobbing in great gulps.

The Knight shook himself free of the pilgrims and went back to his seat in the corner. Aside from the youth's clotted sobs, the room was silent.

"He nearly killed me," Emilio choked.

The others stared blankly at him, not saying a word. The landlord appeared at the kitchen door and looked around.

"It's all right, *papà*," said the landlord's son. "Just a little scuffle."

He helped Emilio to his feet. "Let's go out to the fountain and get you cleaned up. There's blood all over your clothes."

He guided the red-haired youth to the door and led him into the courtyard.

The other customers slowly returned to their places, righting the tables and picking up the scattered knives and cups. The room was soon buzzing with low voices. Eyes darted in the Knight's direction and slid away.

The Knight sat slumped at his table, his head in his hands, silently cursing himself. Why had he lost his temper with that ninny of a boy? It wouldn't help Bec and Tien Nu. He felt sick at heart.

There was a gust of wind as the door swung open. Malaspina stepped across the threshold. He stood there for a moment, leaning on his cane, surveying the room. His eyes picked out the Knight, lingered, then glided on. He said something to his bodyguard and limped across the room to the kitchen door, where he called for the landlord.

"I need to leave a spare horse here—perhaps for a few days."

"Of course, milord. And a room?"

"No. We're travelling on tonight. But I want you to keep an eye out for a runaway slave." Malaspina turned and raised his voice to address the entire company. "All of you. Listen well. I'm looking for a slave boy who escaped from my estate. He's small, with blond hair cut short. Name of Bec. I'm offering a reward—thirty florins."

"And if we see him ...?" asked the landlord.

"Seize him and hold him fast. Then send for me. I'll be moving along the road toward Ponti. If you check the inns along the way, you're sure to find me. My name is Adolfo Malaspina."

"Of course, milord. I'll be on the lookout for the slave. All my family, too—and we're practically the whole town. Eyes everywhere. We'll catch him, milord, if he so much as sets a foot near this place."

Malaspina made another survey of the room, singling out the Knight.

"So, we meet again," he called.

The Knight gazed back, saying nothing.

Malaspina stared at the Knight's face. "Just stay out of my way."

He turned and left the inn.

CHAPTER 35

The Chasm

The stream rushed through a series of gorges, gathering force from brooks and rivulets on either side. Tien Nu led the way, picking a path downward through the jumble of rocks, drenched with spray. In the gathering darkness, he thought it would be easy to slip and twist an ankle.

The torrent passed into a chasm, deep in shadow. They stopped to rest at the top of a waterfall, where the stream slid smoothly over the rim of a rocky ledge and dropped in a ghostly curtain to a pool below—patches of pale foam drifting on the black water.

"Something's following us," whispered Bec.

"What?"

"Shh! There it goes again."

Tien Nu strained his ears, holding his breath. With the rushing water, it was hard to make out anything. Then he heard it. A faint click. One stone against another. It seemed to come from somewhere behind them, not far away.

"I've been hearing it ever since we left the road," said Bec. "At first, I thought it was just my imagination. But now I'm sure of it. We're being tracked."

"By who? Malaspina?"

"Not with his bad leg. It's much too steep."

"What about the bodyguard?"

"That ox? We'd hear him coming miles away. No. Whatever it is, it's pretty light on its feet."

"But who else could it be?"

"Who? Or *what!* There are lions around here."

Tien Nu paused. "Have you ever actually seen one?"

"No. But I've heard lots of stories."

They sat there, listening intently. The moon rose over the top of the chasm, painting the rocky walls with a pallid light. Bec kept swivelling around, peering into the shadows.

There was a sudden splash, followed by a snuffling noise. Bec flattened down on the ground. Tien Nu focused on the noise, then crept to the edge of the waterfall and looked over. In the moonlight he could see a mother goat and a pair of kids lapping at the water in the pool below. The mother lifted her head to sniff the air, then resumed her drinking. After a few minutes, she turned and sprang sure-footed up the side of the ravine, followed by the kids, their hooves clicking on the rocks.

Tien Nu looked back at Bec, eyebrows raised.

"Guess it was only the goats." Bec gave a grin. "My imagination again! It's the dark. I hate it."

They shouldered their packs and set off, following the torrent as it twisted down through the gorge, spray tossed high into the air. They reached an escarpment, where the stream hurtled down a long gulch and swept under a bridge with a hollow roar. Beside the bridge, they could see the rooftops of a village, dark against a gleaming mass of water beyond.

"That must be the river," said Bec.

A path took them down to a road beside the river, where a row of ancient buildings overlooked the water. A profusion of flowers twisted up the walls and drooped over the doors and windows. The place was deathly quiet. All the houses were locked and shuttered, with not a glimmer of light.

The silence was broken by snarls and hisses as a pair of cats streaked across the road. Hannibal struggled to jump out of his sling, his eyes fixed on the spot where the cats had disappeared.

"I don't like this place," said Bec. "Let's keep moving."

The road ran to the end of the village, where it turned into a path that continued by the water. They tramped wearily ahead, not stopping to rest. Beside them glided the river, glistening in the moonlight like a great silvery snake. After a while, Tien Nu fell into an almost trance-like state. He felt himself being swept onward, into a future as dark and obscure as the hills that rose on either side.

"How about stopping up there?" Bec pointed ahead to a place where the river swept around a broad curve that sheltered a marsh. On the bank, a large willow tree drooped over the shallow water.

Tien Nu gave a weary nod. They dropped their bags under the willow and retrieved their capes. Soon they were sound asleep.

The stars peeped through the branches above Tien Nu's head, like tiny sparkling fish tangled in a net. He pushed himself up on his elbows.

There was the river, flowing quietly along in the moonlight. And there was Bec, rolled up in his cape, dead to the world. Hannibal raised his head and gazed briefly at Tien Nu, then snuggled back against Bec's legs.

Was it just a dream?

Tien Nu listened carefully. No, there it was again. A rhythmic rasping noise, like a door swinging on rusty hinges. He looked around, trying to locate the source of the sound.

At the outer edge of the marsh was a long black shape. Tien Nu stared at it. A boat with a pointed prow—caught in the rushes, rubbing against the thick stalks.

Tien Nu staggered to his feet. The boat seemed to be empty. He tucked up his tunic and waded into the marsh, drawing in his breath at the frigid water. He pushed through the rushes and put a hand on the boat. A frayed rope was attached to the bow and some paddles were stored inside. The boat must have gone adrift upstream and come to rest in the marsh.

Tien Nu dragged the boat into shore and tied it to the willow, then settled down again. His sleep was filled with dreams of ships and stars.

CHAPTER 36

The Castle

Bec squinted dubiously at the boat. "Why can't we just walk?"

"We'll get to Ponti a lot quicker," said Tien Nu. "And Malaspina won't be looking for us on the river."

"What do you think, Hannibal?"

The little dog was frisking about in the shallows, tossing up wisps of spray and snatching them with his mouth. He raced back to Bec and pawed at his tunic, panting madly.

"Now you've done it! Spoiled my nice new clothes." Bec laughed and pushed the dog away, brushing the mud off his tunic.

Hannibal bounded over to the boat and scrambled inside, where he sat gazing at them.

Bec sighed. "All right, Scraps. We'll take the boat. But you'll have to show me what to do. I've never handled one of these things before."

Tien Nu gave him a paddle. "You take the bow—that's the front. I'll be in back. No, no! Don't stand up. You can stow your pack with mine—there in the middle. Hold on. Don't start paddling yet. I'll push the boat out further."

Tien Nu waded through the marsh, shunting the boat ahead. When he reached deeper water, he scrambled into the stern and quickly started paddling to prevent the boat from being swept sideways.

"Paddle! Paddle!" he shouted. "Not too deep. Shorter strokes. That's it."

Bec grunted as he leaned into the strokes. "I thought ... this was meant ... to be easy."

The river swept around a bend beneath a gallery of chalky cliffs, then narrowed and pursued a meandering course between the hills. On the right, the path they had been following hugged the bank, occasionally looping away to avoid a swamp or inlet. The sun was full in their faces, and it soon turned hot. They dragged off their tunics and paddled along in their shorts, letting the breeze cool their bodies. Hannibal held his head high, gazing at the countryside and snapping at dragonflies that wandered within reach.

As the sun arced higher in the sky, Bec became increasingly hungry. What little food they'd brought with them had been polished off at breakfast—but it had hardly been enough. Around noon, the river entered a broad valley, where open fields and pastures stretched to hazy hills in the distance.

"Look!" Bec stood up and pointed.

The boat rocked violently. He quickly sat down. "Sorry! It's a castle. Over there."

He pointed again. In the distance, above a grove of trees, some towers glinted in the sunlight.

Tien Nu shaded his eyes. "You're right."

"Do you think it's safe to stop?"

Tien Nu rested his paddle on the thwarts, letting the boat glide. "It won't be safe no matter where we stop—not completely. But we need the food."

Soon they reached a landing place, where a track wound up to a large castle perched on a cliff above the river. The towers and battlements were draped with multi-coloured banners, as if for a celebration.

"What do you say, Scraps?" asked Bec. "Shall we give it a try?"

Tien Nu nodded. "But at the first sign of trouble, we'll take off."

They pulled into the landing place and Bec scrambled out to hold the boat steady. Nearby, some men were shifting goods

from a barge into a donkey-cart. The men glanced at them, gave friendly nods, and went on with their work. A girl about their age was standing beside the donkey, her hand on the bridle. She had green eyes and long auburn hair. She stared at them with undisguised curiosity, examining first Bec, then Tien Nu.

Bec stood there in his sagging shorts, bare-chested, sweating profusely.

"What castle is this?" he asked the girl.

"Fontesecca, of course. Are you here for the wedding?"

"Actually, we didn't know there was one."

"Well, there is," said the girl. "The lord's daughter is getting married. They're at the church right now, but they'll be back later and there'll be a big feast. People are coming from miles around. Everyone's invited."

She glanced at Bec's glistening chest. "But I don't think they'll let you in like this! Slippery as an eel, you are!"

She giggled and put a hand over her mouth.

Bec grinned at her, fanning his face.

"Oh, I've got proper clothes, all right," he said. "But I need to cool down first. My name is Bec, by the way."

"And I'm Francesca."

Bec tied the boat to a bollard, all the while chatting with the girl.

As she talked, her eyes kept wandering to Tien Nu, who was standing awkwardly beside the boat, trying to smooth down his hair.

"Aren't you going to introduce me?" she asked Bec.

"Of course! This is Tien Nu—my best friend in the entire world. Tien Nu, meet Francesca."

Tien Nu flashed a smile and quickly bent over to tousle Hannibal about the neck.

The girl let out a laugh. "Ah, a shy one! Not like you, you cheeky thing. So, what brings you down the river?"

"We're ... ah ... travelling jugglers and acrobats," said Bec.

"Jugglers! Just in time for the celebration. I'm sure you'll be welcome. Come along. I'll bring you to the kitchen." She gave them a look. "But you'd better get dressed first!"

They put on their tunics and shouldered their packs, following the girl up the track to the castle, while Hannibal raced ahead to scatter some geese. They passed through the gate into the courtyard, where a doorway led to an immense kitchen, bustling with people. The aroma of roasting meat almost made Bec faint.

"Look what I fished out of the river!" announced Francesca. "Jugglers, if you please!"

The whole kitchen stopped and stared.

"Well, you've come to the right place," said a tiny man with smears of flour on his face.

"This is Gaston, our head chef," said Francesca. "He'll feed you if you're nice to him. Won't you, Gaston? Not that he wouldn't feed you anyway. He's a soft touch, is our chef."

She wrapped an arm about the little man and planted a kiss on his balding head.

Gaston wriggled free. "Now, you know how busy we are, Francesca. Don't you bother me with your nonsense!"

He motioned toward a table in the corner.

"Put your things down over there and take a seat. Are you hungry?" Gaston glanced at their faces and laughed. "I guess I don't have to ask."

"I'm needed back at the landing, so I'll be off," said Francesca. "You're in good hands with Gaston."

She left the kitchen.

Bread and cheese arrived at the table, along with platters of scrambled eggs and bowls of warm milk. Hannibal got his own bowl of scraps.

As they ate, Bec gazed around the kitchen, which was a hive of activity. Everywhere he looked, people were peeling and chopping, pounding and plucking, rolling out dough, dressing chickens, preparing joints of meat. A man turned a boar on a spit before the fire, sweat dripping from his nose. A clutch of steaming pots hung from hooks in the cavernous fireplace. Servants scurried in and out, carrying cups and spoons and plates and bowls. From all appearances, it was going to be an enormous feast.

A natty man with a trimmed beard entered the kitchen and looked around. He spotted them and came over.

"You must be the new jugglers. Someone told me you'd arrived. A stroke of luck."

Tien Nu got to his feet and made a formal bow. "Yes, milord. My name is Tien Nu, and this is my partner, Bec. We're known as *The Young Dragons*—all-round tumblers, boxers, and magicians."

Bec bowed so low, his forehead almost struck the table.

"Er ... yes," said the man. "We already have some mummers and players. But the dratted tumblers never showed up. Could you fellows take up the slack?"

Tien Nu glanced at Bec. "We could give a display of *quan fa*—acrobatics from the East. Monkey Style and Drunken Style. Something light and entertaining."

"Just what's needed!" said the man. "Anything else?"

"How about a grand magical illusion?" Tien Nu said.

"Marvellous!" said the man. "Everyone loves magic."

He put a finger to his lips. "Now let's see. We'll start with music as the guests arrive. Then the mummers can circulate and keep everyone happy while the first course is served. Once that's over ... hmm ... that would be a good time for the magical illusion. But don't take too long. The players will be waiting to do their act, which will carry us through the second course. After that you can do some kong ... uh ..."

"*Quan fa,*" Tien Nu said.

"Exactly! How does that arrangement sound?"

"Perfect," said Tien Nu.

"Now, as far as payment is concerned, I'm afraid ..."

"No need for that, milord," said Tien Nu. "We'll pass the hat."

"Then it's settled. If you need anything, just let me know. I'll be in the hall, helping to set things up. Through there." He pointed to the door at the end of the kitchen. "Just ask for Raimondo. That's me. I'm the steward."

"Just one thing. Where can we practise, milord?"

Raimondo pursed his lips. "There's a *bocce* court out behind the castle. You can use that."

He hurried off.

"Monkey Style," Bec said. "Did I hear that right?"

Tien Nu nodded.

"So, who's going to be the monkey?"

CHAPTER 37

The Rehearsal

"I knew I'd get stuck with this!" Bec said. "Why can't I do Drunken Style?"

"Because Monkey Style is easier to learn," Tien Nu said.

"Not because you think I'm a monkey."

Tien Nu grinned. "Never crossed my mind."

They were standing in the *bocce* court, which was as flat as a table and fringed with apple trees. Bec looked around and shook his head.

"I don't know, Scraps. I'm not sure I like the idea."

"*Coraggio, amico!* Monkey Style has all the best moves. Anyway, you won't be on your own. I'll be doing it with you. Here, let me show you what it's like."

Tien Nu moved to the centre of the court and squatted down on his haunches. Gibbering loudly, he swivelled from side to side, then plucked something from his armpit, which he popped into his mouth. Finished chewing, he leapt up and loped around the space, knuckles dragging. Then came a series of somersaults, after which he scratched his rear end and let loose with a wild flurry of kicks and strikes, finishing with a back-fist. He cartwheeled into a drop kick, then slid forward into the splits, toppled sideways and whirled his legs up into the air, spinning on his back like a top. On his feet again, he pulled off a dozen handsprings and landed in a low stance, paws raised, chattering brightly.

There was loud applause from some pageboys who had stopped to look.

"Show me again, Scraps," Bec said.

He watched intently as Tien Nu ran through the routine a second time.

"That was actually a bit different," Bec said.

"Smart boy. The beauty of Monkey Style is that you're free to make things up."

Bec wiped a hand over his mouth. "I think I can do it. Watch."

He started at a slow pace, doing his best to reproduce Tien Nu's moves, gradually picking up speed as he went along. He managed to get through the somersaults, the kicks and the strikes and the back-fist, then loped about the court and improvised by swinging from branch to branch in the apple trees. He did a cartwheel followed by the splits, then launched into a back-spin so furious and prolonged that it left him dizzy. He staggered about, jabbering and scratching.

The pages fell about themselves, laughing and slapping each other's backs.

Regaining his balance, Bec let out a high-pitched screech and sprinted across the grass. Grabbing a tree-trunk, he swung around by one arm and flew into some bushes. Out he crawled, pawing at his eyes, then did a series of spinning hook-kicks, which he didn't quite pull off, landing in a heap. He leapt up and scampered crazily around, snatching apple blossoms and scattering them in the air. Finally, he fell into a low stance and let out an ear-splitting howl.

"*Bravo! Fantastico!*" shouted the pages.

Bec grinned and looked at Tien Nu.

Tien Nu smiled back. "Not bad."

They practised the routine again and again, until they were dripping with sweat. Tien Nu explained that the moves were actually fighting techniques, designed to confuse and mislead.

After some time, they flopped down under the trees to cool off.

"What should we wear for the performance?" asked Bec.

"I've got some costumes."

Tien Nu dug into his pack and pulled out a red silk outfit. "The pants don't fit me anymore. But they should work for you."

He handed the outfit to Bec, who held it up for inspection, poking his hand through a rip in the seat of the pants.

"Looks like you were a bit too energetic," Bec said.

"It happened in the middle of a performance, and I had to keep going. Very embarrassing."

Bec laughed. "But I'll bet the ladies loved it."

CHAPTER 38

The Feast

Tien Nu gazed from the courtyard into the great hall of the castle, which was ablaze with torches and candles. The noise was deafening. People of all sizes and shapes were crammed together at long trestle tables arranged around a central space. Servants hustled in and out of the kitchen, carrying platters of food and jugs of beer.

At one end, a minstrel gallery was suspended high above the hall, where some musicians were trying to make themselves heard above the din. At the other end was the head table, sparkling with glassware and silver plates. The bride and groom were seated in the centre, with family members and local dignitaries ranged on either side.

In the candlelight, eyes shone, smiles broadened, and faces grew redder and redder. Jokes were traded back and forth, and bursts of laughter echoed around the hall. Mummers roamed between the tables, wearing the masks of donkeys and goats and rabbits, capering about and poking fun at the guests. Hannibal had joined a posse of dogs foraging for scraps under the tables.

Bec turned to Tien Nu. "Are you nervous?"

"Always—no matter how often I perform. How about you?"

"I'm about to pee myself."

The steward, Raimondo, came over and wiggled his eyebrows: "It's time for you boys to go on."

Bec took a deep breath and scrambled onto the dappled grey pony they'd borrowed from the stables. In his haste, he dropped the handbell he was holding, which fell with a clang to the cobblestones. Tien Nu retrieved the bell and handed it back to Bec.

"Don't worry, they'll be a good audience," he said. "They've had lots to drink."

Raimondo signalled to the minstrel gallery, and a trumpeter stood up and blew a fanfare. The crowd ignored him, laughing and shouting. The man took a deep breath and tried again—blowing on and on, until his cheeks looked fit to burst. Eventually, the crowd quietened down and shifted in their seats to watch.

The steward strutted into the centre of the hall. "Ladies and Lords, friends, neighbours, we are privileged to present something new and unique. A magical spectacle to rival the ancient mysteries of Babilonia. Please welcome our special guests, *The Young Dragons!*"

There was a smattering of applause as Tien Nu entered the hall, wearing a black silk outfit belonging to his father. He was leading the pony, with Bec very straight in the saddle, splendid in his red silk costume and a feathered cap. The pony had leather saddle bags, and her mane and tail were braided with scarlet ribbons. She raised her hooves high as she trotted daintily along.

Bec was ringing the handbell continuously. The sound caught the crowd's attention. They watched as Tien Nu conducted the pony to the open space in the middle, where he swept off his hat, bowed deeply, and retired to the side. Bec was left alone in the centre, seated on the patient little mare, still tolling the bell. A team of pageboys trotted out, dressed in blue livery with floppy hats. They were carrying tall wooden screens, decorated with flowers and peacocks, which they arranged in a tight circle around Bec, hiding him and the pony from the spectators.

Tien Nu circled the screens three times, waving a wand, as Bec's bell continued to ring inside. Finally, he raised his arms high and gave an enormous shout.

"Ajji Majji la Tarajji!"

There was a crash and the bell fell silent.

A hush spread through the hall, everyone staring. The pageboys returned to pick up the screens and carry them outside. There in the centre was the grey pony, with the handbell lying on the floor.

Bec had vanished.

The crowd erupted, jumping to their feet, craning to see. Some kids ran out and searched all around the pony. They scratched their heads, peering up at the rafters, as if Bec might be hiding there.

Amid the uproar, Tien Nu returned to the centre of the hall. He shooed the kids away and took the pony by the bridle, leading her in a circle for all to see. Then he turned toward the end of the hall and once again raised his hands and shouted.

"Ajji Majji la Tarajji!"

A savage cry came from the doorway beneath the minstrel gallery. The audience turned and gaped as a masked lion came racing from the kitchen and leapt over a table, barely clearing the heads of the people sitting there. The lion-man landed in a crouch, shaking his mane. Then he bounded about the hall, roaring and snarling and snatching food from the tables. He did a series of handsprings toward the pony and landed askew in the saddle. Dragging himself upright, he whipped off his mask.

There sat Bec, grinning broadly.

The audience went wild. They stamped their feet and banged the tables, whistling and clapping and roaring their approval. Tien Nu walked among the tables, holding out his hat. The guests dug into their purses and showered him with coins. Tien Nu ran back to the centre, gave an extravagant bow, and led Bec and the pony out into the courtyard.

Bec slipped from the saddle, breathless with excitement.

"Was I okay?"

"You were fine!" Tien Nu said. "They loved it!"

"How did you make him vanish?" asked Francesca, who'd followed them from the hall. "I was watching the whole time."

"You won't tell anyone?" Tien Nu said.

"Cross my heart!"

"Did you count the pageboys when they took away the screens?"

Francesca stared at Tien Nu with widened eyes.

"You mean ..."

"There was an extra pageboy," Tien Nu said.

"That was me!" said Bec. "I helped the others carry off the screens."

"But where did you get the pageboy outfit?" Francesca asked.

"Easy," said Bec. "In the saddle bags."

Meanwhile the troupe of players had launched into their performance. Peals of laughter came rolling through the doorway.

"Let's go in and watch," said Bec.

"Go ahead," Tien Nu said. "I'll take the pony back."

Bec and Francesca returned to the hall to see the show, while Tien Nu led the little horse to the stables.

"How did she do?" asked the groom, stroking the pony on the nose and feeding her a carrot.

"She was perfect," Tien Nu said. "A born performer. She didn't blink an eye, even when my friend jumped on her back."

By the time Tien Nu returned to the hall, the play was almost over. He looked around for Bec, who waved from the corner and came to join him outside.

As the players made their exit, the steward took centre stage once again, raising his hands to silence the crowd. "And now, my friends, please welcome back the favourites of the night, *The Young Dragons,* in a virtuoso display of Eastern martial arts known as *quan fa*—to wit, Drunken Style and Monkey Style!"

Tien Nu bounded into the centre of the hall—this time to a thunderous ovation. He strolled from table to table, peering into the beer jugs, smacking his lips. Finally, he grabbed a jug and drained it, leaning backward until his head almost touched the floor. He righted himself and staggered sideways, fanning his face. He tore off his shirt and flexed his muscles to a chorus of catcalls, then spun around and leapt into the air, kicking wildly and toppling onto his side.

A series of reverse somersaults brought him to his feet, where he tottered back and forth, rubbing his stomach and belching. He lurched toward the wedding table, his arms windmilling about, then abruptly reversed direction, stumbled and fell flat on his back. Rolling onto his stomach, he propelled his body forward in great gasping lurches like a wounded snake. He lay there for a moment, then heaved himself up and staggered to a side table, where he refreshed himself from another jug.

By this time, the crowd were on their feet, clapping and shouting at the top of their voices. Now Bec made his entrance, dressed like a constable, truncheon in hand. He bellowed at Tien Nu, who was wobbling around, then came over and struck at him with his club. Tien Nu swayed to the side, avoiding the blow by a whisker. He casually flung out a fist and smacked Bec across the face, sending him flying. The audience went crazy, howling with laughter.

Bec picked himself up, rubbing his jaw, then launched into an all-out attack, swinging the truncheon and kicking furiously. Tien Nu weaved this way and that, apparently off-balance, miraculously evading the blows and parrying with lightning strikes to face and chest and belly, until Bec toppled to the ground. Tien Nu gazed down at Bec and collapsed on top of him.

Tien Nu lay there for a moment, then sprang to his feet. Bec followed, moving a little more slowly. They bowed to a deafening storm of applause and whistles.

"Why the devil did you hit me so hard?" Bec hissed.

"You almost broke my head, you fool."

Tien Nu retrieved the monkey masks and wigs he'd borrowed from the mummers. He tossed a set to Bec, and they launched into their Monkey Style routines, capering about like madmen, while the crowd laughed and clapped, egging them on.

Suddenly, there was a commotion at the entrance to the hall. Some kind of argument had broken out.

CHAPTER 39

Monkey Style

Bec glanced at the doorway and was stunned to see Malaspina—his bodyguard beside him. He was berating a servant, his voice carrying across the hall: "Blockhead! I have every right to be at the head table."

Bec felt a shiver of fear. He quickly turned and continued with the performance, adjusting his mask to make sure it covered his head and face.

Tien Nu skipped close. "He's here."

"I know."

The steward, Raimondo, hurried over, frowning slightly. He put a restraining hand on the servant's shoulder, then bowed to Malaspina and escorted him and Nozzo to the wedding table.

Heads turned to follow them, and flurries of whispers spread through the hall. Judging from people's expressions, Malaspina was well known by reputation but not well loved.

Nevertheless, the lord of the castle greeted him politely and made room for the two men at the head table, calling for more wine and food.

Bec watched Malaspina from the corner of his eye, waiting for the moment when the man would jump up and shout his name. Yet the moment didn't come. The man piled his plate with food and set about shovelling it into his mouth while he watched the performance.

It dawned on Bec that Malaspina could have no idea who they were. The masks disguised them completely. To him, they were just a couple of mummers, no different from the others scattered about the hall.

Bec felt as if the bonds of fear had suddenly been sprung. Hidden behind the monkey mask, he could do whatever he wanted—Malaspina be damned.

Tien Nu cut short his routine and moved to the side, motioning for Bec to do the same. Bec glanced at him and gave a slight shake of the head. He continued to caper and prance about the hall, twisting his head and emitting yelps and howls, as the crowd laughed and hooted, following every move. On impulse, he approached the wedding table and loped alongside it, chattering at the guests. When he reached Malaspina, he let out a piercing shriek and snatched a chicken

leg from the man's hands, knocking over a glass of wine.

People stood up to watch and clap as Bec danced in front of Malaspina, waving the purloined piece of chicken in his face. The man kept trying to grab it, but each time Bec skipped nimbly out of reach, provoking gales of laughter. Eventually Bec took a bite of chicken and tossed the leg back toward Malaspina, splashing the man with grease.

There was a startled silence, as gravy dripped from Malaspina's nose and chin. Then the hall erupted in hooting and applause. The noise was so loud, Bec thought his eardrums would burst. Malaspina leapt to his feet, shouting and shaking his fist. Yet the more he shouted, the more the crowd roared and laughed.

Malaspina turned to his bodyguard and pointed at the monkey-man. As Nozzo got to his feet, Bec sprinted toward the other end of the hall, setting his sights on the minstrel gallery. A throng of enthusiastic spectators trailed after him, thumping him on the back and pressing money into his hands.

Bec freed himself from the crowd and swarmed up a pillar supporting the gallery. He clambered over the railing at the top, and tumbled into the midst of the startled musicians, who dropped their instruments and backed away.

"Sorry, sorry!" Bec said.

He headed for the door at the rear, stumbling over the instruments on the floor. His foot got caught in a tambourine, which clung to him, jangling crazily. He hopped about, shaking his leg until the tambourine fell off.

Tien Nu climbed into the gallery. "I'm here!"

"Where's Nozzo?" Bec asked.

"Down below," Tien Nu said. "He tried to climb up but couldn't make it. Come on, let's go."

The door at the back of the gallery led to a staircase that took them down to the kitchen.

Francesca was there waiting. "I thought you'd end up here."

"Have you seen the bodyguard?" Bec asked.

"That big man? He came storming in here just now, looking for you. I told him you'd gone outside, and he ran into the courtyard."

"Did he use my name or talk about a runaway?"

Francesca shook her head. "He just asked about the monkey-man."

Bec grinned at Tien Nu. "He doesn't have a clue who we are."

They slipped across to the pantry, where their packs were stored.

Tien Nu paused to gaze at some kitchen scullions in soiled white uniforms, who were rolling a series of barrels toward the door.

"Where are they taking those?" he asked Francesca.

"To a cart outside. They're empty."

"And then where?"

"To a barge at the landing place."

"Perfect!" said Tien Nu.

CHAPTER 40

The Escape

The heavy cart rumbled as the scullions pushed it across the dark courtyard, with the barrels inside rattling and banging against the rails. The yard was full of people, some singing drunkenly, others sagging against the walls or relieving themselves in the corners.

Francesca led the way, helping to guide the cart through the rowdy mob. It took them some time to reach the gateway, where Nozzo emerged from the shadows.

"Hold on there," he said. "Where are you going with that?"

"To the landing," Francesca said. "We're loading a barge for tomorrow."

The scullions stopped and fanned themselves, staring at Nozzo.

"Is that so?" The bodyguard motioned toward the cart. "What's in those barrels?"

Francesca shrugged. "Nothing."

"So why are you taking them to the barge?"

"To return them to the brewery." She gave a smile. "To be filled up again."

Nozzo scowled. "Don't take me for a fool. I need to look inside."

"But the steward said the barrels weren't to be tampered with."

Malaspina stepped from the gateway.

"Now, why would the steward say that?" He glanced at the bodyguard. "Open them up."

"But you don't need to," said Francesca. "Just thump on the lids. You can tell they're empty."

"We'll see," said Malaspina.

Nozzo climbed into the cart, squeezing between the barrels. He hammered on the nearest lid, which boomed like a bass drum.

He looked at Malaspina. "Seems empty, all right."

"They're all like that," Francesca said.

Malaspina gave a tight smile. "So you keep saying."

He nodded at the bodyguard. "Check them all."

Nozzo continued testing the barrels. One after another, they produced the same booming sound. The final barrel was wedged into the back corner. Nozzo tried to reach it but failed.

"Guess there's no point," he said.

Malaspina had been watching Francesca's face. "That's just the one we need to look at."

Nozzo sighed and shifted the barrels around, eventually making his way through.

He pounded on the lid of the barrel, which gave a dull thud.

"This one isn't empty," Nozzo said. "What's inside?"

"Sorry, I forgot," said Francesca. "It's filled with slops from the kitchen."

"Not good enough," Malaspina said. "Open up."

Nozzo tried to remove the lid, but it was hammered tightly down.

"I'll need something to pry it off," he said.

One of the scullions fetched a crowbar that Nozzo used to lever the lid up.

He leaned over to look inside, then recoiled sharply.

"What a stink!"

"Told you so," Francesca said.

"Take a closer look," Malaspina said. "Make sure no one's in there."

Nozzo wrinkled up his nose and poked the crowbar into the putrid mass, raising it and lowering it several times.

"Nothing's here," he said finally.

He banged the lid back into place and got down from the wagon.

The scullions applied their backs to the cart once again. As Malaspina watched, they pushed it through the gateway and headed down the track.

On reaching the landing place, Francesca looked back toward the castle.

"All clear," she said.

"And thank our lucky stars!" Bec took off his floppy white hat and wiped the sweat from his forehead. "I was sure they were going to spot us."

Tien Nu unbuttoned his dirty uniform. "They were so focused on the barrels, they didn't give us a second glance."

He smiled at Francesca. "You played your part just right. They were convinced you were up to something."

"Actually, I was!" she said. "But not what they thought."

"It's the art of distraction," Tien Nu said. "The magician's best friend."

There was a noise on the track behind them.

Out of the darkness came a man in a chequered red and yellow costume—one of the mummers, carrying two packs. A small, very dirty dog trotted along beside him.

"Thanks so much for bringing our packs," said Bec, mussing Hannibal about the head. "Did they give you any trouble at the gate?"

The man shook his head. "I told them it was our equipment."

Tien Nu and Bec stored the packs in their boat and made ready to leave. Bec looked over at Francesca, but she didn't seem to notice. She was gazing at Tien Nu, who was untying the rope.

"Well, anyway," she said, "I just wanted to say goodbye."

She threw her arms around him and kissed him on the lips.

The kitchen boys laughed and clapped. "Well done, Francesca!"

She ran off into the darkness, leaving a trail of giggles in the air.

Tien Nu stood there, rooted to the ground. He glanced at the grinning boys, then at Bec, who shook his head.

"I don't know how you do it, Scraps. Not with a mug like that."

They paddled out to mid-stream. The lights of the castle receded into the distance, then vanished behind the trees. The boat glided down the dark river, which was streaked with moonlight, as the water bubbled and creamed beneath the bow. Swallows raked across the gleaming surface and an owl called from the woods.

Tien Nu felt supremely happy, dizzy from the kiss and the beer. He poked Bec with his paddle.

"What the devil got into you back there? I thought you'd gone crazy, taking on Malaspina like that."

"I really don't know," Bec said. "Usually, the man scares the living daylights out of me. But with my monkey mask on, I felt completely free."

"What you did—it reminded me of the stories about the Monkey King."

"Monkey King?"

"*Sun Wukong*. One of the Immortals. My father used to tell me about him."

"Is he good or bad?"

"Oh, definitely good. But mischievous, crazy! I think maybe his spirit possessed you."

Bec laughed. "I don't need the spirit of the Monkey King to make me crazy."

CHAPTER 41

Scars

The Knight paced along beside the pilgrim wagon, lending a hand whenever it got stuck in the deeply rutted road. The red-haired youth was keeping a safe distance on the other side of the wagon. He'd been quiet the entire day, staying out of the Knight's way. His left eye was swollen shut, the surrounding skin stained a glossy black.

The Knight glanced over at the youth. He paused and waited for the wagon to move ahead, then crossed to the other side. Emilio noticed the Knight approaching from behind and shied away, keeping his eyes on the ground. When the Knight touched him on the shoulder, he jumped and spun around, fists raised.

The Knight held out his hand. "I owe you an apology, my friend. I lost my temper. I was drunk."

The red-haired youth didn't seem to understand.

"Ap ... apology?" he stuttered.

"For last night."

Emilio looked down at the Knight's immense hand.

"You're apologizing for hitting me?"

The Knight nodded.

Emilio shook his head. "You don't need to do that. It was my own fault. I should have kept my big mouth shut."

"We all make mistakes. Come, my friend."

The youth hesitated, then took his hand.

The Knight gripped Emilio's arm and pulled him close, his mouth close to the boy's ear.

"Don't ever pull a stunt like that again," he said.

The wagon shuddered to a halt. They were in a village high in the mountains—no more than a scattering of houses. Ahead, the road made a serpentine descent into the valley, where the river threaded a path between the hills. The driver climbed down and entered a ramshackle inn, calling for the landlady.

The Knight helped unload the bags, then walked back to survey the countryside they'd just passed through. The road ran in a long dusty ribbon over the crests of the hills to the horizon. He stood there silently, letting his eyes drift over the scene—groves, fields, meadows—all bathed in a soft light, not a leaf moving. From the distance came the clank of cowbells and the bark of a dog. The sun was setting in a flawless sky and the evening star had appeared.

The Knight gazed at the star, glimmering with a pearly light. He wondered where Bec and Tien Nu were. He hoped they'd find their way to Ponti. If need be, he'd wait for them there, as long as it took, pilgrimage be damned. It was years since he'd cared about anything so much—cared about anything at all.

A tide of shadow swept across the valley as the sun dropped out of sight. The Knight watched the outlines of the hills dissolving into the liquid sky, then walked back to the inn.

The red-haired youth was seated on a bench in front, a hunk of raw meat pressed to his eye.

"Mind if I join you?" said the Knight.

"No, no. Sit down." Emilio looked surprised, but shifted over to make room.

The Knight gazed at the meat. "Does that help?"

The youth grinned. "Not much. But I'll get the kitchen to cook it up for me later."

He glanced at the Knight, hesitated, then said: "You look like you've been in a few scrapes yourself."

"You mean this?" The Knight touched the scar on his cheek.

Emilio nodded. "How did you get it?"

"It was a gift from my brother. A message, you might say."

"A message? Telling you what?"

"To get out." The Knight pursed his lips. "Very handy with a knife, my brother was. I left home that night."

"And you never went back?"

The Knight shook his head.

Emilio nodded at the man's missing finger. "Did your brother do that, too?"

The Knight held up his hand and wiggled the stump. "No, this happened when I was younger. My cousin and I were trying out some swords—presents from my father. I got carried away and took a swipe at Bernardo. He ducked and struck back. I parried, but the blade slid down and caught me on the hand."

"You must have been pretty angry."

"I was at first, but we made up later. Bernardo was my closest friend—we'd grown up together. He left home not long after I did. Moved on to Ponti, I hear. With any luck, we'll meet again."

"Actually, I've got a scar, too," Emilio said. "In a rather delicate spot."

He widened his eyes. "On my arse."

The Knight struggled not to laugh.

"And worse still," Emilio said, "it was a self-inflicted wound."

"You did it to yourself?"

Emilio nodded gleefully.

"Why in the name of all the saints would you do that?" asked the Knight.

"I was trying to impress a girl."

"By stabbing yourself in the arse?"

"No, no! I was serenading her from the street. When she came out on the balcony, I started climbing up the vines. My dagger kept getting in the way, so I shifted it round to the back. Halfway up something happened."

"You fell!"

"Exactly! A branch broke and I dropped like a stone. The dagger stuck me in the bum."

CHAPTER 42

Roast Pigeon

Bec and Tien Nu continued paddling late into the night, only stopping when a bank of cloud rolled across the moon. They pulled into shore and bedded down in a meadow.

Bec was so tired, he fell asleep almost instantly. At dawn, he was woken by something wet pressing on his mouth and nose, smothering him. He jumped up with a shout. But it was just a cow nuzzling at his face.

"What's the matter?" Tien Nu asked, rolling over.

Bec broke into laughter and pointed at the beast, which was placidly gazing at them.

Tien Nu groaned and got to his feet, rubbing his stomach. "Say, did you bring any food with you from the castle?"

Bec shook his head. "I thought you were going to do it."

"I meant to, *amico*, but I forgot in the rush."

Bec gazed at the animal's swollen udder.

"I may not know much," he said, "but I know how to milk a cow."

They set off with stomachs full of rich, creamy fluid. But the relief was only temporary. Hunger returned in full force as the day wore on. They passed several villages along the way, where the road to Ponti dipped down from the hills. But they didn't dare stop, in case they ran into Malaspina.

Now it was almost dusk, with the light rapidly fading. Ahead they saw a bridge of many arches, which crossed to a walled town on the left bank. A quay extended beside the river, with a string of boats and barges moored alongside.

Bec pointed to what looked like an inn on the quay, propped against the town wall. "Why don't we pull in there and get something to eat. I'm starving."

Tien Nu studied the inn. "I suppose it's as good a place as any. We'll have to stop sooner or later."

They headed for a space at the end of the quay. As they slid alongside, Hannibal scrambled out and scurried to the wall to lift his leg.

Pleasant aromas were wafting down from the inn.

"I'll go and get the food," said Tien Nu. "You'd better stay out of sight."

"But I need to use the privy."

"Is it really that bad?"

Bec made an agonized face.

"All right," Tien Nu laughed. "I'll wait here and keep watch. Just be careful."

Bec headed down the quay. But Hannibal kept running after him, so Tien Nu found some rope and tied him to a bollard. The dog strained against the rope, his tail whisking as he watched his master depart.

"Just stay there," said Bec, turning to shake a finger. "I'll be back soon."

The inn was several stories high, with an enclosed yard at the side. A faded signboard over the door showed an eagle clutching a pigeon. Lights shone through the open windows, and the sound of voices and laughter drifted out.

Several grizzled men were chatting by the door. Bec nodded to them, then poked his head inside and looked around the busy room. No sign of Malaspina or the bodyguard.

"Looking for someone, laddie?" inquired an old man with watery eyes.

"Not really," said Bec. "Just wondering if the food's any good."

"Best this side of Ponti. Try the roast pigeon."

"Ponti—that's where we're headed," Bec said. "Do you know how long it takes to get there?"

"You're in that boat?" The old man glanced down the quay. Bec nodded.

"Four days at most," the man said. "But there's a gorge with rapids not far ahead. You'll have to leave your boat there and take to the road."

Another man chipped in. "You'll see the place when you come to it. There's a path that runs up to the road."

Bec thanked the men and went inside, taking care not to slip on the floor, which was greasy with droppings. He scanned the room again, then made his way to the counter at back.

A lady with a pinched face gave him a sharp look, then took his order, relaying it to the kitchen through a small window behind her.

"Ready in a minute," she told Bec.

He inquired about the privy and was directed down a corridor to the walled yard, where he spotted a privy in the far corner.

He peered inside and quickly retreated, waving his hands at the swarm of flies that descended on him, invading his eyes and ears. His mouth firmly shut, he ducked back in, taking care not to step in the gaping pit. He left the door ajar to get some air and was in the midst of his business, when he heard footsteps approaching.

"Occupied!" he shouted, tugging the door shut.

He quickly finished up. Outside some people were talking in low tones. When he went to open the door, he found it stuck. He pushed harder, almost slipping backward into the pit. But the door wouldn't open. Someone was blocking it.

"Who are you?" demanded a gruff voice. "Identify yourself."

Bec thought quickly. "I'm Giulio ... Giulio Patti. From San Vito."

There was a hurried exchange outside.

"Are you a slave?" asked the voice. "A slave belonging to ... ah ..."

"... Adolfo Malaspina," added a woman.

"I've already told you," said Bec. "I'm Giulio Patti, from San Vito. I'm on my way to Ponti."

The door jerked open. A bald man with a dent in his forehead peered inside. Behind him was the landlady, a lamp in hand, her small eyes glittering in the light.

"Come out," said the bald man. "If you're actually who you say you are, you haven't got anything to worry about."

Bec stepped outside and gazed boldly at them. The landlady held the lamp close to his face as the bald man studied it.

"Matches the description," he said finally. "Right age.

Skinny. Shaved head—with blond hair showing. What do you think?"

"There's no family called Patti in San Vito," the landlady said. "I ought to know. My mother's from there."

Bec silently cursed himself. Of all the villages in the world, why did he have to pick that one?

"If you don't believe me, ask my friend." Bec pointed toward the other side of the yard.

The couple turned to look. Bec dove between them and made a dash for the gate leading out to the quay.

The landlady screamed. "He's getting away!"

Bec collided with a husky young man crossing the yard. He scrambled to his feet, but the bald man was already there. He grabbed Bec around the waist and hoisted him off the ground.

The young man stopped to stare.

"A runaway slave," said the landlady.

"They should all be strung up." The man shook his head and continued to the privy.

The landlady waited until he'd closed the door, then pulled a greasy rag from her apron. She pried open Bec's jaws and stuffed the rag inside. Bec gagged, nearly choking.

The bald man bound Bec's hands behind his back, then

went to work on his ankles, while the woman tied another rag across his mouth.

Bec was lifted sideways and carried into the inn, then tilted at an angle and taken up a long stairway. At the top, they opened a door and dumped him on the floor.

He found himself in a small dark room, with a steeply sloping roof and a shuttered window. Boxes and spare furniture were piled in the corners. His captors stood over him.

The bald man rubbed his chin. "What now?"

"It's too late to do anything tonight," said the landlady. "First thing tomorrow, we'll send someone to find Malaspina. He said he'll be moving along the Ponti road, stopping at all the inns."

The man prodded Bec with his foot. "Stay put, you hear? No tricks or you'll be sorry."

They left the room and shut the door behind them. Bec listened as the key turned in the lock and the footsteps died away. Then he sat up and shunted himself across the floor to the nearest wall, where he rested for a moment.

A long silken thread dropped in front of him, and a tiny spider scuttled onto his cheek. Bec scrunched up his face, trying to shake the spider off. It scooted up inside a nostril and triggered an enormous sneeze. The spider shot out on a stream of snot, which dribbled down over the gag.

Bec closed his eyes, trying to stay calm. He levered himself up the wall, bit by bit, until he was in a standing position. He paused to gain his balance, then hopped over to the window, where he lowered his head and butted open the shutters.

It was almost night outside. Far below was the river, where the light from the inn shone across the dark water. He could see their boat at the end, with Hannibal lying nearby, tied to the bollard. Bec peered at the boat, then looked up and down the quay.

Tien Nu had disappeared.

CHAPTER 43

The Wall

The light drained from the sky as Tien Nu sat on the edge of the quay, legs dangling over the water. He glanced down toward the inn. People were coming and going, but there was no sign of Bec. Something had gone wrong. Bec should be back by now. He'd better go and take a look.

He retrieved his cape and flung it over the packs to hide them, then set off toward the inn. He greeted a group of old men outside and paused on the threshold, peering in.

"Looking for your friend?" asked a man.

Tien Nu gave a start. "Yes. He came in here a while ago."

"Thought as much. You're from that boat down there at the end."

Tien Nu nodded.

"Well, the laddie's still inside," said the old man. "And no wonder. He looked like he could do with a square meal."

Tien Nu thanked the man and ducked through the low doorway. The tables were full of people bent over trenchers piled with meat. A small army of servers hurried about, bearing platters of roast pigeon.

No sign of Bec.

Tien Nu spotted a corridor on the other side of the room and followed it to the yard outside, where he saw a privy. He went over and heard some grunts inside.

"Still at it, Bec? Must be a whole week's worth."

The door inched open. A young man was squatting in the darkness, round eyes gazing upward.

"Sorry," Tien Nu blurted.

As he returned along the corridor, two people came down a flight of stairs.

"What if it isn't him?" a bald man said to the woman behind.

The woman began to reply but stopped when she noticed Tien Nu.

"What can I do for you?" she said sharply.

"I'm looking for my friend. He's about my age, but smaller, with a shaved head."

"What's his name? Giulio? Giulio Patti?"

Tien Nu sensed something was wrong. "No, it's … Angelo."

The landlady's eyes narrowed. "I haven't come across anyone like that."

She gave a curt nod and pushed past him into the corridor. Tien Nu looked up the stairway, where the bald man had paused on the landing. The man gazed back at him, then sat down on the stairs, fiddling with his ring.

"You haven't seen my friend, have you?" Tien Nu asked. "He came in here earlier."

The man's eyes flitted about. "You heard what the lady said."

Tien Nu started to climb the stairs. The bald man shook his head. "It's private up here."

"But I need to find my friend."

The man got to his feet, folding his arms across his chest. "Take off, kid!"

Tien Nu glanced at the man's heavy shoulders, then turned and made his way back outside.

The group of old men had moved on, and the quay was deserted. Tien Nu examined the windows on the upper stories of the inn. Bec must be up there somewhere. But where?

He called Bec's name—softly at first, then more loudly, until some shutters scraped open.

"Quiet! We're trying to get some sleep!"

Tien Nu stood there, wondering what to do. He should

never have let Bec go off on his own. His eye caught a movement at the top of the inn. There—in a window under the roof—a small head.

"Bec?"

The head nodded.

"Can you get out?"

A vigorous shake, side to side.

"Hang on, I'm coming."

But how? It was too dangerous to try and climb up. And he couldn't use the stairway with the bald man sitting there.

He studied the town wall that ran behind the inn, extending along the quay to the main gate. It was almost the same height as the inn roof. A guard tower was built into the wall about halfway to the gate. If he could get up into the tower, he'd be able to use the wall to reach the roof.

He went along the quay and entered the gate, which was unguarded. A narrow alley doubled back to the tower, where he climbed an external stairway and reached the turret, which was strewn with rubbish. He was startled by a noise and peered into a corner. Nestled among some rags was a litter of new-born kittens, wriggling and mewing.

He went to the edge of the turret and peered back along the wall, which ran toward the inn, straight as a die. It was capped by a stone ridge, a few inches wide. On one side was the quay, thirty feet down; on the other side was the alley.

It would be like walking a tightrope.

Tien Nu felt the first stirrings of nausea. He squatted down and lowered his head, waiting for his stomach to settle. Maybe he could crawl along the wall. But that would be a coward's way out—an admission of defeat. He was an acrobat, for pity's sake, someone who'd walked tightropes all his life. He had to do it.

Tien Nu climbed over the parapet onto the ridge. He steeled himself, then set off, one foot in front of the other, arms spread wide. From the corner of his eye, he could see the river gliding smoothly alongside the quay. It made him feel dizzy, as if he were moving himself. He tried to ignore it and focus on the inn ahead.

He noticed something further down the ridge—something small, headed in his direction. A black cat, padding steadily along the wall. The cat stopped about ten feet away and gazed at him, yellow eyes unwavering. Tien Nu slowed to a halt, balancing precariously.

From the turret behind him came the mewing of kittens, louder now.

The cat took several delicate steps forward.

Tien Nu waited.

Suddenly the cat sprang at him, digging its claws into his leg.

Tien Nu gave a cry and leapt back.

He lost his footing and toppled sideways.

CHAPTER 44
The Rescue

Lashes of lightning streaked across Tien Nu's eyeballs—branching, twisting, tailing into blackness, then bursting out in great mushrooms of light.

Somehow his fingers caught hold of the ridge. He hung there, clammy with sweat. The cat was clinging to his calf, letting out shrieks of terror.

Tien Nu glanced down. It was a straight drop to the quay. He imagined the pavement rushing up at him—the sickening crack of bone on granite.

The cat clawed its way up Tien Nu's leg. One of its paws became tangled in his tunic and the creature thrashed about, trying to work itself loose.

Tien Nu's fingers started to slip. He tightened his grip and made to hoist himself back on top. The cat got free and clambered further up his leg, digging its claws into his private parts. A stab of pain shot through Tien Nu's body and propelled him upward. His elbows found the ridge and he rolled onto the top, the cat still clinging to him.

He reached down and grabbed the animal, which hissed and spat at him. Holding it at arm's length, he deposited it on the wall. The cat turned to glare, then resumed its journey toward the kittens in the tower.

Tien Nu looked ahead. The ridge threaded a ghostly path through the darkness toward the inn. The sight blended in his memory with the tightrope strung across the courtyard— his father waiting for him mid-way.

He closed his eyes, pulse throbbing.

Bec's life was at stake.

He pushed himself to his feet and started once again along the ridge, moving slowly and deliberately, trying to ignore the trembling in the pit of his stomach. Step by step, the inn got closer.

Some stonework crumbled underfoot. He vaulted toward the inn and leapt onto the roof. For a moment he stood there, breathing hard.

He looked around to get his bearings, then made his way to the front of the inn, where he peered over the edge at the window below, calling softly several times.

Bec's head emerged, looking downward.

Tien Nu cupped a hand to his mouth. "Numbskull! Up here!"

The head twisted around. Bec's eyes widened.

"Are you alone?" Tien Nu asked.

Bec nodded.

"Move back inside—as far as you can go. I need room."

Bec disappeared.

Tien Nu gazed down at the window, trying to figure out how to reach it.

Some swallows swept over the roof and wheeled into the empty space above the river. Tien Nu listened to their thin cries, trying not to think of the distance to the quay below.

He dropped his legs over the edge of the roof, his feet sliding over the smooth plaster wall, until he was hanging full-length from his hands.

The window was still some distance away.

Now!

He let go of the roof and thrust his legs forcefully inward. He hurtled through the window and hit the floor, shooting across to the wall. He lay there, staring up at the dark ceiling.

Something moved into his field of vision.

Bec's face—a cloth tied across the mouth.

"Mm ... phgh!" said the face.

"Hold on!"

Tien Nu slowly pushed himself to his feet and untied the gag.

"Aaargh!" said Bec, opening his mouth wide.

Tien Nu saw another rag stuffed down his throat. He gently extracted it.

"Great God in heaven above!" spluttered Bec. "I thought I was going to choke."

Tien Nu untied his arms and legs. Bec bent over, hawking and spitting.

"Vile!" he said. "That rag was filthy."

Tien Nu rubbed his rear end and limped to the window. He looked out, confirming what he already knew. There was no way to get back to the roof, much less to climb down.

He went to the door and tried to open it.

"It's locked," said Bec.

Tien Nu put his eye to the keyhole. "Luckily, they took away the key."

"Luckily?"

Tien Nu rummaged around in his pouch and pulled out a thin metal pick. Sliding it into the keyhole, he turned it this way and that, his ear cocked.

A solid click. He tugged the door open an inch.

"And you call *me* a thief!" said Bec.

Tien Nu grinned. "A little something I picked up from my father."

He opened the door some more and gazed down the stairs. "It's going to be tricky. There's a man at the bottom."

The sound of tramping feet came up the stairwell. Tien Nu quietly shut the door and motioned for Bec to flatten himself against the wall. He moved next to Bec, pressing an arm against the door to keep it closed.

The footsteps got louder. A key rattled in the lock.

"That's funny," someone muttered. "I thought I'd locked it."

Tien Nu released his arm, allowing the door to be pushed open. Light streamed into the room. The landlady held up her lamp and entered, peering into the darkness.

Tien Nu sprang out, knocking the lamp from her hand. She gave a startled cry and stumbled, falling to the ground. The lamp sputtered out.

Tien Nu shoved Bec through the doorway and they ran down the stairs, trailed by shouts from above. The bald man was no longer on guard at the bottom. They raced along the corridor into the dining room, as the customers looked up and stared.

Bec skidded on the greasy floor and windmilled about, trying to keep his balance.

His feet flew out from under him and he hit the ground hard.

CHAPTER 45

Adrift

"Get up, you fool!" Tien Nu grabbed Bec's arm and dragged him to his feet. They dashed out the front door.

The bald man was standing outside, a cup of wine in hand, gazing over the river. He glanced around as Tien Nu and Bec tore past him. He took a few steps, squinting after them as they sprinted down the quay.

"Hey, there!" he shouted. "Stop! Stop!"

The landlady appeared at the door, panting heavily, one hand to her chest, her thin face flushed.

"Don't just stand there!"

The bald man put down his wine and set off after them.

Tien Nu reached the boat first. He freed Hannibal while Bec untied the boat and hopped inside. Hannibal scrambled in after him and landed on a paddle resting on the thwart. The paddle flipped upward and flew into the water, where it began to float away. Bec leaned over the side, stretching out, trying to retrieve the paddle. The boat tilted sideways and water spilled inside.

"Let the paddle go!" Tien Nu shouted. "There's no time."

He glanced back to see the bald man pounding down the pavement. Behind him, a crowd was gathering at the doorway of the inn.

"Get going," he said to Bec. "I'll swim out after you."

He unfastened his pouch and threw it into the boat. Bec pushed off from the quay and the boat swung into the river.

Tien Nu turned and faced the bald man, fists raised. The man slowed down, then came to a halt. He looked warily at Tien Nu. His eyes shifted to the boat drifting away.

"That fellow!" said the man, indicating Bec. "He's a slave. There's a big reward. We can split it."

Tien Nu responded with a feint to the head, followed by a punch to the gut.

It was like striking a stone wall.

The man moved toward Tien Nu, arms spread wide.

Move Number One. Run like hell.

Tien Nu dashed to the edge of the quay and peered into the water, trying to gauge its depth. Too dark to tell. He plunged in, keeping the dive shallow. The cold water burst about his ears and bubbled into his nose. He swam underwater, kicking hard, until his lungs nearly burst. He shot to the surface, snorting and coughing.

Around him was an expanse of water—dark and empty. Then the embankment lurched into view. People were clustered on the quay, talking excitedly, pointing at the river.

Where was Bec?

"Over here, Scraps!" came a shout.

Tien Nu turned. The boat was behind him, not far away, revolving slowly. Bec held out a paddle.

"Grab it!"

Tien Nu swam toward the boat and clutched for the paddle, missing it by inches. He lunged a second time and caught the blade with his fingertips. The paddle slipped from Bec's grasp and dropped into the water, where it floated out of reach.

Hannibal peered over the side of the boat, barking sharply. The boat began moving more rapidly as the current took hold.

No time to recover the paddle.

Tien Nu thrashed after the boat and got one hand on the stern as it reached mid-stream. He tried to climb inside, but the boat rocked crazily and almost capsized. He dropped back into the water and hung onto the stern.

They were moving fast now, heading for the bridge, its arches resting on heavy stone piers. The boat yawed sideways as it swept toward one of the piers. Bec beat the water with his hands, trying to bring the boat into line.

The bridge got closer. Tien Nu kicked violently, steering the boat toward the central arch.

Bec stared anxiously ahead as the bridge loomed up.

"More to the left," he shouted. "*Left!* No, no! I mean *right. Right!*"

Hannibal started to gnaw at Tien Nu's fingers gripping the stern.

"No, no, Hannibal," Tien Nu shouted. "Stop! Stop!"

His words were lost in the roar of the water as they slid toward the bridge.

A wild rush and a sudden boom.

The boat was sucked into the archway, dragging Tien Nu under. He fought to keep his head above the surface. The boat shot out the other side in a burst of spray. The force of the torrent wrenched one of Tien Nu's hands loose. He clung on with the other, choking, as water gushed into his mouth. His fingers almost slipped on the wet wood, but somehow he held on, coughing and spitting and blowing. Mucus streamed from his nose, and his eyes and ears were clogged with water.

The current hurried the boat along. They swept around a bend and the town disappeared from view. There was only the night sky above, studded with stars.

"Head for the right bank," Tien Nu shouted. "Paddle with your hands and I'll kick."

Between them, they managed to steer the boat toward a narrow beach, where some fishing craft were pulled up. Tien Nu found his footing on the muddy bottom and pushed the boat into shore, where Bec hopped out and helped to drag the boat up onto the beach.

Tien Nu was chilled to the bone. He stripped off his wet clothes and wrapped himself in his cape, then returned to the shore, where Bec was looking back toward the town, Hannibal at his side.

"Anyone coming after us?" Tien Nu asked.

"Not that I can see."

They waited, gazing at the dark river. The broad expanse of water was quiet and empty.

Bec glanced at Tien Nu. "You risked your life for me back there."

"Actually, I did it for Hannibal. He'd miss you."

"I knew you had a heart deep down."

Tien Nu grinned. "I've always liked dogs."

"So, what now, Scraps?"

"We'd better keep going," Tien Nu said. "But we'll have to walk. The boat's no good without paddles."

Bec went over to the fishing craft, moving from one to the other. He gave an exclamation, reached inside a boat, and brandished a pair of paddles.

"I don't count this as stealing."

CHAPTER 46

Fathers

The river narrowed as they paddled along. In the darkness, it was hard to see where they were going. On several occasions, the boat almost came to grief on sandbars and half-submerged rocks.

"This is far enough, *amico,*" said Tien Nu finally. "Let's pull in over there."

He pointed to a narrow strip of beach ahead.

They gathered some driftwood and built a fire, sheltering under the spreading roots of a gigantic toppled tree. Tien Nu's clothes were still damp, so he draped them over the roots, fending off Hannibal, who kept jumping at them.

He sat down at the fire beside Bec, huddled in his cape.

Bec patted Hannibal, who had wriggled into his lap. He looked at his hands. "Blisters everywhere. How are yours?"

"Not too bad," Tien Nu said. "It's my stomach that's the problem. We haven't eaten a crumb since ... who knows when?"

"Dummy! It was yesterday at the castle—if you don't count the milk."

"Was it really? It feels like weeks ago."

Tien Nu was silent for a moment. "How did those people at the inn know about you—that you're a runaway?"

"Malaspina had passed by and given my description. Seems like he's travelling down the Ponti road, stopping at all the inns."

"Do you think they'll go and tell Malaspina we're on the river?"

"Actually, they might. He'd probably pay for the information."

"So, the river isn't safe any longer."

Bec shrugged. "We can't go much further, anyway. Some old men at the inn told me there's a gorge ahead where you have to leave the boat and take to the road."

"That means Malaspina could be waiting for us there."

"We don't have much choice, Scraps. River or road, it's all the same. He'll keep on hounding us until we get to Ponti."

Tien Nu gazed into the flames, feeling as if the net were closing in. Not for the first time, he wished his father were around to give advice. He'd always been a great escape artist.

Bec threw him a sideways glance. "Penny for your thoughts."

"Actually, I was thinking about my father—wondering how he'd get out of a fix like this."

"What do you suppose he'd do?"

"Don't know. Maybe nothing. My father always said there's no situation so bad that you can't make it worse."

"Worse?"

"By doing something stupid."

Bec laughed. "I think I like your father." He was silent for a moment. "You really miss him, don't you?"

Tien Nu nodded. He tossed some twigs into the fire and watched them flare up, sending sparks spiralling into the darkness.

"What's it like to have a father?" Bec asked.

Tien Nu looked at him. "That's not easy to say. I guess every father's different."

"What was yours like, then?"

"What do you mean?"

"Like ... was he hard on you sometimes?"

"My father ..." Tien Nu blew out a long breath. "Well, my father was a complicated man—full of contradictions. He always told me that family was the most important thing in the world. Yet I know as a fact, he rebelled against his own father and left home when he was young. He said he didn't believe in violence, always quoting Buddha—a holy man he followed. But he made a living by challenging people to fight." Tien Nu rolled his eyes. "Figure that one out! And yes, he could be pretty tough on me sometimes, even though he loved me a lot."

"If he loved you, why would he be tough on you?"

"Maybe he thought the two things went together."

"I'm not sure I understand."

"All right, let me tell you a story."

Tien Nu settled back against his pack. "This happened after we arrived in Venezia, when I was still a kid. My father sent me out to buy some fish. It was the first time he'd let me do it on my own. Venezia is like a maze, with millions of canals and alleys and bridges. It's easy to get lost. But I knew where the fish market was, so everything should have been all right."

He laughed and stretched out his legs. "Should have been! But I ran into a parade in the street, with people singing and dancing and banging drums—somebody's name day. It was so much fun I followed along. They ended up at a wine shop, where they invited me in and offered me some *grappa* to drink. I'd never had any before."

"Trouble!" Bec said.

"The first sip burned all the way down. I thought I was going to die. But I couldn't stop because everyone was

314

watching me. I took another sip, and this time it wasn't so bad. The next one was even better. I started to feel all warm inside, and the people became very friendly. For some reason, they seemed to like me."

"Ugly as you are."

"Do you want to hear the story?"

Bec grinned. "Keep going."

"So, anyway, they kept on pouring *grappa* into my cup, and I kept on pouring it down my throat. I got drunker and drunker—chattering away with everyone, not keeping track of the time. Then I saw my father outside, peering into the wine shop."

"Double trouble!" Bec said.

"When Papa spotted me, his eyes went very wide. He straightened up and walked into the place—slowly and calmly, as if he didn't have a care in the world. He came right up to me and ... *whack!* ... he smacked me across the face. I was so surprised, I didn't say a thing. Then he hugged me and said: 'I thought you were dead, Tien Nu.' I realized he was crying. I could feel his tears trickling down my neck. He told me never to do it again. And I never did."

Tien Nu gave a soft laugh. "That was my father."

"So how did you feel when he hit you?"

"I was angry, of course. But mostly I was embarrassed—because he did it in front of all those people. I was also ashamed, because I knew I'd let him down."

"Because you wanted to please him?"

"Because he'd trusted me to behave like an adult, and I'd gone and done something stupid."

"Did ... did your father beat you very often?"

Tien Nu shook his head. "Actually, he apologized to me later—said he'd lost his head. Somehow, that only made me feel worse."

"Why so?"

"Because it didn't seem right for him to be apologizing, when it was my fault to start with."

Bec was quiet for a while, tracing circles in the sand.

Finally, he looked up. "You loved your father?"

"Very much."

"But still, you'd get angry at him."

"Of course. Just like he'd get angry at me sometimes. It's normal."

"That's just my problem," Bec said. "I don't know what normal is. I only know that Malaspina hates me and beats me for no reason at all."

Tien Nu stayed awake long after Bec had fallen asleep—staring into the dying embers of the fire. Talking about his father had stirred up old memories, making him think of the years they'd spent together, just the two of them, traipsing from place to place.

He realized how little he knew about his father. He'd always been just that—his father. A force of nature, like the sun or the wind, with no interior life. And yet his father must once have been a boy much like himself, full of dreams and hopes, regrets and fears. It was difficult for Tien Nu to imagine what he'd been like.

All he knew was that at the age of fourteen, his father had set off by himself from Samarkand and headed west, relying only on his wits and skill in *quan fa*. He'd had many adventures and close calls, if only half the stories he'd told were true. Somewhere along the way, he'd joined a troupe of jugglers and ended up in Alessandria. And there he'd met Tien Nu's mother, the member of a sprawling family of acrobats, with roots and branches all over the East—Siria, Persia, India. They'd fallen in love and married. Tien Nu was their only child.

His mother died while he was still young, the victim of an epidemic that swept up the Nile with the winter winds.

That was when his father began travelling again. And Tien Nu, barely six years old, had travelled with him.

All these years, in good times and in bad, his father had taken care of him.

Now he was dead.

And Tien Nu was sure it was his fault.

CHAPTER 47

The Spring

The bandit peered through the bushes at the two travellers by the pond across the road. They were toasting bits of bread and cheese over a fire, with their horses hitched to a tree nearby. The sun hadn't set yet, but it was already twilight in the forest.

They made an odd pair, Bosco thought. The older man was tall and lean, while the other was as stocky as a barrel, with a neck and shoulders to match. The first man said little, but when he spoke, it was in a tone that brooked no dissent. The other man listened with a nod and a smile. Master and servant, obviously.

Bosco surveyed the master's fine apparel and the elaborate trappings on his horse. It would be rich pickings—easy, too. The men had unbuckled their swords and left them on the ground near the horses. Their daggers were still in their belts, and the master had a holster of knives strapped to his chest. But he didn't look like a fighter. He'd be too worried about getting his nice clothes dirty. The servant was another story—but he'd follow his master's orders. If all went well, the older man would hand over his pouch without a fuss, and his servant would follow suit. It would be clean and fast, just as Bosco liked it.

He took a last careful look around the site. Then he crept back through the forest to the clearing, where the other bandits were waiting by the stream. The two newcomers—Ugo and Aldo—got to their feet as he approached, looking at him expectantly. He wondered how far they could be trusted. His brother, Beppe, remained seated by the stream, watching him with rounded eyes.

"It's time," Bosco said. "They're eating, so we'll catch them off guard."

He went over to his brother and put a hand on his shoulder. "You wait here, Beppe. We'll be gone for a while. But don't worry, I'll be back soon. Whatever happens, just stay here. Understand? Don't go anywhere."

Beppe folded his hands in his lap, looking up at his brother's face. Bosco squeezed his shoulder and turned to the others.

"Sometimes my brother gets anxious when I leave," he said. "Wanders off to look for me."

"Has he always been like this?" asked Ugo.

"Just since last year. He got knocked about in a fight. But he's getting better, little by little. Right Beppe?"

The brother smiled and nodded, but said nothing.

"Now then," Bosco said briskly. "Everyone ready? It should be easy. Just keep your wits about you."

The bandits left the clearing and made their way through the forest to the bluff overlooking the road. They crouched in the underbrush, swords drawn, gazing down at the two travellers, who had finished eating and were stretched out by the fire.

At a signal from Bosco, they burst across the road, spreading out around the pair.

The master jumped up, dagger in hand, while the big servant struggled to his feet.

"Drop your weapon," said Bosco.

The master gazed impassively at the bandits surrounding him, then opened his hand and let the dagger fall to the ground.

"Smart man," said Bosco. "And that holster—the one with the knives. That's right. Kick everything over here."

The master shunted the weapons across.

"You, too," said Bosco, nodding to the big man.

The servant looked inquiringly at his master. "Give me the word, Signor Malaspina."

"Do as he says, Nozzo," said Malaspina.

Nozzo dropped his dagger to the ground.

Bosco smiled. "Don't play dumb. Send it over here."

The bodyguard glared at him, but followed his instructions.

"Now your pouches. On the ground. Just leave them there."

The two men unfastened their pouches and laid them down.

"Step well back. That's it. Keep moving—right around the fire."

Bosco waited until the two men reached the other side. Then he glanced at Ugo.

"Go get the pouches."

The bandit moved forward, stooping to retrieve them.

Malaspina plunged his bare hand into the fire and whisked up some embers, tossing them into Ugo's face.

The bandit reeled back, howling with pain, frantically brushing off the burning coals. He lurched in front of Bosco, blocking his view.

Malaspina scrambled over to his sword and snatched it. He whirled around to face the bandits.

Bosco stared at him, stunned by the rapid turn of events.

"That's better," said Malaspina, his lips curling.

He waved the tip of his sword. "Drop your weapons."

Bosco stood his ground, his sword held lightly in his hand.

Ugo was on his knees by the pool, splashing water onto his face. He glanced at Malaspina, hesitated for a moment, then grabbed his sword and made a dash for the forest across the road.

Bosco glanced at the other bandit. "Don't make a move."

Aldo nodded nervously.

"Now then," said Bosco, gazing at Malaspina. "We're all gentlemen here. There's no point spilling blood. Let's declare this match a draw. You keep your pouches. I keep your weapons. And we all get to live another day."

"That's not how I see it," said Malaspina. "We return to the *status quo ante*. I want the weapons back."

"Ah, a little Latin for the occasion. Reminds me of my monastery days." Bosco rubbed his chin. "Tell you what. My friend and I will go back to the woods. Once we're there, we'll toss your blades into the road and call it quits, fair and square. But I want your word you won't follow us." His eyes flickered. "I assume you're a man of your word."

Malaspina stared coldly at Bosco. "If you return our weapons, I won't follow you. You have my word. But should we ever meet again, today or any other day, the agreement will be off. It will be every man for himself."

Bosco smiled. "Isn't it always?"

He signalled to Aldo, and the two bandits backed slowly across the road to the trees, where they paused to throw the travellers' weapons onto the road. Then they slipped into the forest and made their way back to the clearing, pausing from time to time to make sure they weren't being followed.

They found Ugo in the clearing, bent over the stream, smearing mud on his face.

"Much help you were," Bosco said.

"And what was I meant to do?" said Ugo. "The man's a devil. Throwing fire at me bare-handed."

Bosco looked around. "Where's Beppe?"

"Don't know. He wasn't here when I got back."

Malaspina and the bodyguard picked up their weapons and extinguished the fire, preparing to depart.

The bushes shook on the other side of the road and Beppe blundered from the forest, looking first in one direction, then the other.

Malaspina squinted at him. "You again! I thought you were gone for good. What do you want now?"

Beppe goggled at Malaspina, his mouth open. He shuffled sideways into the middle of the road, as if unsure which way to go.

Malaspina drew his sword and limped toward him.

Beppe backed away, his lower lip trembling. He stared at the sword, then turned and ran heavily up the road.

Malaspina went after him with great hobbled leaps.

Beppe half turned, his eyes wide with fear.

Malaspina raised his sword and hacked at the man's neck.

Beppe made a gurgling noise and clutched the wound. Blood gushed through his fingers, splattering onto his clothes. He staggered forward and fell to the ground.

Malaspina stood over the man, watching as his lifeblood drained away. Then he turned and limped back to the spring, where the bodyguard was waiting.

They mounted their horses and rode off, leaving Beppe on the road, soaking in his blood.

Night had fallen when Bosco emerged from the woods, peering up and down the road.

"Beppe, where are you? It's all right now. I'm here."

He paused to listen, then crossed the road to the spring, where he prodded the remnants of the fire with a stick. Still warm, he thought. Not long since they'd left.

Bosco frowned, recalling what Malaspina had said.

He turned and called for his brother again.

There was a fluttering in the trees. An owl glided silently across the road, barely visible in the darkness.

Bosco shivered and crossed himself. Bad luck.

He started walking slowly down the road, peering into the bushes on either side, stopping to call every few yards.

No sign of Beppe.

He retraced his steps and went the other way.

There was something in the middle of the road. A crumpled heap.

"God, no!"

He ran to Beppe and knelt by his side.

He lifted his brother's head, cradling it in his arms, while tears trickled down.

"Dear soul, what have they done to you?"

CHAPTER 48

The Ring

Tien Nu was in the prow of a ship, sails billowing, dolphins leaping from the sea ahead. There was a sense of life beginning anew—the coast of Africa just over the horizon. But the dream slipped away, and he was back on the beach where they'd camped last night, his muscles aching, his belly empty.

He lifted his head and looked around. The sky was brightening but the river was still dark. It was too early to set off.

Bec was already up—sitting by the water with Hannibal at his side. He was gazing at something in his hand.

Tien Nu pushed himself to his feet.

"Morning, *amico*."

Bec turned with a start and quickly closed his hand. "Morning, Scraps."

Tien Nu went over and sat down.

"What's that?" He gestured toward Bec's clasped hand.

"Oh, just something ..." Bec uncurled his fingers.

"A ring," said Tien Nu. "Where did you get it?"

"It's from Falco—the bandit that drowned in the cave." He gave Tien Nu a quick glance. "I found it in his pouch. I guess I never told you."

He held the ring up, the slim band glowing in the half-light. "There's something written on the inside. Do you know how to read?"

"Not a lot. But I can give it a try. Let's see."

Tien Nu took the ring and peered at the inner surface, slowly spelling out the letters engraved there.

"I ... A ... M ... M ... I ... R." He paused. "I am Mir. That doesn't make any sense."

He looked at the writing again. "Actually, the letters go all the way around. So, it depends where you start."

He turned the ring. "Now I see it. M ... I ... R ... I ... A ... M. That spells Miriam."

Bec made a choking sound.

Tien Nu glanced up. "What's wrong?"

"Miriam." Bec's voice was hoarse. "That's my mother's name."

"But ... lots of women have that name."

"You don't understand. Falco was a slave from the estate."

Tien Nu stared at him.

"My mother ..." said Bec. "She was the only Miriam there."

"You mean Falco might be ..."

"My father."

There was a long silence.

"Let me get this straight," said Tien Nu. "You believe that bandit came from the castle?"

"I *know* he did, Scraps. I never told you, but he had the Malaspina brand on his arm. Whenever slaves cause trouble, they're branded."

"And you think this ring belonged to your mother?"

"It has my mother's name on it. It's a small ring, a girl's ring. My mother died when she was very young."

"So, you really believe ... Falco could be your father?"

"That's it," said Bec miserably. "I think he's the slave called Fiaccola. Even the name is similar. I heard he'd become a bandit."

"But why would he have your mother's ring?"

"Don't know. She must have given it to him."

Tien Nu scooped up some wet sand and slowly shaped it. "This bandit—what did he look like, anyway? I only got a glimpse of him."

"Dark hair. Long nose. Weasel eyes."

"Like father, like son," Tien Nu said.

Bec broke into a grin. "Especially the eyes."

330

"You know what, Bec? I don't think this man could be your father. You and him ..." Tien Nu shook his head. "... You just don't fit together."

"But what about the ring?"

"The ring doesn't mean that much. Think about it. You don't know for sure it belonged to your mother. Even if it did, the bandit could have stolen it from her. Actually, he could have stolen it from anybody. He was a bandit, Bec. This is a big world. There must be plenty of rings like this."

Bec stared at Tien Nu, his eyes unfocused, his body swaying slightly. He sat there for a long while, not saying a word.

Finally, he got up. "Come on, Hannibal. How about a swim?"

He grabbed a stick and tossed it out into the river, watching as the little dog raced into the water and paddled out to retrieve it. Bec tugged off his clothes and splashed into the river after Hannibal. He swam to the middle of the stream, where he turned over on his back and spouted water into the air. Then he came back toward shore, where he stood up and looked at Tien Nu, water streaming down his face.

"Thanks for the advice, Scraps," he said. "I hope you're right."

CHAPTER 49

The Gorge

As soon as it was light, the two boys set off down the river. The countryside turned bleak as they paddled along, with dark forests crowding the banks and not a village or farmhouse in sight. A sheet of grey cloud covered the sky and the air was chilled.

By late afternoon, the river had become a torrent, twisting between rocky outcrops. Ahead, Tien Nu could see a place where it disappeared into a narrow cleft between the hills. Clouds of mist rose into the air, accompanied by a muted roar.

Bec pointed. "That must be the gorge they talked about. There should be a landing place nearby."

"Let's stop here," Tien Nu said. "Malaspina may be waiting for us."

They found a spot to drag up the boat, and picked their way through the underbrush along the bank. Soon they sighted a beach where several barges were moored.

There was not a soul around. They moved cautiously past the boats and took a well-travelled path up into the forest.

Bec came to a sudden stop, twisting around. "Did you hear something?"

Tien Nu paused to look. "I don't see anything. Just trees and bushes."

Bec gave a quick shiver. "I could swear someone is following us. I get this feeling."

"But if it's Malaspina, wouldn't he show himself?"

"It might not be him."

"Then who?"

"There's a price on my head. It could be anyone."

The path wound up the hill, leading to a ledge that ran into the gorge. Dark cliffs towered on either side, and far below, the river boiled and roared as it raced through a string of chutes and waterfalls. Hannibal nosed about, coming perilously close to the edge. Bec collared him and bundled him into the sling.

The ledge narrowed as they moved into the gorge. Bec led the way, sure-footed as a mountain goat. Tien Nu followed, taking care to avoid the edge. But he couldn't help glancing down, catching glimpses of the white-flecked water as it tumbled over the black rocks.

They reached a place where the path rounded a bulge

in the cliff, leaving little room to pass. Bec flattened himself against the wall and slipped around the outcrop with no difficulty. Tien Nu tried to follow his example but balked when he found himself staring down a sheer drop. Loose dirt trickled from beneath his feet and disappeared into the thundering void. He fixed his gaze on the opposite side of the gorge and inched sideways along the narrow ledge.

Bec was waiting for him on the other side. He turned and grinned, then nodded ahead. The gorge opened into a forested valley, where a massive stone bridge spanned the river. The water foamed and tossed as it surged from the gorge and swept on toward the bridge.

On the right, a road emerged from the forest and ran along a high embankment to the bridge, where it crossed the river and vanished into the trees on the other side.

Tien Nu surveyed the area, feeling uneasy.

"It's a good spot for an ambush," he said. "That bridge could hide an entire army. And who knows what's in the forest?"

"What should we do?"

"Let's go and take a closer look. There's good cover all the way to the bridge."

They followed the path down to the river, through a dense grove of evergreens.

The air was cool and full of mist, and the ground was soggy underfoot. In no time they were drenched. Hannibal huddled in his sling, whiskers drooping, fur plastered to the skin.

The path continued along the bank of the river to a second landing place, where more barges were pulled up. Beyond this point, the path petered out. Large puddles lay on the ground where the mist had collected.

Tien Nu dodged through the trees and scrambled up the side of the steep embankment, which was thick with long-stemmed grass and poppies. He lay on his belly in some bushes beside the road, and Bec flopped down beside him. There was no one in sight—not on the road, not on the bridge.

"Malaspina could be hiding in the forest—on this side or the other," Tien Nu said. "Let's wait until dusk. It'll be safer to cross the bridge then."

They settled down in the bushes, taking turns to keep watch. As day came to an end, the sky began to clear. The sun broke through and briefly streamed across the valley, before dropping behind the mountains.

Deep shadow descended on the river.

Bec nudged Tien Nu. "Let's do it now, before the moon comes up. I'll go first."

He shouldered his pack and scurried out onto the road.

As Bec reached the bridge, Tien Nu glanced back toward the forest.

Something moved in the gap where the road emerged from the trees.

CHAPTER 50

The Bridge

Two men on horseback appeared, pale against the dark forest. They swept along the embankment toward the bridge. Tien Nu wriggled backward down the slope, clinging to the coarse grass. Halfway down he stopped, not daring to move further.

The horsemen came to a halt on the road above.

"I could swear I saw someone on the bridge," said Malaspina.

"There's no one there now."

"Go and check. They could be hiding here, right under our noses."

Tien Nu watched as the bodyguard dismounted and plodded onto the bridge. He waited tensely, wondering if Bec had made it across in time.

Nozzo came back. "Nothing on the bridge or the other side. I checked everywhere."

"How about under the bridge?"

The ground trembled as the big man lowered himself down the embankment, no more than a few feet away. Tien Nu pressed himself into the tall grass, holding his breath. His heartbeat was so loud, he was sure the man could hear it.

There was a sudden flurry and an oath. Nozzo slid down the steep slope, landing with a splash in the pool at the base.

Malaspina let out a curse. "Clumsy oaf! Get back up here."

There was more splashing as the big man found his footing and waded out of the pool. He clambered up the embankment, his boot trampling on Tien Nu's outstretched hand. Tien Nu gritted his teeth, stifling a gasp. When Nozzo reached the top, he dragged off his boots and upended them, pouring out the water.

"Sooner or later, they'll have to use this bridge," said Malaspina. "There's no way a boat can pass through the gorge. That's what the people from the inn said."

Nozzo went to the edge of the embankment and gazed down at the water.

"Maybe they didn't know about the gorge and got drowned."

Malaspina shook his head. "They're not that stupid. We'll take a look at the road ahead. They may have crossed the bridge before we got here."

The bodyguard mounted his horse and followed Malaspina onto the bridge.

Tien Nu lay there for several long minutes. There was not a sound, only the steady rush of water. It was hard to tell whether the men were still there. He inched his way to the top and peered out through the bushes.

The bridge was empty. So was the road on the other side.

The men had gone.

But where was Bec? There was nowhere to hide on the bridge, which was hardly wide enough for a single cart. He must have made it across.

Tien Nu crept onto the bridge, keeping his head below the parapet.

Something plopped into his path, making him jump.

"Quiet!" hissed Bec. "Keep going."

They ran to the other side and took cover in the underbrush.

"Where were you, *amico?*" Tien Nu asked. "I thought for sure they'd catch you."

"I was in the middle of the bridge when I spotted them. There was no way to get across in time—and no turning back. So, it was over the side or nothing. Luckily, there's a ledge down there. I hung on for dear life, praying they wouldn't notice me."

Bec puffed out his cheeks. "*Porca vacca!* What a close call!

Poor Hannibal was squashed against the wall. I was sure he was going to give me away. But he didn't make a sound, did you little fellow?"

He scratched Hannibal behind the ears. "I saw the bodyguard barrelling down the embankment. The blockhead! If he'd bothered to look up, he would have spotted me. I was in plain sight, clinging to the side of the bridge."

"Monkey boy!" Tien Nu shook his head. "Always in a fix."

"It's not as if I try. It just happens."

They waited to make sure Malaspina wasn't still around, then hurried up the road into the trees.

CHAPTER 51
The Village

Tien Nu pushed away a branch that had sprung back into his face. The track was overgrown and hard to make out in the darkness. From time to time, he stumbled over roots that snaked across the way.

"The village can't be far now."

Bec gave a sigh. "That's what you said hours ago."

They had been walking for what seemed forever. After leaving the bridge, they'd followed the road into the forest, keeping to the verges in case Malaspina doubled back. They came to an open space at the top of a hill where, across the valley, they saw moonlight glinting off some roofs.

"Why don't we head over there?" Tien Nu said. "Maybe we can find some food and a place to sleep."

Bec gazed at the distant rooftops. "But how do we get there?"

They searched further along the road and came across a

track that led in the direction of the village.

Bec peered down the dark way. "Maybe we should just stay on the road."

"It'll be safer in the village."

"If you say so, Scraps."

The track plunged down through the forest, descending ever deeper into the valley. They trudged along in silence, too tired to talk. After some time, the track levelled off and crossed a swampy area, then began to climb again. They stumbled blindly upward as bushes crowded the track, catching at their arms and legs. Hannibal shrank into the sling, keeping his head down.

Some lighter patches appeared through the dense foliage, and soon they emerged in a grassy glade that was swimming with moonlight. All around were half-ruined houses, choked with vines and thistles. Doorways and windows gaped open, branches poking through holes in the roofs.

The village was deserted.

Bec gave a shiver. "This place is full of ghosts."

"You and your ghosts!" said Tien Nu. "There's nobody here. Anyway, it's too late to go back now. We'll have to make the best of it."

Bec pulled a face and looked around, staring at the

chapel at the end of the clearing. The walls were still intact, but part of the roof was missing.

"Let's head over there," he said. "At least it'll keep the ghosts away."

They started moving across the clearing.

"Stop! Stop!" shouted Bec.

Tien Nu froze and looked down. At his feet was a mass of white flowers that rimmed a shadowy opening, several feet wide. He caught a glimmer of water far below.

An old well, partially collapsed.

They gave it a wide berth and continued toward the chapel.

Hannibal pricked up his ears, sniffing the air. In the distance, they heard ragged barking. It came from the woods beyond the church.

"Wild dogs," said Bec, coming to a stop.

The noises got louder—a cacophony of barks—some high and sharp, others booming.

"Sounds like a whole pack," Tien Nu said. "As bad as wolves."

"Worse," said Bec. "No fear of people."

They waited, listening intently.

A dark stream of animals poured around the corner of the chapel and headed for them.

"Don't move," Bec said.

The dogs raced across the clearing—all legs and jaws and glistening teeth. At their head was a massive black-and-tan with a wolf-like snout. He bounded along, slobber flying from his mouth. A few feet away, he skidded to a halt. The other dogs, close behind, piled into one another.

The wolf dog held his distance, springing right and left, emitting deep-throated growls. From time to time, he lunged at them, jaws snapping, but each time pulled up short. The rest of the dogs—at least a dozen—spread out around them, yelping and barking. A mongrel with a torn ear dashed forward and nipped Bec's ankle. Hannibal snarled at him, almost leaping from his sling, and the dog backed off.

"Well, now, isn't this is a pretty sight."

Malaspina was at the edge of the clearing, an unpleasant smile creasing his face. Nozzo emerged from the trees behind him.

Bec and Tien Nu stood rooted to the spot. The dogs glanced nervously at the riders but showed no signs of leaving.

Malaspina dismounted and drew out his cane. He moved toward them, taking his time. The dogs growled and shuffled uneasily as he approached, their eyes darting between him and the two boys.

The man stopped a few feet from the ring of animals.

He glanced at Bec, then shifted his gaze to the dogs, fixing on the black-and-tan. He sprang forward and struck the dog on the spine with his iron-tipped cane. The beast let out a howl and sank to the ground, his legs jerking convulsively.

The other dogs fell silent, inching back. Malaspina turned toward Bec, who was staring at him, eyes wide, apparently frozen.

Tien Nu dropped his pack and stepped into the man's path.

"Get out of the way," Malaspina said. "This is none of your business."

Tien Nu didn't move.

Malaspina's lips curled. "Think again, dear boy. This slave isn't worth dying for."

"He's my friend."

"Friend!" Malaspina gave a soft laugh. "And what is that worth?"

"Don't you know?"

"Silly, brave boy. Head stuffed with old heroic tales. But you're making a mistake. I know this slave well. He's a liar and a coward."

Tien Nu said nothing.

"I'll give you one last chance to step aside—and thirty florins, to boot. Otherwise, you'll share his fate."

Tien Nu dropped into a fighting stance, fists raised.

Malaspina lunged at him, striking out with his cane, but the Tartar skipped away. As if on a signal, the dogs turned and scrambled in all directions, leaving the wolf dog twitching on the ground.

Tien Nu shouted to Bec. "Run!"

Bec awoke from his stupor and made a dash for the forest. A small dog skittered into his path, and Bec tripped over him and fell. The bodyguard ran up and grabbed him, twisting his arm behind his back.

Bec cried out, struggling to get free, but Nozzo held him fast. Hannibal wriggled from his sling and launched himself at the bodyguard, snapping at his legs. The big man connected with a kick that sent Hannibal flying to the side, yowling in pain. He scrambled off into the underbrush.

Tien Nu launched a spinning kick that forced the bodyguard to stumble back, stepping into the old well. The man gave a shout and dropped down, letting go of Bec. He clung to the rim, as Bec rolled away.

With two great leaps, Malaspina caught up with Bec and pinned him down—boot on his neck, cane raised. "Don't move or I'll smash your skull."

He looked at Tien Nu. "Stop, if you value his life."

Tien Nu glanced down at Bec, whose mouth was a jagged line, eyes half-closed.

He lowered his fists.

"That's a good boy," said Malaspina.

The man shifted his full weight onto Bec's throat. The boy made a choking sound, then went limp.

Malaspina turned to Nozzo, who was dragging himself from the well.

"Clumsy dolt! Get over here and tie them up. And don't make a mess of it."

The big man retrieved some rope from the saddlebags. He bound Tien Nu's wrists and ankles, then did the same for Bec, who was slowly regaining consciousness.

Malaspina gazed at the wolf dog, still writhing on the ground. He lashed down with his cane, striking again and again until the dog was still.

Nozzo dragged Tien Nu and Bec into the chapel, which was strewn with dead branches and leaves. He cleared a path to the inner wall, then checked their bonds and disappeared outside. There was a brief exchange of words as the men settled down for the night. Then silence.

"Sorry, Scraps," said Bec in a hoarse whisper. "I was scared stiff."

"Not to worry. How's the neck?"

"I think my singing days are over."

"No cloud without a silver lining. Get some sleep, knucklehead. We'll need our wits about us tomorrow."

"Have you seen Hannibal?"

"He ran off into the bushes."

"Well, at least he's safe."

Tien Nu's ankles were bound so tightly he could hardly feel his feet. He moved his legs around until the rope loosened a little, then leaned back against the wall and fell into a troubled sleep.

CHAPTER 52

The Amulet

Tien Nu's eyes flew open. A face was looking down at him.

"Wake up!" hissed a voice.

Tien Nu closed his eyes and opened them again. The face was still there, a shadowy oval framed by curls.

He gave a start of recognition.

Curly—the bandit boy.

"What ... where did you come from?" Tien Nu whispered.

"I've been following you—all the way from Montecavo. Didn't know, did you?"

Tien Nu glanced at Bec, who was still asleep. "How about untying me?"

"First I want my amulet back."

"Your what?"

"Shh! Not so loud." The bandit looked toward the doorway. "My amulet. It came off during our fight—when I knocked you out." A smile flitted across his face. "I went back to look for it, but it wasn't there. You must have taken it."

Tien Nu suddenly remembered the tiny bag he'd found that night, tangled in his clothes. Where had he put it? Somewhere in his pack.

"I'll give it back," he said. "But you've got to untie me first."

"Not on your life," said Curly. "Look. I'm doing you a favour. I could just search through your things."

Tien Nu struggled to sit up. "All right. I've got your amulet in my pack. But it's outside with those men."

The bandit gazed warily at him. "This isn't a trick?"

"Take a look. Our packs aren't here."

Curly glanced around the chapel and made a face. He crept to the doorway, paused there for a moment, then vanished outside.

There was the sound of horses snuffling.

Curly came back shouldering two packs, bent almost double under the weight. "I wasn't sure which one to take, so I brought them both."

"Just as well. It's the big one."

The bandit opened the pack and started rummaging about.

"It'd be faster if you let me do it," Tien Nu said.

Curly shook his head.

"Aha!" He held up a little leather bag, gazing at it happily.

He deftly knotted the cord and hung it around his neck.

He gave Tien Nu an amused look. "I could leave you like this. But don't worry, I won't."

He pulled out a knife and crouched down to cut the ropes on Tien Nu's hands, his lips pressed in concentration.

Tien Nu gazed at the boy's face, wondering about the hook-shaped scar on his cheek. The neck of his tunic drooped open, and Tien Nu caught sight of his chest, which was bound tightly about with lengths of cloth.

He stared, trying to make sense of what he saw.

Curly finished sawing at Tien Nu's wrists. "Now, your feet. Lord, but this rope is thick. There we go."

Tien Nu rolled over, rubbing his ankles.

"Thanks," he said. "Are you alone? Where are your friends—the two big men?"

"Those two!" Curly said. "No friends of mine."

There was a grunt from outside the church. They gazed at the door, listening. No further sound.

"I need to get going." Curly nodded toward Bec. "You can untie him yourself."

Curly scaled the crumbling stone wall to an open section of the roof, turned to throw Tien Nu a smile, and vanished over the top.

Tien Nu shook Bec awake. "I'll explain later," he hissed.

He tried to untie Bec's wrists, but his fingers were too stiff. He dug into his pack and found his knife. In a moment Bec was free, rubbing his arms and legs.

"Your pack's here," said Tien Nu.

He began clambering up the wall. A stone came loose and clattered to the ground.

He froze.

"What's that?" said a high-pitched voice outside.

"Go and see, you clod!"

Tien Nu reached the top of the wall and Bec started up after him. The bodyguard loomed in the doorway, peering into the darkness.

"Hey! Stop!" he squealed.

Bec lost his footing and slid to the floor.

Nozzo made for him, crashing over the debris. Bec scrambled up the wall and grabbed Tien Nu's outstretched hand.

The bodyguard caught him by the ankle. Tien Nu gave a heave. The foot slipped from the man's grasp and Bec came shooting up.

Tien Nu lost his balance and fell backwards over the top, landing in the bushes on the other side. Bec jumped down after him. They could hear the bodyguard grunting as he scaled the wall, egged on by Malaspina.

Something brushed against Bec's legs.

"Hannibal!" he said. "Where have you been?"

"Quick," Tien Nu said. "This way."

They pushed through the dense undergrowth, dodging trees and stumbling over stones. Hannibal darted between their legs, tripping them up. Brambles caught at their tunics and lashed their faces and arms.

Behind them came a wild thrashing, as the bodyguard dropped from the wall and started through the bushes. After a while, his shouts receded into the distance. The forest thinned out and a little moonlight trickled through the branches. They were startled by a hoarse scream. But it was only a fox, who stared from a distance, then loped away through the trees.

The land began to rise, growing ever steeper as they struggled upward. They came across a path that wound through a labyrinth of massive boulders and emerged on a cliff overlooking a broad valley. The moon was setting, and the sky was full of stars.

"We've lost them," Tien Nu said.

"Thank God!" Bec collapsed on the ground.

Hannibal came over and licked his face.

"Enough, boy, enough! I'm glad to see you, too." Bec looked at Tien Nu. "How did you manage to get free?"

"It was that bandit, Curly. The one from the cave. He's been following us—all the way from Montecavo. He wanted to get his amulet back."

Tien Nu related how the bag had gotten tangled in his tunic.

"So, he's the one who's been on our trail," Bec said.

"Only he isn't a boy. He's ... she's a girl."

Bec stared at him. "A girl? Are you sure?"

"I could see her breasts when she bent over."

"So, you took a good look."

Tien Nu grinned. "Couldn't help it. But actually, her chest was all bound up."

"*Mio Dio!* What kind of girl is this?"

"Actually, I thought she was ... kind of nice." Tien Nu stopped short. He could feel the blood rushing to his face.

Bec laughed. "Don't fool yourself, Scraps. Someone like that wouldn't think twice about slitting your throat."

"No, honestly. She didn't seem that way."

"Mushbrain."

"Fathead! What do you know about it?"

A grin split Bec's face. "When it comes to girls ..."

CHAPTER 53

The Hollow

The birds were chirping and calling in the trees, as if summoning the world to a new day. Bec opened one eye and looked around. The sky was growing lighter, but Tien Nu was still fast asleep. Hannibal had migrated from Bec's side during the night and now lay tucked in the Tartar's arms.

Bec rolled over and tried to go back to sleep. But it was no use. He couldn't help thinking about what had happened last night, how Malaspina had taken him out without even a fight. He had to do something about it. Maybe *quan fa* would help.

He got up and found a flat area on the ledge and started practising what he remembered of the Monkey Style. He did the same moves over and over—spinning back-fist, hook kick, drop-kick ...

"Not bad," said a voice.

Bec looked around. The Tartar was sitting up, Hannibal in his lap, both watching him.

"But is it good enough?" Bec asked.

"For what?"

"To take on Malaspina."

Tien Nu raised his eyebrows.

"I feel terrible about what happened last night," said Bec. "I acted like a little kid, scared of a bogeyman."

"I thought you were over that, *amico*—that you weren't afraid of him anymore."

"I thought so, too, after the wedding. But as soon as I saw Malaspina again, the old fear came back, as bad as ever. I guess it's because I didn't have a mask on."

"It can't be just the mask," Tien Nu said. "It's what's inside. That's what counts."

"But what can I do about that?"

"You need to practise."

"Practise? You mean *quan fa*?"

"No, practise in your mind."

"That sounds hard."

"Not really. You just sit down and let your mind go quiet. Think about what you want to do, what you want to be. Get a picture in your mind. Remember how you felt at the wedding—

calm and free. How you weren't afraid to take on Malaspina, how good it made you feel. Don't try to force it. Just be patient and let it happen."

"Do you really think that'll work?"

"It works for me. Why not give it a try?"

"You mean, right now?"

"What better time?"

Bec said nothing, gazing at him.

"All right, Scraps," he said finally. "But you'll have to let me do it by myself. I can't have you hanging around, staring at me."

"Right. I'll leave you in peace. I'll be over there, airing out the things in my pack. They've gotten a bit damp."

Bec sat down and watched as Tien Nu opened his pack and took out all the items, spreading them on the ground. Then he closed his eyes and imagined putting on the monkey mask, with its impish eyes and broad grinning mouth. He could feel his own lips curling up—releasing something in his chest and throat. His breathing became easy and relaxed. A kind of tingling crept through his body, making all his limbs feel light. For a while, he seemed to float in the air, perfectly free, without a fear in the world. Then he came gently down to earth.

He opened his eyes. He had no idea how much time had passed—or whether he'd done anything worthwhile. He hadn't followed Tien Nu's instructions very carefully. Maybe he'd just fallen asleep.

He got up and stretched.

Tien Nu turned to look. "Did it work?"

Bec didn't want to disappoint him, so he grinned and nodded.

"I'm now a monkey, through and through."

They set off along the path. After a while, they came across a spring trickling from some rocks and stopped to take a drink.

"You're quite the sight." Tien Nu stared at Bec's face, which was scratched and streaked with grime.

"You don't look that great yourself. There's a big scrape over your eye. Just there."

Tien Nu dabbed at his forehead, then splashed some water on it.

"My stomach's aching," said Bec. "I need food."

"Maybe we can find some berries. There should be bushes around here somewhere."

They continued along the path, which followed the crests of the hills, with valleys falling away on either side. They passed the remains of old castles and fortifications. But there was not a living soul. And not a single berry to be found.

The sun was sinking below the hills when they came to a steep escarpment. The path forked, with one branch plunging into the ravine, while the other continued into a stretch of woods. Bec went to the edge to look over, then gestured for Tien Nu to come and see. At the bottom of the ravine was the glimmer of a fire, with a figure crouched beside it.

"Someone's camping down there," Tien Nu said.

"Could be a shepherd who'd share his food," Bec said. "Should we go down and check?"

"It's worth a try. But we'd better keep out of sight until we're sure who it is."

They crept down the zigzag path, making as little noise as possible. As they descended, their view of the campsite was blocked by a rocky ledge. All Bec could see was a thin ribbon of smoke rising into the air. On reaching the ledge, they crawled to the rim and peered over. Some ten feet below was the fire.

"Curly," Bec whispered.

The girl was using a knife to turn some partridges on a makeshift spit. The smell of roasting meat drifted up and tickled his nose.

Out of the corner of his eye, Bec saw something move. He glanced across the hollow. A lithe body was crouched on a jutting rock, gazing down at the girl.

A mountain lion. Poised to strike.

Bec jumped up and shouted. "Look out! There's a lion! A lion!"

Startled, the animal glanced in his direction, hesitated for a second, then sprang down toward the girl. She dropped her knife and turned, just enough to throw off the lion's aim. It hurtled by her shoulder and landed in the fire, knocking over the spit. It gave a howl of pain and scrambled from the flames to the other side.

Grabbing her knapsack, the girl dashed to the fringe of the hollow.

The lion turned to follow her.

Tien Nu tore off his pack and leapt down to the ground, scooping up Curly's knife. He vaulted over the fire and threw himself at the lion, grabbing it from behind, arms clamped around its belly. The lion twisted back its head, jaws snapping at his face. It rolled over in the sand, trying to throw him off. But Tien Nu hung on. They tumbled over and over, throwing up clouds of dust, the snarls of the lion blending with Tien Nu's grunts.

Suddenly, the struggle was at an end. The pair lay motionless, their bodies in a tight embrace. Tien Nu was clinging to the lion's back, his face pressed into the nape of the

neck, his teeth clamped onto the skin.

"Scraps!" Bec ran over, tugging at his shoulder.

Tien Nu stirred and looked dazedly around. With an effort, he disentangled himself from the lion, releasing his hold on the knife, which was deep in the lion's belly. He rolled onto his side and tried to get up, but his legs buckled under him.

"Is it dead?" Tien Nu croaked. "Better make sure."

Bec gazed warily at the lion, then went over and pulled the knife from the body. The blade was glistening with fluid, and the hilt was covered in blood. The lion started to move, pawing the ground in fits and starts. It turned its head and looked at Bec, its glazed eyes staring through half-closed lids.

The lion snarled and raised itself on its front legs, struggling to get up. Bec shouted and jumped back. But the lion's legs gave way. Gritting his teeth, Bec raised the knife and plunged it into the animal's side. The blade struck a rib, glanced off, and slid into the organs. Bec pushed until the knife could go no further. The lion jerked violently several times, arching its back. Then it relaxed and the legs stopped moving. Bec knelt down beside the animal, his face contorted.

"Well done," said Tien Nu.

Bec attempted to pull out the knife, but it was lodged firmly in the lion's body. He tried wrenching it out with both hands, without success. Blood was boiling up from the wound, covering his fingers. He let go of the knife, leaned to one side, and retched. There was so little in his stomach that almost nothing came out except acid.

He wiped his face and looked at the lion. It lay on the ground, quite still, its golden coat splattered with blood. A foul smell filled the air.

"It's dead," he said in a shaky voice. "I finished it off."

He reached out and touched the animal, feeling the lean muscles under the skin.

Suddenly, he remembered the girl and gazed around.

"Curly," he shouted. "Where are you? Come back. The lion is dead."

There was laughter from somewhere high above. Bec looked up to see the girl disappearing over the edge of the ravine.

"Guess that's all the thanks we'll get."

"She's not the kind to bow and scrape," Tien Nu said.

"Like I told you. A crook."

Tien Nu laughed and turned his gaze back to the lion. "Good and dead."

He got up and braced his foot against the body. With an effort, he pulled out the knife, wiping it on the sand.

"It's yours, Bec," he said, holding out the knife. "A trophy."

"But it belongs to that girl."

"If she wants it, she'll have to come back and ask for it."

Bec grinned. "And ask politely!"

CHAPTER 54

The River

"Ponti!" shouted the driver, pointing ahead. The wagon stopped at the crest of the hill, waiting for the pilgrims to catch up. The Knight stood there, taking in the view.

The river ran dark through the valley, where a long bridge crossed to the city on the other bank, close to the remains of an ancient bridge that had fallen into ruin. The Knight gazed across the water at the winding tiers of walls and battlements, the bristling towers and belfries, black against the setting sun. He remembered passing through here as a young man. It had been his first taste of the wider world.

At the entrance to the bridge was a small stone house, where a couple of men sat on a bench by the door. When they noticed the wagon at the top of the hill, they got to their feet and ambled into the road.

The Knight gave the driver an inquiring glance.

"Soldiers from Ponti," said the driver. "That's their outpost down there. They collect the tolls for the bridge and keep an eye out for contraband and undesirables."

The Knight rubbed the stump of his little finger, thinking about Bec and Tien Nu. They'd have to cross the bridge to reach Ponti. The soldiers could give them trouble, chase them away, even arrest them.

"Could you take my baggage to the hostel in Ponti?" he said, fishing for a coin. "I'll wait here for a while and see whether those two servants of mine don't show up."

"Your decision," said the driver, pocketing the money. "Personally, I wouldn't want to spend the night out here. I've heard stories about this place. People say ..."

"I think I can manage," said the Knight.

The driver gave him a glance. "Well, I suppose you can. I'll make sure your things are stored safely at the hostel."

He slapped the reins and the wagon jolted slowly down the slope, coming to a stop by the outpost at the bottom. A soldier climbed into the back of the wagon and poked among the bags, while the other soldier talked with the driver, who doled out some money for the tolls.

Satisfied by his inspection, the soldier hopped down and gave a nod to the driver, waving them through. The wagon rumbled onto the bridge, followed by the pilgrims. The soldiers watched until they reached the other side, then turned back to the outpost. One of them glanced up the hill and spotted the Knight standing in the road at the top. The soldier nudged his companion, who looked up and stared at the huge figure. They exchanged a few words, then went inside the outpost, closing the door behind them. Soon the flicker of a fire showed through the windows.

The Knight heard someone approaching from behind and turned to look. A big man with a broad-brimmed hat came tramping along the road, his long hair greased with sweat. He was carrying a large pack.

"Greetings, milord," he wheezed, tipping his hat. "Bosco is my name. I'm looking for two men on horseback. Master and servant. The master's lean as a switch and dressed in blue. The servant is younger and built like an ox."

The Knight pursed his lips. "I ran into some men of that description several nights ago—at an inn this side of Montecavo. But I haven't laid eyes on them since."

"Were they travelling this way—to Ponti?"

"To the best of my knowledge."

Bosco tipped his hat once again, grunting his thanks. He trudged down the hill toward the bridge. The Knight gazed after him, wondering what he wanted with Malaspina.

The man pounded on the door of the outpost and a soldier appeared, who shook his head and pointed to a clearing halfway up the hill, beside the road. Bosco retraced his steps to the clearing, where he built a fire, apparently settling in for the night.

The cold was seeping into the Knight's bones. Wrapping himself in his cape, he eased himself down on the grassy bank at the side of the road. He was drifting in and out of sleep when he heard the muffled sound of hoof beats. He sat up and listened. A horse was approaching from the direction of the bridge—moving slowly, stopping from time to time. The Knight peered into the darkness but couldn't make out anything. A waning moon had risen in the sky, but the road was thick with shadows.

Soon the silhouette of horse and rider appeared. The rider stopped, seeming to search for something. Then he moved forward until he was level with the Knight.

"Who's there?" he called. "Show yourself, if you're an honest man."

The Knight rose to his feet. "And who is asking, pray tell?"

"Someone who has the right to know."

"And who is that?"

"Someone who is waiting for an answer."

The Knight was silent. He heard the rasp of a sword being drawn.

"I don't wish you any harm, stranger," said the voice. "But unless you tell me who you are, I must conclude that you're a robber and a cutthroat who lies in wait for honest men."

"No one calls me a cutthroat," said the Knight. "Take it back."

The figure slipped from the horse and stood in the road—sword in hand, legs astride. The Knight stepped from the shadows. In the moonlight, he could see the glint of the man's eyes. He was small and neatly built—shorter than the Knight by nearly a foot—and dressed in military apparel.

"Your choice," said the soldier. "Yield or suffer your fate."

The Knight could not help smiling. For such a little man, these were brave words.

"God be my witness," the Knight said, moving closer. "You've brought this on your own head. Apologize or fight."

"I only apologize to those I've wronged. Unless I'm greatly mistaken, it's no offence to flush out a scoundrel in the dead of night."

"So, I'm a scoundrel now! If I were a little runt like you, I'd watch what I say."

"Runt is it! Better than a great lumbering oaf."

The Knight's fist shot out and struck the soldier in the chest, knocking him down.

He gazed at the little man lying at his feet.

"An apology wouldn't be amiss."

The soldier grabbed the Knight's ankle, jerking hard. The Knight lost his balance and stumbled to the ground.

"A little trick my granny taught me," said the soldier, springing to his feet.

He held the point of his sword to the Knight's throat.

"Now then," he said. "A word of explanation would do no harm."

"Only a fool explains to a fool," said the Knight.

He grasped the blade of the man's sword in his bare hand and wrested it from his grip, tossing it away. He heaved himself up and charged at the soldier, who skipped nimbly to one side, extending a foot. The Knight tripped and went flying, but grabbed the soldier as he fell and dragged him down.

The little man scrambled away to a safe distance. The Knight pushed himself to his feet and stood there in the moonlight.

The soldier eyed him up and down.

"I see you are a Knight," he said finally. "Perhaps we got off to a bad start. My name is Bernardo Tavello. Who might you be?"

There was a silence. "Did I hear right? Bernardo Tavello?"

"The same."

"I am Cristoforo Malaspina."

It was the soldier's turn to be silent.

"I know that name," he said finally. "It belongs to an old friend of mine. Don't play games with me, stranger."

"Games?" The Knight grabbed the little man and hoisted him in the air, staring into his eyes. "Look at me, Bernardo. It's me, Cristofo."

"The Cristofo I knew was a mere slip of a lad, not a hairy giant," said the man with dignity, feet dangling. "Now, if you could restore me to my normal earthbound state, I might take a better look at you."

The Knight gently lowered him to the ground.

"Bernardo, you must remember this." The Knight held up his right hand, displaying the stump of his little finger. "It happened when we were sparring."

The soldier stared.

"Remember? How could I forget? Damned if you didn't deserve it! You nearly chopped off my arm."

Bernardo stood there, chin out, shoulders thrown back.

The Knight gazed at the little rooster of a man. "Bernardo, you dunce. You haven't changed a bit. Scrappy and headstrong as ever."

CHAPTER 55

A Surprise

"Come sit over here in the moonlight, where I can see you better," Bernardo said, drawing the Knight further along the bank.

"So, you're a soldier now," said the Knight, settling down beside him.

"For nearly fifteen years," said Bernardo. "I left Scarmagno not long after you did. You know how it was after your father died. With Adolfo in charge, things went from bad to worse."

"My brother never did anything by halves."

"Once you'd left, I knew he'd find a way to get rid of me as well. I didn't hang around to see how he'd accomplish it."

"I should never have run away like that," said the Knight. "I deserted you and ... everyone."

"Don't blame yourself, Cristofo. You didn't have much choice."

"Adolfo always hated me—from the time I was just a boy.

I could never understand why."

"Jealousy, my friend—the green-eyed demon. Your father loved you best and he didn't try to hide it. Every time he sent a fond glance your way, it was like a knife twisting in Adolfo's gut. You were wise to leave. Your brother would have killed you."

"As it was, he left his mark." The Knight touched the scar on his face. "So, what have you been doing all this time?"

"Leaving Scarmagno was a blessing in disguise," said Bernardo. "When I reached Ponti, I discovered they needed soldiers and weren't too fussy where they found them. I liked the work and stayed on. I'm now commander of the forces. Married, too. Five children—three of them still alive."

"You've been busy."

Bernardo smiled. "All this, thanks to Adolfo. If it weren't for him, who knows where I might have ended up."

They sat there silently, as frogs chirred and trilled in the ditches.

"So, what brings you out here at this hour?" asked Cristofo.

"That was *my* question, remember?"

"But seriously ..."

"Well ..." Bernardo took off his hat and ran a hand through his thinning hair. "This morning I set out to make a tour of our defences. I was delayed on route and didn't reach the outpost below until after nightfall. I found the soldiers huddled by the fire, chattering like madmen. They said they'd seen an ogre in the woods up here."

He glanced at the Knight. "The half-wits! I didn't give their story much credence, but I thought I'd come up and take a look. And lo and behold, I came across an ogre all right, skulking in the bushes. But I don't see any bones lying about."

Bernardo laughed and patted the Knight on the arm. "But what have you been up to yourself?"

"Not much to boast about," said Cristofo. "After leaving the castle, I found my way to Sicilia, where I entered the services of a great lord and became a knight. But I was restless. I heard there were fortunes to be made in the Terra Santa and headed there. And there I stayed for almost ten years—doing one thing and another—making a few enemies along the way. Then one night I was caught in an ambush, carved up like a Christmas goose, and left for dead. By some miracle I survived. But two members of my household died that night—Daud and Bakr—just boys. They were like sons to me."

He looked down at his great hands, turning them over.

"For months afterward, everything stank of death—my hands, my clothes, my hair. I dreamed of death. I ate it, drank it, shat it. So, I decided to leave the Terra Santa and return home, thinking that Adolfo would be dead by now. He didn't seem like the long-lived sort."

"Or so you hoped," said Bernardo.

Cristofo gave a wry smile. "But when I reached Montecavo, I heard Adolfo was very much alive. And by all accounts, his temper hadn't improved with age. There was no point going back to Scarmagno while he was still in charge. It would just stir up trouble—for me, for everyone."

Bernardo paused, gazing at the Knight. "And so ... did you hear about Miriam?"

"Miriam?" The Knight sat up, his voice changing. "No, nothing—not since I left home. I asked about her in Montecavo, but no one could give me any news." He paused. "You know how things were between Miriam and me. You were the only one I ever told."

"You didn't hear what happened?"

Cristofo held very still. He shook his head.

"You didn't know she had a child—some eight months after you left?"

"A child?"

"A boy."

The Knight was quiet for a moment, then spoke in a low voice. "Is Miriam still there at the castle?"

Bernardo slowly shook his head. "She passed away while giving birth, God rest her soul. But I hear the boy is alive and well. A slave, like his mother."

"Eight months? The child was born eight months after I left?"

The little man nodded.

Cristofo covered his face with his hands.

"I think you have a son, my friend."

CHAPTER 56

Surgery

The outpost was small and stuffy—ringing with the snores of soldiers. The Knight sat by the fireplace, wrapped in his cape. The meagre glow from the embers cast deep shadows in the corners—shadows filled with ghosts of the past.

Cristofo thought about the night when he'd left the castle, all those years ago. He'd been a different person then, sixteen years old, on the brink of manhood, but still a boy at heart, fiercely independent, courageous to a fault, head filled with crazy dreams, hopelessly in love. People had warned him about Adolfo, telling him to leave while he had the chance. But he was stubborn, unwilling to let his eldest brother dictate his future, determined to find a way to marry Miriam.

Then came the fateful night. He was returning to the castle from the village by the river, well-fortified with wine. They were waiting for him in the trees by the meadow—

Adolfo and four others. He didn't stand a chance. They overpowered him and dragged him by the heels into a clearing, where they pinned him down, spread-eagled.

Adolfo stood over him, gazing into his face.

"I told you, didn't I?" he said softly. "Gave you due warning—plenty of time to arrange your affairs." He shook his head. "But you didn't want to listen, dear brother. Pig-headed, as always."

Adolfo drew a knife from the holster on his chest. He held it up, examining the blade, then knelt down beside Cristofo.

"Some messages can be sent in words," he said. "Others require deeds."

Cristofo stared up at his brother, not knowing what he planned to do, knowing only that he was capable of anything.

Adolfo gave a quiet laugh, seeing the expression on his brother's face. "Not so brave now, are we? Don't worry. One quick cut and it's done."

He paused to let the words sink in.

Cristofo wrestled one arm free and grappled with the man next to him. But the others fell on him, stifling his efforts.

"Hold his head and don't let him move," Adolfo said.

Cristofo stiffened as he felt the blade cut into his skin, carving a line from ear to mouth.

Adolfo cocked his head, gazing at his handiwork.

"Very pretty you look, dear brother."

He bent over Cristofo's face, until their lips almost touched.

"Get out of here," he murmured. "I never want to see you again."

The Knight groaned, troubled by the memory, pushing it away. But more ghosts came crowding in.

He was in the servant's quarters, where Miriam was sleeping. He gently touched her shoulder.

"Wake up," he whispered.

Miriam's eyes flew open. She stared at Cristofo's shrouded face, then glanced at the others asleep in the room.

They crept out to the yard and huddled on a bench in the shadows.

Cristofo threw back his hood and showed his face, all bloody.

Miriam gasped, crying out. Cristofo quickly hushed her and recounted what had happened.

"And you have to leave tonight?" she asked.

Cristofo nodded, holding her hands.

"And not return?"

"Not as long as Adolfo is here."

"I'll kill that man myself," Miriam said. "Poison him ... stab him in his sleep."

"You're very brave. But there isn't time."

"Then I'll come with you."

"That will only make things worse. Adolfo will hound us to the ends of the earth. And he'll kill us both."

Miriam clung to him, quietly sobbing.

CHAPTER 57

The Peddler

Tien Nu and Bec set out before sunrise, with the stars still glimmering in the sky. They climbed back up the ravine and followed the path into the woods. Not far along, they came to the road, which was overarched with branches, dark as a tunnel. They dropped their packs and sat down.

"We should be getting close to Ponti," Tien Nu said, gazing down the empty way. "It's days since we left the pilgrims."

"Four in all," Bec said, counting on his fingers.

"They must have reached the city by now. The Knight said they'd be staying there for a while, visiting the shrines. So maybe we'll run into them."

"Do you think the Knight would take us back?"

Tien Nu shook his head. "Not after the way we left him."

"It wasn't as if we wanted to, Scraps," Bec said. "It was all because of Malaspina."

"I'm not sure he'll see it that way."

There was a jangling sound from the direction of Ponti. Hannibal began to bark, his whiskers quivering. Bec scooped him up and shushed him. Down the road, they saw a haystack swaying slowly toward them, accompanied by a chorus of clatters and clanks. As it approached, the haystack turned into a donkey bearing a mountain of metal goods—tin pots, frying pans, saucepans—with large wicker baskets slung over either flank. Leading the donkey was a peddler in a voluminous cloak made of multi-coloured scraps—red, green, yellow, blue. The peddler stopped to greet them, gazing curiously at their faces as he leaned on his staff.

"Where to, my friends?" he asked. "What destination? Journey's end?"

"We're going to Ponti," Bec said.

"Ah! Yes! Of course! Indeed!"

"Is it very far away?" asked Tien Nu.

The peddler stroked his long grey beard, then recited in a singsong voice: "Not as far as the evening star. Not as near as the wax in your ear. Near-far, far-near. Far for a snail, near for a deer."

Tien Nu grinned and thought for a moment. "A snail has only one foot, and a deer has four. But people have two feet, so we need to know more."

The bearded man laughed and clapped. "*Bravissimo!* We have a poet in our midst."

"But what about Ponti?" Tien Nu said. "Can we get there today?"

The man waggled his head: "If you move at a crawl, your chances are small. If you go in a dash, you'll be there in a flash."

"You mean, by this morning?"

"Give or take. Take or give. Speaking of which ..." The peddler nodded toward his donkey. "... Can I sell you something?"

"Have you got any food?" asked Bec.

"A pot for your kitchen, a patch for your coat. But nothing to nibble, unless you're a goat."

Bec laughed. "My teeth aren't that good."

"Pity!" The peddler raised his hat. "Well, my friends, I'll be toddling on. *Buongiorno, arrivederci, addio!*"

He tapped the donkey with his staff. The mobile haystack came to life and resumed its stately march, the pots and pans swinging to and fro, clanging in time.

Tien Nu and Bec watched the peddler disappear down the road, then shouldered their packs and headed in the other direction. After a while, the woods came to an end, and they passed into a valley of well-tended fields—a sure sign a town was nearby. As they crossed the valley, the sun rose over the mountains, setting afire the dew in the fields.

They climbed the hill on the other side, stopping on the ridge. Below, the river ran through a broad valley, where a bridge crossed to a city on the opposite bank, its towers and palaces shining in the morning light.

"Ponti!" Bec said. "I can't believe we're finally here."

He turned to Tien Nu, extending a hand. "We've done it, Scraps! Didn't I say we'd make a good team?"

"Rats like us." Tien Nu laughed and shook his hand.

Bec looked back at the valley, then pointed with his chin. "What's that over there—just beyond the hill?"

Tien Nu gazed at the sheet of silver extending to the horizon, so bright it merged with the sky.

"It's the sea," he said. "The Mediterraneo."

"*Mio Dio!* It looks like it goes on forever."

"Almost. Until it reaches Africa."

"Africa. That's the place where you were born."

Tien Nu nodded, a lump rising unexpectedly in his throat.

A shout came from behind.

Tien Nu glanced over his shoulder. "*Merda!*"

Nozzo was pointing at them from the valley below, calling to his master, who had dismounted to relieve himself by the road.

CHAPTER 58

Revenge

Bec dashed down the slope toward the Ponti bridge, with Tien Nu and Hannibal not far behind. Halfway down, he noticed a big man standing in a clearing on the left—one of the bandits from the cave. The man stared at him as he raced by.

He had almost reached the stone house at the bottom, when the bodyguard charged over the crest of the hill. Hoofbeats hammered in Bec's ears. He dodged to the side. A hand grasped his shoulder and dragged him along the road, his feet scraping over the stony surface. His tunic ripped and he dropped to the ground.

Nozzo jumped from his horse and yanked Bec up. He wrapped his massive arms around Bec's chest, squeezing hard. Bec fought back, struggling and kicking. The man's rancid odour enveloped Bec, making him feel sick.

The bodyguard gave a sudden cry, and his grip loosened

slightly. Bec glanced down to see Hannibal clinging to Nozzo's leg, his claws digging into the flesh. The man swore and hopped clumsily around, still holding Bec, until he finally shook off the dog. Hannibal scurried over to the stone house, barking at the door.

Tien Nu shrugged off his pack and circled around Nozzo. The bodyguard turned with him, using Bec as a shield.

"Bloody coward!" Tien Nu hissed. "Let him go."

Nozzo only tightened his grip.

Tien Nu feinted to the left, then reversed and dove at the man's legs. Nozzo saw him coming and unleashed a powerful kick. His heavy boot connected with Tien Nu's head and sent him sprawling. He lay there unmoving, blood pouring from a gash in his forehead.

Malaspina rode up and dismounted, sliding his cane from its sheath. Bec stared at him as he approached, his body turning cold. Malaspina stopped a few feet away, gazing at Bec, pinned helplessly in Nozzo's arms.

"Release the slave," he told the bodyguard.

Nozzo looked at him.

"Let him go, I said."

The bodyguard did as he was told. Bec stood there, facing his master.

"Now, hit me." The man gave a mocking smile and spread out his arms. "Go on! Show me what you're made of."

Bec wanted to lash out, to drive a fist into the man's grinning teeth. But he was incapable of movement.

"Just as I thought," Malaspina said. "You're the same snivelling little coward you've always been."

With one hand, he seized Bec and dragged him back toward his horse. Bec stumbled along behind him like a child. He tried to recapture the sense of freedom he'd felt at the wedding. But it was no use. His fear was too intense.

So, this is how it ends, he thought. All his dreams, his hopes for the future, snuffed in an instant. He looked back at the Tartar, who was lying unconscious on the ground. Tien Nu, his friend, who'd do anything for him, who'd risked his life to save him more than once.

A spark of anger flared in Bec's chest. Anger at Malaspina for his malevolence and cruelty, which now threatened Tien Nu as well as himself. Anger at Nozzo for being the willing instrument of Malaspina's venom. But most of all, anger at himself—for letting his friend down.

The anger intensified and spread, blazing into a fury that swept through his entire body, shocking his muscles back to life, driving out his fear.

In a kind of frenzy, Bec whirled about and broke Malaspina's grip. He grabbed the man's cane and danced out of reach, skipping from foot to foot, taunting his master, daring him to retrieve his stick.

Malaspina's face darkened. "Don't think you can get away with this."

He moved forward. "Hand it over."

Bec swung the cane about like a club, smashing the man's legs.

Malaspina fell hard. He lay on the road, breathing heavily, then slowly pushed himself up.

Bec watched his master hobble to his feet, seeing the pain in his face.

Malaspina was a man like any other man. Not invincible. Flesh and blood.

He remembered something the Tartar had said, and almost laughed.

Move Number Two. Ring the Temple Bells.

With a cry, he vaulted forward and kicked Malaspina squarely in the groin.

The man let out a gasp and doubled over. He dropped to the ground, writhing in pain.

Bec turned to help Tien Nu, who was still sprawled on

the ground. But Nozzo blocked his way, arms spread wide. Bec dodged from side to side, trying to slip past. The big man mirrored his moves, then dove forward and caught him. He tossed the cane aside and lifted Bec over his head, slamming him to the ground.

Bec lay there, struggling for breath. When Nozzo reached down to grab him, he scuttled through his legs and leapt onto his back, clinging like a monkey. The bodyguard bellowed, trying to shake him off. Bec coiled his legs about the man's waist and held on tight, pounding his right ear with a fist.

Nozzo twisted his head away and Bec slipped an arm under his chin. He locked in the chokehold with his other arm and pressed upward into the neck, squeezing with all his might. The man gave a hoarse cry and swayed back and forth, trying to pry the arms loose.

Every muscle in Bec's body strained. He let out a feral screech, summoning powers he had no idea he possessed. His hands were slippery with sweat. He closed his eyes and imagined the arms of a great ape wrapped around Nozzo's neck, cutting off the flow of blood to the brain.

The bodyguard made a guttural sound. His legs buckled and gave way. He dropped to the ground like a felled tree, dead to the world.

Bec untangled himself and glanced around.

Tien Nu was back on his feet, still unsteady, his face marbled with blood.

Malaspina was approaching him from behind, sword in hand.

"Scraps! Behind you!"

Tien Nu wheeled around as Malaspina plunged forward. The blade cut through the Tartar's tunic and sliced across his chest.

Malaspina turned and charged again. Tien Nu dodged to the side. He seized the man's outstretched arm and swung it down and around and up as far as it would go, pressing it against the shoulder joint, forcing the man to his knees.

There was a sharp crack and Malaspina let out a howl. He dropped the sword and rolled over, clutching his shoulder. Tien Nu kicked the sword away and fell on the man, pinning him to the ground.

"Stop!"

The Knight was standing bare-chested in the doorway of the little house. Behind him, some rumpled soldiers were strapping on their swords.

"Leave him be," the Knight said to Tien Nu. "You've done enough."

Tien Nu gazed at the Knight, eyes wide. Then he nodded and slowly got to his feet. His face and hair were clotted with blood, and a crimson stain was spreading on his tunic. He touched his chest and grimaced, then stumbled to the side of the road.

One of the soldiers—a mere wisp of a man—was staring at Bec. The soldier whispered something to the Knight.

"Yes, that's him, Bernardo," said the Knight.

The little soldier came over to Bec and put a hand on his shoulder.

"Don't touch him," Malaspina shouted, struggling up. "That's my slave! Don't you know who I am?"

"But my good man, you are on Ponti lands," Bernardo said. "The writ of Scarmagno does not run here."

"Writ? What writ?" said Malaspina. "I claim him by the force of my right arm."

Bernardo gave him a look. "That arm's not worth a pot of piss."

He nodded to the other soldiers, who drew their swords.

The little man stepped forward, chest puffed out. "By the authority vested in me by the Republic of Ponti, I order you to leave."

Malaspina's eyes slid back and forth between Bernardo and the soldiers. He gave a thin smile, managed a shrug, then limped back to his horse. The bodyguard got to his feet, eyes still bleary. He lumbered after his master and helped him climb into the saddle.

Malaspina stared across the road at the Knight.

"I don't know who you are," he called, "or why you have chosen to meddle in my affairs. But you may be sure I will remember you. One day our paths will cross again."

The Knight stood there, gazing in silence at the man.

"As for you," said Malaspina, turning his eyes to Bec. "I swear on the blood of Christ that I will track you down and kill you."

He nudged his horse around and started up the hill, followed by the bodyguard. Suddenly he twisted in the saddle, his left arm raised.

A knife spun toward Bec.

The Knight threw himself in front of Bec. He landed on the road, the blade embedded in his side. He lay there gasping, as Bec knelt down beside him.

Malaspina gazed at the scene, his lips curled in satisfaction. He slapped the reins of his horse and cantered off.

Bosco was waiting for him halfway up the hill. The bandit drew his dagger and shouted at Malaspina as he approached. His face was distorted, veins standing out in his neck.

Malaspina stared at him. "You, again! I thought you were dead."

He dug in his spurs and the horse leapt forward. Bosco shuffled to the side, dagger in hand. As the horse approached, he sprang out with a cry, his huge body flying through the air. When he fell to the ground, his hand was empty.

The horse slowed to a trot, then stopped. Malaspina sagged in the saddle, his hand slack on the reins. With a grunt, he pulled the dagger from his chest where it had lodged, wiping it on his thigh.

"What are you gawking at, you imbecile?" he said to the bodyguard, who had ridden up beside him.

He turned to Bosco, now standing by the road.

"Lucky blow, my friend. But it will take more than that to kill me."

Even as Malaspina spoke, he listed to the side. He dropped the dagger and probed the wound, gazing curiously at the blood on his hand, then started slipping sideways. He made no effort to stop himself, but only glanced back at Bosco, a dazed expression on his face. His body toppled to the ground, one foot trapped in the stirrup. His leg jerked spastically, trying to free itself. Then it stopped moving. Malaspina lay there quietly, his arms splayed out.

Bosco gave a great cry. "That was for my brother!"

Malaspina's horse took fright at the shout and bolted up the hill, dragging the man with him, one foot still tangled in the stirrup. The bodyguard stared dumbly as his master disappeared over the crest. He roused himself and galloped after him.

Bosco watched them go, then vanished into the woods.

CHAPTER 59

The Truth

The Knight gripped the knife in his side and pulled it out. He lay there, exhausted by the effort, letting the knife slide to the ground.

Bernardo crouched down beside him. He examined the wound, wiping away the blood with a scrap of cloth Bec had ripped from his tunic.

The Knight stiffened as the fingers moved about. His eyes turned to the little man.

"How bad is it?"

Bernardo's face was grave. "We'll get you inside."

The soldiers helped carry the Knight into the outpost, where they laid him on a pallet.

The Knight was panting heavily, barely able to speak.

He looked at Bernardo. "You need ... to ask him."

The soldier nodded and turned to Bec.

"My dear young man," he said. "There's something that needs to be cleared up. You're a slave from Castello Scarmagno, is that correct?"

Bec stared at him, then looked at the Knight.

"It's all right," the Knight said. "Bernardo ... is a friend."

"Yes," said Bec in a small voice. "I'm a slave from Scarmagno. Or I was."

"And how old are you?"

"I'm ... I'm just fourteen."

"Not sixteen?"

"No. That's what I told the Knight. But it isn't true."

"And who, pray tell, is your mother?" Bernardo asked.

"Her name is Miriam. She lived on the estate. She died when I was born."

"And your father?"

Bec's eyes narrowed. "I don't know who my father is."

Bernardo paused. "I believe you have found him."

"No, I haven't," Bec said bitterly.

"You don't understand," Bernardo said. "Cristofo is your father."

"Cristofo?"

The Knight and Bernardo exchanged glances.

"You tell him," Bernardo said.

"Bec ..." The Knight struggled to get the words out. "I am your father."

Bec stared at him, then shook his head.

"That's not possible," he said, turning away. "You're making fun of me."

"No, no, Bec. Look at me. I'm really your father." The Knight reached for Bec's arm.

Bec shook him off. He dug into his pouch and produced the ring he'd found in Falco's possession.

"What about this?" he said, almost choking.

The Knight stared at the ring. He took it from Bec and lifted it to the light, gazing at the inscription inside.

"Where ... where did you get this?"

"So, you know about it?" said Bec.

"This ring ..." The Knight gave a ragged cough, then pressed on. "I gave it to your mother. But she never wore it. She was afraid ... what people would say. Then someone stole it. We never knew who."

Bec was gazing wide-eyed at the Knight. "I know who stole the ring. And for a while I even thought ..." He stopped and shook his head. "But now it seems crazy."

"Bec ... I know I am your father. I am Adolfo Malaspina's ... youngest brother. I grew up at the castle. Your mother and I ...

we fell in love. But we kept it a secret. She even pretended to dislike me. Adolfo was obsessed ... with your mother. He would have hurt her ... if he had found out."

A ripple of pain crossed the Knight's face.

"You ... you were born ... months after I left Scarmagno," he continued. "I never knew your mother ... was pregnant. Never knew about you. Not until I met Bernardo last night."

Bec stood there, staring. "So, this isn't a trick?"

"Would I play a trick on you?'

A smile crept to Bec's lips.

"Not a trick like this," said the Knight. "Not here ... not now."

"No," said Bec. "I don't believe you would."

He swallowed hard and knelt down beside the pallet.

"Father."

The Knight laid a hand on Bec's head.

"My son."

The hand slipped down and the Knight's eyes closed.

Bernardo gently pulled Bec away. "We need to move your father into town."

Bec nodded and looked around for Tien Nu, then went to the door and gazed outside.

The Tartar's pack was lying in the road, but its owner was nowhere to be seen.

CHAPTER 60

The Tightrope

Darkness. Vast and cold.

Falling, falling, falling.

Tien Nu dropped into a field of stars, whirls of light bursting on all sides, streaming out around him, white, yellow, silver—filmy as goldfish tails. Spinning, twirling, tumbling, pulsing, blooming into whirlpools of light. All in perfect silence.

Falling, falling, falling.

Sounds—the hum of the crowd, the roll of a drum, the cries of vendors.

His father standing in the middle of the tightrope, waiting for him.

Tien Nu danced along the rope, his arms extended. He came up behind his father and vaulted onto his shoulders. Straightening up, he threw his arms high as the crowd roared its approval. His father started to cross toward the other side—step by step—the rope swaying beneath his feet. The crowd turned quiet, all eyes on them. Tien Nu relaxed, his feet gripping his father's shoulders.

From below came a shrill cry: "Whoo! Whoo! Whoo!"

Tien Nu glanced down. A small boy was racing across the courtyard. He made a beeline for a cluster of pigeons on the side. The birds edged away as he ran into their midst, shouting at the top of his voice. The boy tried to grab a pigeon, which fluttered upward in alarm. With a clamour of wings, the entire flock took off, flapping in all directions, confused by the flaming torches and the drifting smoke.

A pigeon blundered into his father's face and clawed at his eyes. His father wobbled as the tightrope switched wildly back and forth. Tien Nu was thrown to one side, then the other. He toppled over. Somehow his father grabbed him as he fell. They fell together, his father holding him tight.

There was a crash.

His father hit the ground first, clasping Tien Nu in his arms, shielding him.

Darkness again.

Tien Nu gave a groan.

"Quick," said a voice. "He's coming to."

But Tien Nu sank back, clinging to what he'd seen.

The accident was not his fault. It wasn't anyone's fault. Just a small boy chasing some birds.

His father had saved him—and died in doing so.

There was nothing more to know.

Tien Nu drifted to consciousness.

Smoke.

Blood.

He opened his eyes.

"Dammit, Scraps," said Bec. "I know how you like to sleep, but this is going too far."

Tien Nu gazed at Bec, then reached out and touched his face. "You're real."

"Of course, I'm real, you dummy. And get your finger out of my eye."

Tien Nu patted the bandages on his chest and winced.

"I remember now. Malaspina did this to me."

"And now he's dead," Bec said. "Good riddance."

"Did I ... did I kill him?"

"No, no," said Bec. "It was Bosco—the big bandit from the cave."

Tien Nu was silent for a moment. "I only recall going to the side of the road."

"That's were we found you—hidden in the grass. You were bleeding like a stuck pig. Blood everywhere. I guess you Tartars have lots to spare."

Tien Nu grinned feebly. "More blood than brains."

He tried to prop himself up, but his arms folded under him, weak as blades of grass.

Bec put a hand under Tien Nu's head and lifted it, bringing a bowl to his mouth.

"Drink some."

"What is it?"

"Don't you trust me?"

"No."

He took a sip anyway. Chicken broth.

He coughed most of it up.

"Where are we?" he asked, looking around.

"In Ponti," said Bec. "The pilgrim hostel. We brought you here yesterday."

"Yesterday! Have I been asleep that long?"

"We wondered if you'd ever wake up."

Tien Nu remembered something. "The Knight. I saw him. He was there at the bridge, wasn't he?"

Bec nodded, gesturing toward the other side of the room.

Tien Nu raised his head, peering into the shadows. In the

wavering light of the fireplace, he saw the Knight, stretched out on a pallet.

"What happened?"

"Malaspina threw a knife at me," said Bec. "But the Knight leapt out in front and took the knife himself."

"Is he ...?"

Bec pressed his lips together. "They don't think he's going to make it."

He paused to clear his throat.

"I've got something to tell you, Scraps," he said. "It's about my father."

CHAPTER 61

Death

The Knight's condition gradually worsened. By the third morning, his fever was so high he was hardly able to speak. A priest was called to administer the final rites.

Sister Cecilia shooed Tien Nu and Bec away when the priest arrived. They waited in the hallway outside the infirmary.

After a while, the door opened and the priest came out, followed by the young nun.

Bec jumped up. "Can we go back in?"

Sister Cecilia nodded. "But stay by the door. I need to wash him first. It won't take long."

"How is he doing?"

"Not well, I'm afraid. The fever is burning him up."

The nun filled a basin with water and returned to the Knight's bed, while Bec and Tien Nu found stools inside the door. She dipped a cloth in the basin and started wiping the Knight's face.

Cristofo opened his eyes and gazed up at the nun. He began speaking in a low voice—so low that Tien Nu couldn't hear what he was saying.

Sister Cecilia looked startled and bent over to listen. Her face softened and she murmured something to the Knight. They talked for a while, then Cristofo fell silent, gazing at her, his eyes filled with tears.

The nun put a hand on his forehead, and he closed his eyes.

She came back to the boys. "You can go and sit with him now."

"What did he say?" asked Bec.

Sister Cecilia placed the basin and cloth on a table by the door. "Actually, he's seeing things. It's the fever. He thought I was someone called Miriam. He told me he still loved me. Begged my forgiveness."

She shook her head and smiled. "So, what could I do? I told him I forgave him. I'm sure that's what Miriam would have wanted."

"Miriam ..." Bec stumbled to a halt. "That was my mother."

"And so, you ... you're ..."

"Cristofo's son."

Sister Cecilia gazed at him. "Ah! Now I understand. You have the same look about the eyes."

Tien Nu and Bec carried their stools to the Knight's bedside, while the nun busied herself with other patients. Cristofo was breathing heavily, his eyes closed, his head jerking from side to side. His face was flushed and the scar on his face had turned a livid white.

The Knight seemed to sense their presence. He turned toward them and opened his eyes—then mumbled something incomprehensible. He gestured, continuing to talk, trying to make himself understood.

Tien Nu bent over the Knight, listening.

"He's speaking Arabic."

"Can you understand him?"

Tien Nu nodded. "It's what I spoke in Alessandria."

Cristofo reached out and tugged at the boy's sleeve. Tien Nu listened some more, translating as the Knight talked.

"He thinks we're some other people—Daud and Bakr. He says he's sorry. That he tried to save us."

The Knight stopped talking. He looked back and forth between Tien Nu and Bec, his eyes pleading.

Tien Nu started speaking to Cristofo in Arabic—a language he hadn't used for years. He didn't know where the words were coming from, didn't know exactly what he was saying. But the words flowed freely, as if from a distant place.

The Knight listened intently to Tien Nu, his head slightly raised, barely breathing. He interrupted to ask a question. Tien Nu waited until he was finished, then spoke some more—talking quietly.

When Tien Nu stopped, Cristofo let out a long uneven breath. He whispered something to the boy, then nodded toward Bec and repeated the same words.

He lay back and closed his eyes. His breathing became more regular. After a while he fell into a deep sleep.

Sister Cecilia had come by to watch. "Whatever did you tell him?"

"I hardly know myself," Tien Nu said. "It just came out."

The nun raised an eyebrow. "Well, whatever it was, it seems to have done him some good."

And so it had.

Throughout the day, the Knight's fever gradually eased, and by the evening his forehead was cool. He was able to sit up and drink some soup. He slept through the night, as Bec and Tien Nu took turns watching over him.

When the first light of day came through the windows, Bernardo arrived to stay with the Knight. Bec and Tien Nu went to the refectory to get something to eat.

"I've been meaning to ask you ..." Bec broke off a chunk of

bread. "What did you actually say to the Knight yesterday?"

"It was very strange," Tien Nu said. "I felt as if other people were talking through me. There were two voices. And they were speaking directly to the Knight—ignoring me completely, as if I wasn't there."

"And what did they say?"

"All sorts of things. But mainly that the Knight shouldn't worry—that they were safe and happy. That someday he'd be with them."

"And what did the Knight say?"

"That he understood. That he was glad to see them."

"But he didn't see them, Scraps. There was no one else there. Just me and you."

"Honestly, *amico,* I don't know. I just don't know."

CHAPTER 62

The Dancer

"Get out of here!" roared the Knight, pushing himself up on his elbows. "Haven't you fellows got anything better to do? Staring at me as if I'm on my deathbed."

Tien Nu turned to Bec. "Do you think he's getting better?"

Bec pursed his mouth. "Hard to say."

The Knight sank back onto the pallet, pulling the sheet up to his chin. "You're a pair of jokers. I'd be better off on my own."

"So he can lie here and feel sorry for himself," Bec said.

The Knight gave a grimace. "At least no one would keep on asking me how I feel."

Sister Cecilia entered the room and came over to the bed. "And how do you feel this morning, Cristofo?"

The Knight sighed.

"He's fine, sister," said Bec. "He just needs something for his bowels. Something powerful."

"What!" The Knight sat up straight—then made a shooing motion with his hand. "Scoundrels! Get out of here! Walk around the town. See the sights. Go on, you heard me."

"All right, all right! Come on, Hannibal."

But the little dog remained where he was, curled up beside the Knight.

"I've never been in a place like this," Bec said, as they walked about the town. "It's immense. All I'd ever seen before were the shabby little places up the valley."

Even Tien Nu was impressed. He hadn't expected to find so many people in the streets, the mix of nationalities and languages, the throngs of buskers and beggars, the shops and markets stocked with goods from every corner of the world. It was almost like Venezia.

"What's going on over there?" Bec pointed down a side street to a square where a crowd had gathered.

"Don't know," said Tien Nu. "Let's take a look."

As they approached, they heard music—the sound of fiddle, flute, and drum. But the square was so tightly packed, they couldn't see much of anything. They climbed to the top of a wall on the side to get a better view.

In the centre of the square, a slim girl in a long dress

was dancing to the accompaniment of three musicians. Her shining black hair was pulled back into a bun, and her large dark eyes were painted with kohl, contrasting with her scarlet lips and the roses in her hair. The music was fast and intricate, and the girl's feet kept time, deftly following the rhythm as she whirled and swayed, her hands high above her head.

Tien Nu watched the girl, mesmerized by the performance. He'd seen many dancers in his travels, but none that matched this. There was a snake-like fluidity to her movements—a silky menace that sent shivers up his back. He didn't recognize the girl, yet something about her seemed familiar. He racked his memory, but without success—which seemed strange. If he had actually laid eyes on her before, he could hardly have forgotten her.

Then he noticed something.

He grabbed Bec's arm, almost choking in the effort to get his words out.

"That's *her* ... the bandit!"

"Curly?" Bec stared at the dancer for a moment, then let out a laugh. "No! That's not possible. You're imagining things."

"But it *is* Curly. I'm sure, *amico*. Look at the scar on her cheek."

Bec squinted at the dancer as she whirled about. "*Mio*

Dio! I believe you could be right!"

The tempo of the music slowed, and the dancer threw a glance at the two boys on the wall. She plucked a flower from her hair and tossed it in their direction, high over the heads of the crowd. Tien Nu reached out and caught it, nearly falling from his perch.

"It's Curly, all right.' he said. "She's seen us. I bet she wants her knife back."

Bec patted his belt. "If she thinks she's going to get it easily, she's in for a surprise."

The performance ended with loud applause. Curly bowed and collected the money tossed at her feet. She said a word to the musicians, then made her way through the crowd to the sidelines, where Bec and Tien Nu were waiting.

"We meet again!" she said.

"Small world," said Bec.

Curly held out her hand, palm up. "So, where's my knife?"

"What knife?"

Curly stared at him, then transferred her gaze to Tien Nu. "You know what I'm talking about."

Tien Nu shook his head, smiling innocently.

"You two are even dumber than I thought," Curly said.

"You'll have to explain it to us," Bec said.

Curly gave an impatient shake of the head. "I dropped my knife at the campfire that night. One of you must have picked it up. So, where is it?"

Bec turned to Tien Nu. "Did you hear 'please'? Or maybe 'thank you for killing that lion'?"

Curly tapped her foot. "It's my knife. Why should I have to beg for it?"

"Because it's mine now." Bec lifted his hand from his belt, revealing the weapon's handle. "And I like it."

"Of course, you do," said Curly. "It's not just any knife. I got it in Damascus."

Tien Nu gazed at her. "Is that where you're from?"

"Wouldn't you like to know!"

Bec folded his arms across his chest. "We're still waiting."

"All right, all right!" Curly said. "If you want some thanks, here it is. I'm glad you killed that lion. I could have done it myself—but that's neither here nor there. Between the two of you, you managed to pull it off. *Bravo! Bravissimo!* Now, can I have my knife back?"

"I still didn't hear 'please,'" said Bec.

Curly stepped forward, leaning into his face.

"And you won't be hearing 'please,'" she said. "It's not my style to grovel."

"And you won't be getting the knife," Bec said. "It's not my style to be bullied."

They stood there, staring into each other's eyes.

Curly finally gave a snort and looked at Tien Nu. "Can't you do something with this idiot?"

Tien Nu shrugged. "It's his knife now. He's the one to decide."

"So, that's the way it is," Curly said quietly.

She turned and walked away, one hand clutching the folds in her dress. She joined the musicians, and they disappeared down the street.

"I can't believe you didn't give her back the knife," Tien Nu said. "I thought you were just joking around, but you'd turn it over in the end."

"Why should I?" said Bec. "She was so rude—treating us like dirt. Well, she can do without the blessed knife. I don't know what's so special about it, anyway."

"Steel from Damascus," said Tien Nu. "It's famous."

"Is that so?" Bec reached for the knife to take a look.

"Where is it?" he said, fumbling in his belt.

He patted his tunic, then stared at the ground. But there was no knife in sight.

"It's gone," he said.

Tien Nu grinned. "And guess who took it."

CHAPTER 63

Chess

"Aren't you ever going to make a move?" Bec asked.

"Don't rush me," growled the Knight.

He stared at the chessboard, then glanced at Tien Nu across the table.

"Take your time," the Tartar said.

"It's no good," the Knight said eventually. "I'm trapped, no matter what I do."

He laid the black king on its side and shook his head. "I thought you said you always lose."

"I usually do," Tien Nu said.

"That's twice in a row you've drubbed me."

"I'd only played with my father before."

"Was he any good?"

"Don't know. But he always won."

"He was good."

The Knight stood up and stretched, his face registering a twinge of pain.

"Damn wound! It's taking its time to heal."

He looked at Bec. "When are you going to learn how to play?"

"When you teach me."

Cristofo poked his chin toward the Tartar. "There's your teacher."

Tien Nu shook his head. "Asks too many questions."

"How else can I learn?" Bec said.

"By watching and analyzing," said the Knight.

"Analyzing?"

"Figuring it out."

Bec grinned. "That I can do."

The Knight's eyes flicked over to Tien Nu. "Another match?"

"Sure, if you like."

After a while, Bec yawned and got up, wandering around the room of the inn where they were staying. He drew the Knight's sword from its scabbard and tried it out, sending a shard of light dancing around the walls.

"Stop fidgeting," said the Knight. "You're distracting me."

Bec laughed. "Go easy on the old man, Scraps. He's suffering."

"I'm not so old I can't throttle you with one hand," said the Knight. "Now, be quiet!"

Bec put the sword away and glanced back at the chess game. The Knight was hunched over the board, his forehead creased. Tien Nu was waiting for him to make his move, hands resting lightly on his knees, as patient as a cat.

Bec gazed at the two of them, companionable in their silence. His father and his friend. His chest suddenly tightened, and he felt his eyes brim with tears. He coughed and drew an arm across his face.

Cristofo captured Tien Nu's bishop, then leaned back with a grunt.

"So, when are we going to head off again?" Bec asked.

"Not until I'm fully healed," Cristofo said. "There's no rush, now that the pilgrims have found a man to replace me."

"Any idea where we'll go?"

"I'm not sure—Roma, Alessandria, the Terra Santa." The Knight shrugged. "Bernardo would like me to stay here for a while. He says he has plenty of work."

Tien Nu threw a glance at the Knight, then dropped his eyes. Bec wondered what was going through his mind.

Ever since they'd reached Ponti, he and Tien Nu hadn't discussed what came next. They weren't exactly avoiding the subject—but neither of them was in any rush to raise it. Originally, they'd talked about travelling around as a team—

The Young Dragons. But now that Bec had found his father, that plan seemed to be on hold.

"So, you'll be staying with us, Scraps?" Bec asked.

There was a brief silence. "Is that an invitation?"

"Since when do you need an invitation?"

"Since when do you need to ask me if I'm staying?"

Tien Nu returned his gaze to the chessboard. After a minute, he reached out and moved his knight.

"Dammit!" Cristofo stared at the board, then gave a sigh and moved his queen.

"Why do that?"

"Desperation."

The Tartar slid his rook across the board. "Check."

"There it is," said Cristofo. "Will I ever learn?"

"Only by watching and analyzing," said Bec.

"Scoundrel! No respect for your elders."

The Knight pushed himself slowly to his feet. "Well, that's enough humiliation for today. Come on, Hannibal. Time to go and visit Bernardo."

The little dog leapt up and ran to the door.

Tien Nu watched them leave, then gathered up the chess pieces.

Bec went over to the window and looked out, his forearms

resting on the sill. The inn was located on the outskirts of
Ponti, where the river met the sea. He stared at the expanse
of water stretching into the distance, on and on, as far as he
could see. It was enough to make him feel dizzy.

Tien Nu joined him at the window, and for a while they stood there, side by side, gazing silently outward, as the sunlight danced on the waves.

Eventually, Bec nudged his friend. "Where would you like to go, Scraps, once we start travelling again?"

"Every time I look at the sea, I think of Africa," Tien Nu said. "My mother's family should still be there—in Alessandria— aunts and uncles, and a whole tribe of cousins."

"Are they much like you?"

Tien Nu laughed. "Worse."

"That's hard to believe."

"You haven't seen anything yet, *amico*."

Bec paused. "But no matter what, we'll stick together, right?"

"You have other ideas?"

"Not really." Bec grinned. "Until something better turns up."

Acknowledgments

This book has had a gestation period far longer than the average elephant, and along the way many people have helped ease its passage into the world.

Foremost among these are the members of my family who have soldiered through untold drafts and offered sage advice. To my daughter and son, Shannon and Michael, and my sisters, Maureen and Patsy, a heartfelt thanks. And yes, despite appearances, I did always listen, though it sometimes took a while before the advice sank in.

At an early stage, the members of Marsha Skrypuch's online writing group gently disabused me of many a crazy idea. And at a later stage, Sylvia McNicoll guided me skillfully through the process of producing a viable draft. My colleague, Kent McNeil, read the manuscript with an eagle eye and offered encouragement. In bringing the work to completion,

Beverley Brenna of Red Deer Press showed a deft and experienced editorial hand that greatly enhanced the text, while humouring a few of my residual follies.

And last but not least, I owe a profound thanks to Mary Ann, my beloved spouse and partner in crime, who has long wondered if it would ever really end.

The signs on the post read:

GR 654 — VITRY le FRANÇOIS 1ʰ30

GR14 — Vitry-en-Perthois - 1 km

GR654 - Saint Jacques de Compostelle
GR145 - VIA FRANCIGENA — Vitry-le-François

424

Interview with Brian Slattery

How did you begin to craft this narrative?

I have no clue where the inspiration for this book came from—although I've wanted to write an adventure story from the time I was a teenager, scribbling ideas and scenes in various notebooks. I only know that one day I got the idea for a tale in which several characters took parallel journeys along a pilgrimage route, weaving in and out of each other's lives at various points along the way. I felt certain from the start that one of the characters would be a young slave escaping from his vicious master, and that another would be a wandering acrobat and martial artist, who'd recently lost his father. I also knew that the story would take place in medieval times, because it needed a setting in which there were no cars or trains or planes, much less cell phones, televisions, or computers. Other than that, I didn't have a very clear idea where the novel would go and just started to write.

Somehow the story took off on its own, leading me along many a winding path and sometimes over precipices. Characters popped out of nowhere and took on surprising attributes and did surprising things. They became so numerous and lively that they threatened to sink the entire enterprise, and had to be culled. The plot itself became quite twisty and complicated, and also had to be pared down. But the basic kernel of the story has remained the same throughout. The result, for better or worse, is what you have in front of you.

Bec and Tien Nu are both going on a journey to Ponti. Have your own travels helped you in developing this story?
I cut my teeth on long-distance travel in my twenties, as a volunteer working with refugees in Tanzania. I fell in love with the place and lived there for some six years. Almost every holiday was devoted to hitch-hiking around the countries of East and Central Africa. I often spent as much time trudging along dusty roads as I did getting lifts, due to the scarcity of traffic. Along the way, I met any number of friendly and generous people, who shared with me their life stories and whatever else they had to offer in the way of food and accommodation. I was impressed by their optimism and irrepressible good humour in the face of

adversity, and by the stories and adventures they related. I also had a few adventures of my own, some of which have found their way into this book. However, I'm sorry to say that I've never been chased cross-country by a vicious psychopath, nor have I killed a lion while armed only with a knife.

More recently, I've done a good deal of hiking in Europe with various family members, and I'm currently in the midst of a long-distance hike by stages along the Via Francigena, which runs from Canterbury to Rome. All this hodge-podge of experience has been poured into the stew that forms this book—which hopefully makes it more savoury, rather than simply indigestible.

Tien Nu is a superb acrobat, well versed in kung fu, and Bec demonstrates his enthusiasm for tumbling and daring feats. What influenced your characterizations here?
My book is indebted to the great martial artists of Asia, such as Bruce Lee, Donnie Yen, Jackie Chan, Michelle Yeoh, and Jet Li, whose remarkable athleticism has expanded our notions of what the human body and spirit are capable of. I was also influenced by Mark Salzman's wonderful book, *Iron and Silk,* which describes his experiences as a martial artist in China. My training in Tae Kwon Do under the tutelage of Master Chris

Park has made me keenly aware of how difficult it is to reach the levels attained by Tien Nu, who makes it all look easy. It also taught me the first rule in street-fighting—run like hell!

Historical fiction has the advantage of bringing readers into new and surprising settings, while also telling a good story. Can you talk about how you balance these two goals— crafting a setting, and telling a story?

My novel stands in a long line of historical adventure tales, in which strict factual accuracy has never been allowed to get in the way of a good story. The strongest influence throughout has been Robert Louis Stevenson, whose novels, *Treasure Island* and *Kidnapped,* have been a constant source of inspiration. No less important has been Alexandre Dumas's classic work, *The Three Musketeers,* as well as the ever-green tales of Robin Hood, as related superbly by Rosemary Sutcliff in *The Chronicles of Robin Hood,* all of which I devoured when I was young and have returned to many times over the years. Less well-known, but just as funny and exciting, are Sir Arthur Conan Doyle's tales of Brigadier Gerard. I've also learned much from the martial arts stories of Louis Cha, such as *The Deer and the Cauldron,* with their distinctive blend of the natural and the supernatural, and their strong vein of comedy.

The engrossing novels by Michelle Paver have left their marks on my own work, notably the two series: *Wolf Brother* and *Gods and Warriors*. Last but not least, I am indebted to the historical novels of Arturo Pérez-Reverte, especially *Captain Alatriste* and its successors, which feature a striking array of heroes and villains and darkly gripping plots.

Both Bec and Tien Nu think a great deal about their parentage—Bec hoping to discover the name of the father he never knew, and Tien Nu grappling with guilt over his own father's untimely death. What was the impetus to include this preoccupation for both characters?

Actually, the story came to me first; the themes, such as they are, emerged later. It was only when I was deep into the writing did it dawn on me how certain common elements could be found in the inner journeys of my characters. I suppose a more savvy writer would have noticed this from the start, but I was writing from the gut, struggling to put into words the feelings and ideas that I found gripping and enthralling and appalling. At a certain point, my characters took over and forged ahead on their own—with me just tagging along, trying to keep up. At no point did I consciously intend to explore any particular themes or to advance certain ideas. Whether any such themes run through the story—and what they might signify—is a matter for each reader to discover on their own.

The novel takes place in medieval times, yet the characters speak like modern people. Discuss your choices here.

In reality, the characters in the novel would have spoken a local version of medieval Italian, which obviously wouldn't work in the book. I could have made a stab at "medieval-speak," the antique-sounding English that some authors employ, but to my ear this has the effect of making the characters seem formal and stiff and quaint, if not downright comical, which gives the reader entirely the wrong impression. Normal medieval speech was just as informal and flexible and salty as modern English. I wanted readers to relate to the characters without the obstacle posed by antiquated language, and so I've used a neutral version of modern English, with a few Italian words thrown in, while avoiding any distinctively contemporary expressions. I hope that Bec and Tien Nu and the Knight sound nearly as fresh and lively to modern readers as they would have sounded to one another.

Is the setting of the novel imaginary, or or are the places real?

The novel is set in the province of Liguria in northern Italy

during the late Middle Ages, when the famous Silk Roads (and sea routes) between China, the Middle East, and the West were flourishing. The river that features in the novel is based on the Magra river, which runs southward into the Mediterranean, not far from the modern city of La Spezia. But many features of the river and its surroundings have been changed—and the reader will look in vain for the towns of Montecavo and Ponti. Nevertheless, large parts of this region were actually controlled by members of the powerful Malaspina family, who built a number of important castles there—even if Adolfo Malaspina and the Castello Scarmagno are creatures of my imagination. The valley of the Magra river was a major route for medieval pilgrims travelling southward to Rome, and the same route forms part of the modern trail known as the Via Francigena, mentioned earlier.

Tien Nu comes from a family with roots in China, Persia, and Egypt, and Bec's maternal family stems from Circassia on the Black Sea. Could two boys with such different backgrounds actually have met in medieval Italy?

There was a significant amount of East–West travel in the late medieval period, as exemplified by the Venetian merchant, Marco Polo, the Berber scholar and explorer, Ibn Battuta, and

the great Chinese Admiral, Zheng He, all of whom embarked on voyages that encompassed large portions of the Eurasian and African continents and their surrounding seas. So it's no great stretch to suppose that the wanderings of Tien Nu and his father brought them to Venice, which had extensive trading relations with Alexandria and other Middle Eastern ports. For those interested, I'd recommend the fascinating work of Janet L. Abu-Lughod, *Before European Hegemony: The World System A.D. 1250–1350*, and Peter Frankopan's sweeping book, *The Silk Roads: A New History of the World*.

Slaves were not uncommon in northern Italy in this era, even if the absolute numbers were not great. Some of these slaves came from regions bordering on the Black Sea—such as Circassia, where Bec's mother and grandmother were captured and taken for sale to Genoa, eventually ending up in the Malaspina household. For a good general account, see the Wikipedia article, "Slavery in medieval Europe." Scholarly works include Hannah Barker's book, *That Most Precious Merchandise: The Mediterranean Trade in Black Sea Slaves, 1260–1500*, and the massive study by Charles Verlinden, *L'Esclavage dans l'Europe médiévale*.

Thank you for these responses, Brian!